THE MANKILLER OF POOJEGAI

Walter Satterthwait
(Photo by Kelly Lange)

THE MANKILLER OF POOJEGAI AND OTHER STORIES

by Walter Satterthwait

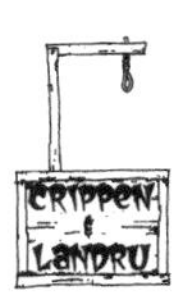

Crippen & Landru Publishers
Norfolk, Virginia
2007

Cover design by Gail Cross
Crippen & Landru logo by Eric D. Greene

ISBN (signed, limited clothbound edition): 978-1-932009-62-4
ISBN (trade softcover edition): 978-1-932009-65-1

FIRST EDITION

Printed in the United States of America on acid-free paper

Crippen & Landru Publishers
P.O. Box 9315
Norfolk, VA 23505
USA

Contents

INTRODUCTION

In the introduction to one of his slim volumes of poetry, Edgar Allan Poe complained that because of pressing commercial concerns, he had been unable to give to poetry the attention he felt it deserved. I feel much the same way about short stories—I love to write them, but I haven't been able to write as many as I would've liked. Either I'm more-or-less gainfully employed at tending or managing a bar, or I'm working against a deadline on a novel.

There was a time, not terribly long ago, when a writer might be able to make a living of sorts by writing short stories. There were fewer writers then, and there were perhaps hundreds of outlets: the pulps, including any number of mystery magazines; the "family" magazines, like *Redbook*, *Collier's*, and *The Saturday Evening Post*; and, later, the slick, expensive men's magazines, like *Playboy* and *Hustler* and *Penthouse*. Most of these markets have dried up.

Which is a great pity.

The short story, I think, can do things that a novel cannot. For one thing, it can pull off a terrific twist ending. O'Henry, de Maupassant, and John Collier were all famous for theirs. Many novels have a kind of twist ending as well, but in my opinion these can never be as effective as the final twists in a short story, simply because of the shorter span of reading time that leads up to it. The twist at the end of Bierce's short "An Occurrence at Owl Creek Bridge" is exactly the same twist at the end of Golding's long *Pincher Martin*; but the short story leaves us surprised, horrified, and yet delighted. The novel leaves us—leaves me—vaguely irritated.

In its small compass, a short story can reveal a significant, penetrating truth; or it can open up, despite its size, a universe of possibilities. I think of Stephen Crane's "The Open Boat," of Hemingway's "Big Two-Hearted River," of Joyce's "Dubliners," of Borges's "Ficciones," of almost anything by Chekov or Nabokov. One short story, written by Mr. Poe himself, "The Murders in the Rue Morgue," essentially invented the mystery story—

you've got your detective, your bumbling sidekick, your clues, your red herrings, your deduction, and, at last, your brilliant solution.

I'm not, of course, comparing the stories in this volume to any of these. My short stories were written, in a way, to scratch an individual itch. Someone once said that most writers write the book they write because they want to read that particular book, and no one has written it yet. The same, for me, is true of short stories.

Ernie Bulow, of Buffalo Medicine Press, has published an anthology called *The Gold of Mayani*, a collection of my stories about a young African constable, Andrew Mbutu, all of which were originally published in Alfred Hitchcock's Mystery Magazine. The first of these stories is repeated in this book. The rest of the stories included here, I'm ashamed to admit, are the rest of the stories I've written. Some of them have been republished in various anthologies, but they've never been together under one cover before. I'm grateful to Doug Greene of Crippen and Landru for scooping them up off the streets and giving them a home.

I hope you enjoy them.

A Conflict of Interests

(Published in *Alfred Hitchcock's Mystery Magazine*, November 1982)

This story contains, I think, the first decent writing I ever did.

I had written my second novel, The Aegean Affair, *in Kenya; and, ever since, I had wanted to write a book about Africa. My then-agent argued against it–no one wanted to read books set in Africa, she said. Then Wilbur Smith came along and did quite well with Africa, so I got a new agent. I told her I wanted to write about Africa. She told me that Wilbur Smith had Africa all sewed up.*

She also told me, several times, that she was unable to sell the proposals I was writing. I left her, too, and for a while I didn't write anything at all.

Around that time I started reading Nicholas Freeling, a writer with whom I fell in love. He had been, I understand, a chef; and at some point following WWII, after stealing food to feed his family, he was arrested. When he turned to writing, he used the name of the judge who sentenced him, Van der Valk, as the name of his detective, an Amsterdam cop. Mr. Freeling had basically educated himself; but, unlike most autodidacts, he had done a superb job. He was cultured and funny and wise, and I admired his writing enormously.

Reading him made me want to write again. And, because it seemed to me then that I'd never be able to sell anything, no matter what it was, I decided that I might as well write exactly what I wanted to write. So, finally, I wrote about Africa, and a young African constable. The writing, as should be obvious to anyone who's read us both, was very heavily influenced by the rhythms and textures of Mr. Freeling's work. And this is, I think, a Good Thing.

Constable Kobari whipped the steering wheel to the right with his usual disregard for the laws of physics. Pebbles pinging against the undercarriage, the Toyota Land Cruiser swooped through the gates at the entrance to the compound, bounced and bucked up the rutted dirt drive.

Sitting beside Kobari, Sergeant Andrew Mbutu sighed. Kobari had seen

Bullit eleven times and was unable to circle the block without imagining himself Steve McQueen.

There were three cars parked before the broad veranda: the major's celebrated red Land Rover, a second police Toyota, and a rusted grey Citroen 2-CV sagging slightly to the left, wounded. Constable Kobari discovered his brakes and the Land Cruiser came to a teeth-clicking halt an inch from the Citroen's rear fender.

Kobari nodded to the 2-CV and said in Swahili, "Doctor Murmajee is already here."

Andrew grunted. "He enjoys this. It's his only opportunity to examine Europeans. They never come to him when they're alive."

He opened the door and stepped out into the relentless sun.

The rains had stopped two weeks ago; the winds off the ocean two days ago, inexplicably; the morning air was as hot and thick as broth. Andrew's uniform, cardboard crisp when he put it on—Mary believed devoutly in starch—was limp now, clinging, after only an hour.

Baton under his arm, he led the way. To the left, the garden was crowded with color: bougainvillaea, flame tree, jacaranda, jasmine.

"They live well," Kobari said behind him. Meaning the *Wazungu*, the Europeans.

"A half acre for flowers," Andrew said over his shoulder. "Who can eat flowers?"

He was in a foul mood. Awake for hours last night, this bloody miserable heat, tossing in his own oily sweat. Sheet clumping up beneath him, sticking. And throughout it all Mary placidly asleep beside him. Infuriating. In the next room, the children, too. A conspiracy.

And then this morning, Mary and the children at church, he hadn't yet finished the leftover porridge when Kobari came pounding at the door, bellowing about a murder, chief wanted him there right away. Not a tourist either; no one cares when visiting *Wazungu* kill each other off, the Italians were doing it all the time down in Mombasa, a hobby with them apparently. No, a local European, and one of the big ones. Bound to be messy. Politics.

Which meant the C.I.D. would send someone expendable: the way Andrew's luck was running, probably that great idiot, Moi.

The front door was open. Andrew took off his sunglasses, tucked them away in his shirt pocket, stepped inside.

A most imposing house indeed. Enormous main room, overhead the soaring *makouti* roof of mangrove pole and thatch. White walls, framed painting, tribal masks, spears, rows of bookshelves, rows of display cases stuffed with trinkets: enough frippery for a museum. And, amid the bric-a-brac, quite a gathering.

On the left, Constable Gona, thick arms crossed, baton jutting from left armpit. Very big for a Kikuyu tribesman, and very sullen: he resented Andrew's unlikely success, Andrew having come from the wrong tribe, the Giriyama.

Beside him to the right, sitting on the sofa with his hands folded atop his lap, an old man in a long white Arab *kanzu*. The Somali house servant. No resentment there, nor fear either. Well-accustomed to the police, Somalis, a fine distinguished history of cattle raids and brigandry.

Next, standing with a notebook in his hand, chubby Doctor Murmajee wearing the familiar drooping black suit, the familiar smarmy smile.

And last of course the host. The major, rather the worse for wear. Fully dressed, sprawled on his back across a Persian carpet that had absorbed a considerable amount of blood.

The doctor first.

Murmajee's shining round face beamed as he held out his hand. "*Jambo*, Sergeant Mbutu! Such a very great pleasure to see you again."

Like most Asians, Murmajee spoke English in a singsong that Andrew normally found amusing, attractive even. Today he found it grating. Everything was grating today.

"Doctor," he said, and nodded. "How did he die?"

Murmajee giggled. "Straight to business, yes, Sergeant? Oh my, very proper, yes, as it should be." He stepped over to the body and squatted down awkwardly beside it. "Here, you see," pointing to the wound at the neck. A few flies buzzing, industrious. "One good slash, yes, only one, but very strong, of course, and the carotid is severed. Also, of course, the trachea, but the carotid is quite enough, oh my yes. The poor chap bled very thoroughly to death." He grinned up at Andrew with a mixture of pride and pleasure. A small boy showing off an expensive new toy.

"A *panga*?" Andrew asked him. A long-bladed bush knife, the favorite weapon of house thieves.

"A *panga*, yes," said Murmajee, rising from the floor with the slow caution of the overweight. "Very likely, yes, a *panga*."

"Only the one wound on the neck? Nothing else?"

"No, nothing else. No, not as yet." Hinting that the autopsy would disclose a multitude of wonders.

"When did it happen?"

"From the rigor and the lividity, oh my, I should say, yes, possibly four hours ago, possibly six hours. Possibly, yes."

Andrew looked at his watch. Eight o'clock. So between two and four in the morning. Possibly.

"The autopsy, of course, will tell me more," said Murmajee. Practically wringing his hands with anticipation. Loved to open up these Europeans. "There *will* be an autopsy, yes, Sergeant?"

"Of course," Andrew told him. "You are finished here, however, are you not? Good. After the C.I.D. arrives, the body will be moved to the station house."

As grinning Murmajee bustled out, Andrew turned to Constable Kobari. "Get the blanket from the back of the Land Cruiser." He nodded to the body. "Cover him."

Andrew crossed to room to Constable Gona. "Who found him?"

"The Somali," Gona said, with a jerk of his head toward the old man. "But he won't talk."

Andrew glanced down at the house servant, saw the fresh welt across the man's cheek. Recognized it. The Township's desperadoes and layabouts had given it a name: *baton burn*. He turned to Gona. "You hit him?"

Gona glared at him, guilt generating defiance. "He wouldn't talk. The major's wallet was missing."

Bloody idiot.

For an improbable moment Andrew found himself wishing for absolute power, the sort that absolutely corrupts. How agreeable to turn to a nearby lackey and drawl, "Take this buffoon outside and shoot him."

He sighed. "Who called us in?"

"The German woman in the next house. The Somali went and brought her. She called from here."

"And where is she now?"

"I sent her home. She said she heard nothing last night." Enjoyed giving orders. Especially to Europeans. Especially to European women.

Constable Kobari reappeared, unfurled the blanket, draped it carefully over the body. It seemed a ceremonial act, and created a moment of silence. Andrew broke it, speaking to Gona: "You go outside. Wait for the C.I.D."

Gona pursed his lips for a bit, then stalked off. Thwacking the baton against his thigh. Fuming. Good. Imbecile.

Andrew looked down at the Somali servant. Silent, impassive, carved from wood.

Andrew sighed again. He tugged the handkerchief from his back pocket, mopped his face, the back of his neck. Took off his garrison cap, wiped the inner brim. Returned handkerchief to pocket. Held the cap.

Diplomacy required here. Despite the heat. Damn these Somalis.

He pulled a chair, leather and chrome, over to the sofa and sat down facing the servant. The old man stared through him for a moment, then lowered his eyes.

"*M'zee*," said Andrew, using the honorific granted to elders. "I am Sergeant Mbutu. And your name?" A matter of form; Andrew knew it already. There were only three hundred resident Europeans in the Township; their doings, and those of their households, provided the remaining twenty thousand citizens—Africans, Arabs, Asians—with one of their few consistently reliable sources of amusement.

Silence. "*M'zee?*" Andrew said.

Grudgingly: "Farah." Still looking down. Voice smoky with age but strong.

"*M'zee*, you have been with the *bwana* major for many years?" Form again.

The eyes flicked up, something in them. Pride? The old man nodded. "*Hamsini*." Fifty. The old man swallowed then; eyes began to go murky.

Careful. These old colonial servants, a lifetime with the *bwana*, boys together: a relationship longer and more intricate than marriage. Can't have this one weeping; shame would silence him forever. "Then you know of course," businesslike, reasonable, "that Major Hollister was a *bwana mkubwa*, a very important man. And you must know that this death will make a great *kelele* not only here, but even as far as Nairobi. There will be government people, newspaper people, and everyone will ask questions, and more questions, and it will go on forever unless we discover who did this thing."

The eyes shifted slightly. Narrowed: wary. Got him.

"And so," said Andrew, "to avoid these troubles for you and for myself, it would be best, I think, if you were to tell me what you know."

For a moment the Somali said nothing. Then, abruptly, he gave Andrew a single nod. Accepting.

"Good. First I must ask you if you know who did this."

Small shake of the head. "No."

"Last night, did you hear or see anything at all?" No.

"You sleep in one of the outbuildings?" A nod. Yes.

"Ah," said Andrew. "Then did you not hear the major's Land Rover return?"

"Yes. That I heard."

Old fool. "And when did it return?"
"Late."
Bloody hell. Like pulling teeth. "Could you not be more precise, *m'zee?*"
"After the sixth hour." After midnight.
"How do you know this?"
"The car awoke me. I could not sleep until after the sixth hour. The heat."
"Yes, truly, it is intolerable. But you do not know for how long you slept before the car awoke you?" No.
"The major was alone? You heard no one with him?" No.
"You slept well, *m'zee?*"
"No. Very poorly."
"Yes, of course, the heat." Andrew nodded. "Now tell me please about this morning, *m'zee*."
Like the rest, it came in installments. The old man had got up, washed, dressed. Had gone to the front door, found it unlocked, entered the house, discovered the *bwana* lying in blood.
The old man's throat was tightening again. Back to this later. "*M'zee*," Andrew said, "was the front door often unlocked when you came to the house in the morning?"
"Sometimes."
"Sometimes. When exactly?"
"Sometimes the *bwana* major would let the dog enter the house."
"Dog?" said Andrew. And then he realized: certainly, all the English kept dogs. Man's best friend. Filthy beasts. "The dog remained in the yard at night?"
The old man nodded. "That is so."
"Where is it now?"
A shrug. "I do not know." And manifestly did not care.
Could've slipped away while the old man was off fetching the German woman. Still ...
Andrew turned to Kobari. "Get Gona. Search the yard for this dog."

Its head burst open, another *panga* clout, the dog lay on the smooth unruffled lawn beside the stone wall, perhaps fifty meters from the rear of the house. Constable Kobari—his grandfather had been a famous hunter—pointed to the dry grass against the wall. "Two of them, Sergeant. They came over the wall and landed here." The wall was only five feet high, designed to stop not thieves but curiosity. (Had failed to stop that as well, of course. Walls make chatter: Giriyama saying.) "Both men about the same size, big but not too big. Not fat. Wearing sandals. You see? These marks in the earth?"

Andrew, who saw nothing, nodded sagely. "The dog attacks them and they kill it. And then?"

Kobari shrugged. "The ground is too hard for me to say. But Gona found the window where they broke in." He pointed. "That one, beside the metal door. The kitchen window."

Andrew nodded. "The land on the other side of the wall is municipal property, yes?"

"Yes," said Kobari, and nodded sadly. "Very rocky." He meant, no spoor.

Flies busy on the dog as well: giddy, can't believe their luck. With the toe of his shoe—gingerly, he disliked dogs living or dead, they frightened him—Andrew prodded a paw. Stiff.

Kobari said: "A big animal, eh, Sergeant? What do they call them?" Convinced that two years of university had provided Andrew with the answer to every question.

To this one it had. "Ridgebacks," he said. "From Zimbabwe." He looked up. "Check on the other side of the wall. Perhaps you'll be lucky. I'll speak a bit more with the house servant."

But it was not to be. The Criminal Investigation Directorate, in the person of Cadet Inspector Moi, had arrived.

The major's body had been wrapped, trussed, carted to the wagon, driven away. In the kitchen, the men of the Technical Unit murmured and tittered, burying appliances beneath mountains of fingerprint powder. Outside, Kobari searched beyond the wall, Gona within it; two additional constables were stationed now at the compound's entrance, where they gossiped with the crowd they were supposed to drive away.

"Seems fairly straightforward," said Cadet Inspector Moi when Andrew finished his report. "The villains climb over the wall, break in through the back window. Crowbar, eh? Major Hollister comes home, finds them lurking about, they kill him. Simple conflict of interests, eh?" He chuckled.

Inspector Moi—Kikuyu, like Gona, like most of the constabulary—had spent an exchange year at Scotland Yard and had returned to Africa as English as the Queen, and approximately as competent a policeman. A few inches taller than Andrew, a few years older, he sported a lime green safari suit and a small goatee, precisely trimmed, vaguely obscene.

"There are a few more questions," Andrew said, "I should like to ask the house servant."

A complacent smile. "Not to worry, Sergeant. I'll carry on from here. You could put me in the picture, though, about this major fellow." Moi came from a coastal town to the south, and was unfamiliar with local mythology. "Used to be in the constabulary himself, did he?"

Andrew nodded. "The G.S.U." The paramilitary branch. "He retired when his wife died, a few years after Independence."

"Bit of a boozer from all accounts," said Moi. "Womanizer too, hmm?"

There had always been women, true. Primarily tourist ladies and Somali prostitutes—Major Hollister was one of the rare Europeans who mingled openly with the Township's African population; as a consequence, despite his background (colonial, wealthy) few of the others tainted themselves with his company. And there had always been drink. Inevitable, perhaps, in a retired military man living alone.

But it was only recently, only within the last few months, that both seemed to have gotten out of hand. The major was drinking more often, more heavily, for longer periods; he was more frequently seen at the casino and at the Delight, where the Somali women gathered. There had been reports of arguments, of scenes caused; rumors even of a fight. Everything hushed up, straightened away, before the police arrived: they may have deplored him, the other Europeans, but in the end he was still a member of the club. Official action, scandal, Just Wouldn't Do.

Andrew explained this to Cadet Inspector Moi, adding, "He had become self-destructive. As though he had lost control, as though he had crossed some sort of line and knew there was no going back."

"Very interesting," said Moi through a faint smile. "Did he have family?"

Tersely (and sod you, cadet inspector): Two sons, one running a safari camp up-country, on Lake Turkana; the other a businessman here in the Township, imports.

"Yes," said Moi. "Well, as I say, it all seems cut and dried. Thieves, isn't it. Thing to do now is learn what they took." He turned to the Somali servant. "*You.*" Speaking Swahili for the first time. He waved an indifferent hand at the Africana about the room. "This is all *takataka.*" Trash. "Where did Major Hollister keep the valuable things?"

As the old man led Moi to the major's bedroom, Andrew wandered hands-in-pockets round the room. An abundance of stuff here, but nothing to interest a house thief.

On the top of one display case he found an ebony-framed black and white photograph of the major and, presumably, his wife. Taken out of doors, broad sweep of lawn behind them; she young and serious, darkhaired and slender in a white dress (its hem stirred faintly by the long-ago breeze); he young and tall and lean in uniform beside her, grinning hugely, radiating vigor. A remarkable people, the colonials: able to swagger even while standing still.

Beside the picture lay a small wooden *hirizi*, a magic charm, about five inches long and shaped like a phallus. Masai, by its markings. Andrew sniffed in distaste. *Takataka* was right.

He set it back as Moi and the house servant returned to the room.

"Well," announced the cadet inspector. "That's it, then. This lad tells me the major kept five or six thousand shillings in the bedroom drawer. Gone now. So's the jewelry belonged to the wife. We'll start picking up a few of the likely boys a little later—shouldn't be too hard to trace the lolly. I'm off to chat up this German woman. Meantime, you run round to the major's son and let him know what's happened."

Andrew began a protest, bit it off.

But Moi had noticed: smiled. "You're good with the Europeans. One of the advantages, eh, of being such a clever fellow."

Africans would have flung themselves to the dirt, shrieking and hissing, tearing at their clothes, their hair. Mrs. Hollister, who was standing, dropped a glass of lemonade to the patio. Mr. Hollister, who was sitting, jerked back his head and said, "No."

"But how?" asked Mrs. Hollister.

Andrew told them.

"Oh *no*," she said, her face twisting. Thin, moderately pretty, topped with a swirl of red hair. Gauzy pale green blouse, loose dark green skirt. She walked over to her husband, put her hand on his shoulder. "Oh, David."

Mr. Hollister gaped. Long-legged and bony and blond. White shirt, white pants. He pulled himself up out of the chair. His wife stood beside it, her hand on his arm as though supporting him.

"I'm sorry," said Andrew.

"The *bastards*!" snarled Mr. Hollister.

Startled, Andrew blinked.

"My God, Sergeant, can't people do anything to *stop* this filth?" Raging, leaning toward Andrew, leaning over him.

"*Bwana* Hollister—" Backing up. Flustered, flushed, suddenly returned to mission school, eight years old and helpless.

"This is the third time this month! The Freemans, down the road, the bloody buggers have broken in there *twice* this year. *Damn* it, Sergeant!"

Mrs. Hollister said a single word: "*David.*" Clipped, cool, commanding.

It stopped him. He looked at her quickly, spun around, stalked away. Stopped several yards off with his back to them and shoved his hands into his pockets. Stood there, taking deep, ragged breaths.

Mrs. Hollister said, "I'm so very sorry, Sergeant. ... this has been a dreadful shock for us."

"Of course." A curt nod, stiffly formal. He was furious: at the Englishman for attacking, at himself for retreating, at the woman for ending the contest.

"We only just saw him a few nights ago," she said. "It seems impossible that all that ... extraordinary vitality of his could be ... well, that it could be gone."

Andrew nodded, quiescent, letting his self-control return.

"And we've all been so concerned about these thefts," she said, with a glance at her husband. Not anxiety, merely a kind of casual attention, a busy mother checking to see that the son playing in the yard hasn't wandered too close to the well. "We were robbed ourselves only a few months ago."

Andrew looked at her. "Oh yes?"

She frowned slightly, puzzled at his interest. "But surely, Sergeant," she said, "you can't be thinking that that's in any way connected to this?"

"I very much doubt it. You reported the incident?" Knowing they hadn't; he read the robbery reports before he read the newspaper.

"No. No, we didn't. Nothing of any great value was taken. David and I—well ..." She hesitated.

"Yes?"

"Well, we thought at the time that perhaps the *ayah*, the nursemaid, was in some way responsible. She had a key, you see, and the things that were missing were mine. Some earrings. A gold bracelet. But we had no real proof that the girl was involved. I shouldn't like to see her get into trouble with the police. We let her go, of course, but we felt that should be the end of it."

"Yes. And when exactly did this happen?"

"Two months ago, perhaps a bit longer."

"And could you give me, please, the *ayah's* name?"

"But Alysha can't possible have been involved in this."

A cough, to the right. Mr. Hollister, returning to civilization. "Sergeant?"

"Yes." Deadly cold.

Mr. Hollister's face was drawn, his long body ungainly and slack, an ill-fitting suit. "Well, you know ... Damn it. Sergeant, I really am terribly sorry."

The outburst of a child, and so a child's apology. Despite himself, Andrew warmed to the man. "Not at all, *Bwana* Hollister. The shock."

"Yes. Well. Still. Jumping at you that way. I really am sorry."

"Not at all." Very gracious, very pleased with the man and with himself.

"But Karen's quite right, you know." In a tired voice. "About Alysha. Be impossible for her to have anything to do with this."

"Of course, of course. I want merely to question her. Could you tell me where she lives?"

"I'm afraid not. I've heard she's moved." He looked at his wife.

"I can't see what good it will do, really," she said to Andrew. "But I was told she works as a bar girl now. At the Delight."

"Ah," said Andrew. "She is Somali?"

"Why yes," said Mrs. Hollister. "Yes she is."

The heat had burned the crowd away from the compound's entrance. Cadet Inspector Moi was still encloistered with the German woman next door. The old house servant was out hunting beer for Constable Kobari, whose search beyond the wall had produced nothing and who was now the sole constable sweltering at the gate. Inside the house, someone had rolled up the Persian carpet and set it along the entranceway wall. Major Hollister still grinned, roguish, from the small photograph on the display case; but the Masai charm was gone.

"Yes," said the old man, back on the sofa. Andrew stood next to the display case. "Yes, I took the *hirizi*."

"Why?" Andrew asked him. The charm itself a trifle, its theft provided him a purchase on the old man.

The Somali shrugged. "The *bwana* major, he told me once that when he died it would be mine."

"Why would you want such a thing?"

"It is a thing of very great *dawa*." Medicine.

"What sort of *dawa*?" Growing curious.

The old man looked at Andrew, said nothing.

"*M'zee*," said Andrew. "I have treated you with the respect you deserve. Please do the same with me."

"I may keep the *hirizi*?"

"Perhaps. Tell me."

Slowly, bit by bit, the old man did.

For a year after the death of his wife, the major secluded himself in the house, drinking heavily, speaking to no one but the Somali, and little enough to him. When at last he reentered the world and found himself with a woman once again, a tourist woman, he learned that he could no longer function. The local European doctor—German, pragmatic—prescribed patience, Time would prepare the cure. Never a man to await Time's unfolding, the major sought out a Masai *mchawi*, a sorcerer, famed for his success with such cases, and from him obtained the charm. Its efficacy, according to the Somali, had been immediate and awesome.

Andrew nodded. "Who knew of this?"

The Somali shrugged. "Everyone knew. The *hirizi* is famous, many people wanted to buy it. The *bwana* major had very many women."

"Tell me this, *m'zee*," said Andrew. "In the past few months, did the *bwana* major have one woman in particular?"

A blink of the eyes, quick as a gecko's. "I do not know." Lying. As expected.

Andrew looked for a moment at the yellowed photograph of the major. Then he turned to the Somali and asked the question he had come here to ask. Clearly, from his face, the old man understood that Andrew already knew the answer.

Andrew sighed. He was tired, hot, hungry, and he had ahead of him a large unpleasantness.

"The dog, you see," said Andrew. "Obviously it had been killed by someone it knew. A ridgeback, a big animal, fearless—they were once used to hunt lions. Even two men with *pangas* would be extremely fortunate to stop it with a single blow. Without themselves being hurt somehow, without in any way disturbing the lawn. Furthermore, of course, the dog never barked that night."

Echoes of Conan Doyle, but hollow: Andrew was not enjoying this. "Now it is a sad fact," he said, "that most of the Europeans in the Township avoided the major. The majority of his acquaintances were Africans. It is conceivable that the dog may have been familiar with one of these. But any of them who knew the major well would know of the major's Masai *hirizi*, a thing apparently much coveted. I believe that any of these men, having killed him, would doubtless take the charm.

"An African woman," he said, "would, of course, have no interest in the charm." He cleared his throat. "But could a woman, no matter how strong, have killed the dog with one slash of a *panga?* Could a woman kill the major, a man familiar with weapons and physical combat?"

Andrew sat back. "I spoke with the *ayah*, Alysha, not an hour ago. She insists she stole nothing from your house."

"Well, of course," said Mr. Hollister, testy. They sat out on the shaded patio, on opposite sides of the table. Mrs. Hollister was in the bedroom, resting. "That's what you'd expect any of them to say, isn't it? They all steal, surely you know that."

Andrew nodded. "Many of them do. But because suspicion falls first on them, they steal only those items whose absence will not be noticed. Or, if noticed, will cause no great concern. Silverware. Bits of clothes. *Takataka*. But expensive jewelry? No, very unlikely. At best they will lose their employment, at worst they will face the police. No, I believe the woman. I believe you took your wife's jewelry and made the theft appear Alysha's."

"Why on earth would I do that?"

Wretched, hating this, Andrew said, "Your wife bears a remarkable resemblance to your mother, *Bwana* Hollister."

The man sagged; suddenly the spirit left him. His shoulders slumped, his eyes slowly closed. So the eyes of the Somali servant when Andrew asked what color hair had the woman in the photograph.

Andrew said: "I imagine you felt that the *ayah* suspected something. You knew how these women gossip, you contrived to have her removed."

Ironically, she had suspected nothing. A disagreeable girl, transparently vindictive; but even spite had been unable to invent the truth. She could tell Andrew only that the major often visited while the husband was away.

Andrew took a deep breath. "I don't know when you learned of their affair, I don't know how long you carried this with you, or why you decided to end it, but I know you did, *Bwana* Hollister. I know you killed him."

The eyes opened and met Andrew's. "You've no proof." Sulky, petulant: the child again.

"Someone will have seen you near the major's house." Likely someone had; likely Andrew would never find him. "The Somali knows. Eventually it will come out. But *Bwana* Hollister, the sooner you admit to this, the better it will go for you. At the moment, you can claim diminished capacity, extenuating circumstances ..."

Extenuating circumstances, yes, but diminished capacity? The man hadn't forgotten crowbar and *panga*. Hadn't forgotten to kill the dog, create thieves by the wall, steal the money, the jewelry. A child's cunning, but cunning nonetheless.

And finally what jury would, or could, allow him forgiveness? Patricide.

In Africa still the Primal Crime: mythic. Awe it could produce; forgiveness never. No, he was doomed. Oedipus.

Andrew said, "Your father welcomed death, I think."

A moment of absolute stillness. (The Giriyama storytellers: "as when even the trees stop breathing.")

Then a flicker, a whirr: and movement and sound returned.

Andrew had never seen a European weep before. The surprise now was its inevitability.

The man tried to control it. He swallowed, shielded his blinking eyes with his hands. But in only a few moments it was controlling him: an explosion of sobs came coughing harsh and rasping, staccato. He coiled forward, fists balled against his eyes, elbows tight against his chest, body clenching, unclenching. And then he began to rock, slowly, slowly, up and down, in time to the rise and fall of wailing.

Andrew looked away, but there was no *away*.

After a while it subsided. Bent forward, face still hidden, the man drew long deep halting breaths. Andrew rose, conscious of his own breathing. He walked round the table, touched him on the shoulder. "Come," he said, and started at the sound of his own voice.

Silence. Another staggered breath. And then the other stood. Tall and awkward and lost.

As he drove the Land Cruiser down the drive, Andrew saw the woman in the rearview mirror. A tiny figure at the front door, arms folded beneath her breasts. Watching them.

She had known, of course. Probably since last night: doubtless the man had told her afterward. Seeking revenge, and absolution, and solace.

Andrew glanced at his watch. One o'clock. Overhead, the sun burned on, relentless still.

A Matter of Pride

(*Alfred Hitchcock's Mystery Magazine*, May 1984)

Sometime in the early '80s I signed with a new agent, Dominick Able, who was not only able, but charming and smart. He tried to sell a proposal of mine about a slightly-less-than-entirely-competent private detective, a man named Grober. (I had stolen the last name from a good friend of mine.) Despite Dominick's best efforts, this proposal was never picked up. I put together a new proposal, a novel called The Gold of Mayani, *featuring my African constable, Andrew Mbutu. Dominick sold it to St. Martin's Press. Before I left for Greece, where I planned to write it, I gave Grober another shot, in this story. He also shows up later in my second Joshua Croft novel,* At Ease With the Dead.

YOU KNOW it's going to be a bad day when you wake up, face down, in an alley.

It took Grober a while, however, to realize where he was. When he opened grainy eyes to the muddled light of dawn, his mind was suddenly very busy contending with a truly spectacular interior display: little parachutes of pain were opening at the top of his head and fluttering down through his brain, their canopies trembling against his temples and against his jaws before they landed with a startling thud at the base of his skull.

He pushed himself to his knees, felt suddenly sick, and waited there a moment, breathing deeply through an opened mouth. Then, slowly, he sat down in the dirt. He looked around him.

A battered green dumpster; a narrow wooden gate, closed; brown adobe walls on either side. He recognized the place: the alley behind the Purple Hogan, the Santa Fe bar to which, last night, he had tailed Hubbard Baylor.

He shook his head, trying to clear it. A big mistake—the parachutes became packing crates. Teeth grinding, he reached up and felt, gently, the top of his head. And found a long narrow lump, tender and aflame.

This was all beginning to make a kind of dreadful sense. With the chill of certain and irrevocable disaster settling over him, he moved his hand to his back pocket, pushed aside his blue windbreaker, and felt for his wallet. ...

Danny was sitting back in his office chair reading a copy of *Soldier of Fortune* magazine, his snakeskin boots perched atop his desk. He was wearing fawn-colored slacks, a pale blue shirt, a bolo tie, and a suede sport coat that looked soft enough to spread on bread. Danny dressed exactly like what he was, a Western Lawman: in his case, a lieutenant in the Violent Crimes Unit of the Santa Fe Police Department. No one could have guessed that he, like Grober, had been born and raised in New York City.

"I see by your outfit," said Grober, "that you are a cowboy."

Glancing up from the magazine, Danny said, "You look terrific."

"Thanks," Grober said, closing the door to the squad room.

"You're losing about a pint of blood through each eye."

"I had a rough night. Mind if I sit down?"

Danny shrugged. "The chair belongs to the city. Who am I to say no?" As Grober sat, Danny said, "Instead of drinking, you ever considered just sticking your thumbs into your eyeballs when you get up in the morning? Save you a lot of money on bar bills and give you the same effect."

"I wasn't drinking," Grober said, stretching the truth a bit for drama's sake. "I was sapped and rolled last night."

"Oh yeah?" said Danny, looking down, turning a page of the magazine. "Some twelve-year-old runaway take a dislike to you?"

"It happened here in Santa Fe. You want to hear about it or not?"

Danny studied the magazine. "Sergeant Martinez, outside, can fill out the report."

"Sergeant Martinez isn't my brother."

"No," Danny said, flipping another page. "No such luck."

Grober waited. Finally, Danny sighed. He closed the magazine, tossed it to his desk top, and swung his legs to the floor. "Where'd it happen?"

"The Purple Hogan."

Danny raised an eyebrow. "Pretty upscale place for a mugging."

"In the alley, outside."

Danny nodded. "That sounds more like your style. What time?"

"Around one this morning."

"See the perp?"

"Perp," Grober said. "Nifty. That's police talk, right?"

"Yes or no."

"No."

"Rolled, you said. What'd they get?"

"Everything. Wallet, car keys. My gun."

"That stupid little Baur? You haven't got a permit for that thing, Phil."

"I don't need a permit in New Mexico."

"Only if the weapon is in plain sight."

"I had it Scotch-taped to my forehead. Look, Danny, I'm not in a wonderful mood this morning. I've got a knot on my skull the size of a beef burrito, I've been robbed, they got all my money, they got my car–"

"Your car?"

"–so I'm not really ready to hear you read statutes at me. Yeah, my car."

"Where was it parked?"

"In the lot around the corner."

"How'd they know which car would fit the keys they stole?"

"I don't know. I've been wondering about it myself." He shrugged. "Maybe they tried the keys on every car in the lot until they came to mine."

Danny frowned. "That doesn't play too well. How'd they know the car was in the lot?"

"I don't know."

"Someone bops a guy, rolls him, he's not going to hang around diddling with a bunch of cars."

"I said I don't know."

"Were you working?"

"Yeah. Tailing a guy."

"What guy?"

Grober shook his head. "He didn't do it."

"The name."

Grober smiled. "Or what? Rubber hose time, Danny?"

Danny made a face. "You've got some nerve, Phil. You come in here, you want special attention, Sergeant Martinez isn't good enough for you, but I ask you for a little simple cooperation and you clam up on me."

"I give you the guy, I blow the investigation."

"*Investigation*" Danny snorted; he was good at snorting. "Who're you, Philo Vance? Some wife wants eight- by-tens of her husband and the chippy he's been jumping, so she can shaft him in court. That's an investigation?"

"One thing you could do, you know. I mean, I can see you're busy and all, but you *could* put my car on the list before some booster's mechanic hacks it up and carts it to Juarez."

Danny laughed. "Yeah. Yeah, right, Phil. There's this terrifically hot market for '72 Pintos in Mexico."

Grober nodded. "I'm glad I could bring a little fun into your life, Danny."

"They're a real prestige item down there. Especially the kind like yours, with that classy coat hanger antenna. Executive- style."

"Maybe you were right. Maybe I should've talked to Sergeant Martinez."
"I think he's already got a Pinto," Danny said, and laughed again.
The telephone on Danny's desk rang. Still grinning, Danny leaned forward and picked up the receiver. "Lieutenant Grober," he said, sitting back in his chair. "Yeah ... yeah ... Is that right?" He looked quickly up at Grober. "Yeah, I know where–right here in my office. Thanks, Ed. Appreciate it."
He hung up. "That was Sergeant Munsen," he said. "A couple of uniforms found your car. The DMV got your name from the tags."
Surprised, Grober said, "Where was it?"
"A few blocks from the Purple Hogan. Some kid spotted it and told his mother."
"His mother? Why? Is the car okay?"
"It's not the car so much. It's what was inside."
Grober felt a flutter of unease. "What was that?"
"A stiff. Shot twice in the forehead. A Baur .25 was on the passenger's seat. According to his papers, it was a guy named Baylor. Ring any bells?"
"Oh great," Grober said, slumping back in his chair. "That is just peachy."
"Wouldn't be the guy you were tailing, would it?"
Grober's headache had returned. He rubbed his temples with his fingertips.
"Just peachy."
"Maybe you better tell me about this case of yours."
Grober nodded. "Maybe I better."

She had come into Grober's office yesterday, tall and dark, capped with a helmet of black hair, full breasted but lean as a whippet. She was wearing leather sandals, a flouncy ruffled peasant skirt, several pounds of Navaho silver, and a Danskin top so tight that one good deep breath would have given her thread poisoning. Right hand wielding a brown cigarette, left resting atop the large brown leather bag slung from her shoulder, she looked around Grober's office with airy distaste and turned to him and said, "Are you Mr. Grober?" From her voice, she had gone to one of those Eastern colleges that teach women how to wear tweeds and talk with their teeth clenched.
Belatedly remembering to stand, Grober said, "Yes."
"I'm Winnifred Gail." She said the name as though she were granting a boon.
"Yes?" said Grober.

"The Gail Gallery. In Santa Fe."

"Oh, right," said Grober, who had never heard of the place. "Sure. What brings you to Albuquerque, Miss Gail?"

"Miz."

"Right. Miz." He smiled again, but wondered exactly how big a pain in the neck this woman was likely to be.

"I'm looking for a private investigator."

"Well," he said, smiling his heartiest smile, "it looks like you found one. Have a seat."

She inspected the client's chair for a moment as though she might find some crispy creature lounging on the Naugahyde, then sat down, settling her purse in her lap, crossing her long legs beneath the peasant skirt. She leaned forward and tapped her cigarette against the ashtray on Grober's desk. Her fingernails were long and sharp, painted the color of arterial blood.

Grober sat. "So. What can I do for you."

She inhaled on her cigarette. "I'd like you to locate a man for me."

Grober said, smiling again, "You have a particular man in mind?"

She smiled at him, briefly, bleakly. "Under different circumstances, Mr. Grober, I'm sure I'd find your puckish sense of humor infinitely entertaining. But at the moment, as it happens, I'm in something of a hurry. So suppose we just take my amusement as given, shall we, and dispense with the wit. Yes, a particular man. His name is Hubbard Baylor. Shall I spell that for you?"

A very major pain in the neck, it looked like; but business had been slow lately. Grober picked up his Erasermate. "Two b's in Hubbard?"

She nodded; Grober wrote the name down on his legal pad. He said, "Last known address?"

She gave it, an expensive subdivision on Sante Fe's west side.

"Description?"

"I've a photograph." She rummaged through her purse, found the photograph, held it out. Grober stood up and reached across the desk. "That was taken last week," she said.

It showed two people standing at poolside, arms around each other's waists, both smiling at the camera: Winnifred Gail in a bikini that could fit into an egg cup, and a tall, extravagantly muscled man in a brief swimsuit that could fit into another. His blond hair was artfully tousled, his grin was crowded with shiny teeth, and his heavy jaw looked strong enough to plow a furrow across the state of Indiana.

"He keeps in shape," Grober frowned.

"He works out with weights."

"Swell."

"I should warn you," she said, "that he can be rather a violent man. I've seen him fly into a rage over virtually nothing."

Grober reminded himself to load the Baur. If it came to rage- time, a few .25 slugs in the pecs might slow this bozo down a bit. "Why is it you want to locate him, Ms. Gail?"

Her lips compressed. "I'm not entirely sure," she said, "that that's any of your business." She leaned forward and stabbed her cigarette out in Grober's ashtray.

Grober sighed. "Ms. Gail, I've got a license to think about here. If I'm going to run a trace on somebody, I've got to have a reason, or I could be open to a charge of violating his privacy."

"He stole something from me," she said simply.

"What?"

"A particular piece of art."

"Bigger than a breadbox? Look, you probably want it back, whatever it is. And unless you give me some idea what we're talking about, I could be tripping over the thing all day and never know it."

"I don't want you to approach Hubbard," she said. "Not at all. If you find him, I want you to report to me immediately."

"I don't have any problems with that." He glanced down at the photograph on his desk. The man's bicep was a shade larger than Grober's thigh. "But I'd still like to know what he took."

She frowned. "You're an awfully inquisitive man, Mr. Grober."

"Yeah. In a private detective, that's what you call a selling point."

Her eyes narrowed for a moment, considering; then she said, "Do you know anything about Hopi art?"

"I used to," he said. "But it's all slipped away. Why don't you refresh my memory."

"At the moment," she said, "Hopi art is selling extraordinarily well. Not so much the modern stuff, although that's not doing badly, but the antiquities, pottery and ceremonial objects from Awatovi, the ancestral Hopi city. Three months ago an Awatovi bowl sold in Munich for forty thousand dollars."

"Wait a minute," Grober said. "One bowl? Forty thousand dollars?"

She smiled, amused. "These pieces are appreciating now at an annual rate of over fifty percent, Mr. Grober. They're an excellent investment opportunity."

"Uh-huh. I guess I better tell my broker to dump the AT&T. Okay, so he stole one of these bowls?"

She shook her head. "A *talaotsumsime.*"

"Oh. Right. And what would that be?"

"A small stick figure, carved from cottonwood root. It represents one of the Hopi deities, and dates back to the thirteenth century."

"And what's it worth?"

"I'd been offered thirty thousand."

Grober nodded. Forty thousand for a bowl, why not thirty thousand for a bundle of sticks. Clearly, he was in the wrong business. "Did you go to the cops?"

"No."

"How come?"

"For one thing, the provenance of the piece, the history of ownership, is ... well, I suppose you could call it a trifle murky. The piece is quite genuine—I've had it authenticated—and, naturally, the manner in which I obtained it was perfectly legitimate. But there appear to be a few niggling questions about the manner in which it was originally obtained."

"It's hot, you mean."

"No. I do not mean."

"Warm?"

"I said, merely, that a few questions existed, nothing important, certainly nothing illegal. But there's been quite a lot of controversy recently about the market in Hopi ceremonials. I thought it best to move with discretion in my purchase of the piece, and in the arrangements for subsequent sale. Except for the man from whom I bought it, the man who appraised it, and the client to whom I promised it, only Hubbard knew I had it in my possession."

"And you want to keep it that way."

"Exactly."

"You're sure Baylor stole it?"

"I'm positive. Two days ago. Monday night."

"And he disappeared right afterward?"

"Yes. I tried calling him at his house, but there was no answer. When I drove over, his car was gone. I've made enquiries, discreetly, but no one seems to know where he's gone."

"Could he sell the thing?"

"Certainly. But Hubbard's a collector, it's more likely he plans to keep it. He's independently wealthy, and hardly needs the money he'd obtain."

"You don't have any idea where he could be?"

"None. But he does have a friend in Coreyville, a woman. An old flame of sorts, apparently. They keep in touch, Hubbard told me, and she might know."

"Name and address?"

"Bonnie Little. She runs a restaurant there, I understand, on Main Street." She smiled. "It's called Little's Vittles, if you can believe that. She lives above it."

"Why not just call her up and ask her where he is?"

"If Hubbard has spoken to her, I'm sure he's told her not to discuss anything about him with me."

Grober nodded.

"Incidentally," she said, "I think it would be wise not to mention to the Little woman that you're a private investigator. I don't know how Hubbard would react if he learned of it. Perhaps with violence, perhaps by hiding himself still more deeply. You might tell her that you're an old friend of his—he has a host of colorful characters in his background. You could use that photograph to establish your bona fides, so to speak."

Grober nodded absently; he was trying to picture himself as a colorful character.

"Is there anything else you need to know?" she asked him.

"A few more things," he said. "But first, I'm a little curious about why you didn't go to a Santa Fe P.I. Why come down here to me?"

She smiled. "Santa Fe's a small town, Mr. Grober. I'd rather no one there learned that Hubbard has done this to me. A matter of pride, more than anything else."

Grober nodded.

He opened the bottom desk drawer and reached in for a contract. He always had the clients sign a contract; it didn't necessarily keep them, or him, honest; but it kept everyone more or less legal.

She said, "I imagine you'll want a retainer of some sort. What would be reasonable?"

Taking a chance, Grober added fifty dollars to his daily rate, one hundred, and doubled it.

She agreed.

A mining town until its coal seam dwindled away, a ghost town for forty years afterward, Coreyville had become an artists' colony in the early seventies when a group of sculptors and weavers and painters had purchased land at cut-rate prices. Since then, speculators had moved in, and now, if you wanted to describe yourself as a Coreyville artist, you could pay thirty- five thousand dollars for a clapboard house with no plumbing that had, at the turn of the century, cost three dollars and fifty cents. And wasn't, in Grober's opinion, worth that much then or now.

It was an ugly town, locked between drab conical hills spotted with drab conical junipers. The frame houses, all huddled tightly together, still seemed coated with coal dust and soot.

Signs of progress, however, were available. There were boutiques that displayed Navaho pottery crafted by artisans from Newark, New Jersey, who had read extensively about the Navahos. There was a Wild West saloon that offered Japanese beer. There were eateries that supplied food—*quiche, sushi, pasta al pesto*—that would have made the long-departed miners scratch their heads, at prices that would have made them roll in merriment across the quaint hardwood floors.

Little's Vittles was such a place. A small room, low- ceilinged, it held about ten tables, atop each of which was a white tablecloth and an unlit candle in a red glass bowl. Only three of the tables were occupied when Grober arrived at one thirty that afternoon. He chose the first table by the door, sat down, and examined the menu.

The woman who came to take his order was in her mid-twenties, petite, fine-boned, and wore straight blonde hair down past her shoulders. She also wore a plaid cotton shirt, big denim overalls, a plain white apron, and workboots. Grober was not favorably impressed; in his opinion, bib overalls should be worn only by people named Elmer.

Using his cowboy accent—he was, after all, working undercover—he ordered the teriyaki burger. (Six ninety-five, but it came with organic french fries.) When he finished eating, and the woman returned with his check, he said to her, "'Scuse me, ma'am, but your name wouldn't be Bonnie Little, now would it?"

She smiled the way people do when a stranger knows their name, with a blend of puzzlement and pleasure. "Yes. But how ..."

Grober grinned. "Friend of mine up to Santa Fe, Hubbard Baylor, he told me if I ever passed through Coreyville, I ought to stop by, grab some grub, and look you up."

The puzzlement vanished from the smile, leaving only the pleasure. "Do you know Hubbard well?"

"Shoot yes, ma'am. Hub and I go back to the Flood."

The puzzlement returned, her eyebrows knitting. "Hub?"

Grober chuckled uneasily. "Well, yeah, that's what we used to call him down at the gym. Didn't ole Hub never tell you?"

She shook her head, smiling again. "And your name is ..."

"Billy Bob Gibson, ma'am. No relation to Hoot." Chuckling genially now, Grober stood. "Right pleased to meet you."

"I'm pleased to meet *you*, Mr. Gibson." She offered her hand.

"Billy Bob," said Grober expansively, warming to his role. "*Billy Bob.* Don't nobody call me Mr. Gibson, although there's a few owlhoots call me a hell of a lot worse. 'Scuse my language now."

She laughed. "Are you in Coreyville on business, Billy Bob?"

"Nope, thing of it is, I'm on my way to Albuquerque to take a look-see at a passel of fillies for sale down there. Thought I'd stop in, give me hellos. Say now, come to think, you heard anything from ole Hub lately? He plumb dropped outta sight."

She frowned. "But ..." Her frown deepened.

Grober laughed, knowing that somehow he'd made a mistake, trying to bury it beneath a flood of heartiness. "Now ain't that just like ole Hub?"

She was frowning still, looking at him uncertainly. "Are you sure," she said, "that you're a friend of Hubbard's?"

"Well, course I am, ma'am. Lemme show you." Grateful for the opportunity to establish his bona fides, he tugged his wallet from his back pocket, took from it the photograph given him by Winnifred Gail, handed it to her. "Snapped that last week out to my place. That Hub, he takes a good picture, now don't he?"

"Last week," she said, looking up.

"Yep. Gave a little barbecue, had a few folks over. Roasted an ox."

She frowned again, quickly, sharply, and handed back the photograph. She said, "I'm sorry, Mr. Gibson, but I can't help you."

"How's that?" he said, sliding the wallet into his pocket.

"I don't know where Hubbard is."

She was distant now, and cold, and Grober didn't know why.

"Well now," he began.

"I'm sorry," she snapped. "I can't help you. Your bill comes to seven fifty, Mr. Gibson. Will that be cash or charge?"

Time to bail out. "Cash, I reckon."

Grober walked down to the lot where he'd parked the Pinto, got into it, started it, and drove it slowly back toward the restaurant. He parked across the street—in the shade, where, from the restaurant, she would be unlikely to see him inside the car.

Something had put a burr under her saddle. (Remnants of Billy Bob were still coloring Grober's thought.) What had it been? The picture? But she'd been suspicious, closing up, even before she saw it.

He reached over, popped open the glove compartment, took out the pint of V.O., uncapped it, and had himself a hit. He settled back and began to wait. A car passed him, heading south, toward Albuquerque.

At three o'clock, after the restaurant's last customers had left, Bonnie Little hung a CLOSED sign on the window, then crossed the room and disappeared behind the swinging doors that led to the kitchen.

Time passed, and with it some more cars, most of them heading north, toward Santa Fe. Up the street, a motorcyclist in a leather jacket and a white helmet emerged from an alley, climbed aboard a big multi-cylindered Honda, revved it up, and set off for Albuquerque, racing past Grober with a roar.

Idiot, Grober thought. He lifted the bottle of V.O., stopped himself ... something about the motorcyclist.

Damn. It had been a woman. And bulky jeans, leather workboots. Bonnie Little?

He pulled himself from the car, stalked across the street, pounded at the restaurant's door.

The Hispanic cook, when he finally came, told Grober that Bonnie Little had just left, on her motorcycle.

Grober walked back to the car. He had blown it—she must have spotted him. And there was no way the Pinto could catch up to her machine. The only thing he could do now was wait.

Grober got a big kick out of Cyril Draper. Cyril was something called an amateur sleuth, and he was forever going on vacations to tiny English villages where, between sets of tennis and bridge, he invariably stumbled into a murder investigation. His current investigation concerned the mysterious death (cyanide, bonbons) of Lord Harcourt of Lower Rumple. Cyril had just gathered all the suspects together in the Harcourts' library—Colonel Pottering; Dr. Llewelyn, the vicar; Gwendolyn Montrose; Teddy Semple-Smythe; Naomi Withers (Grober's bet); and Lady Harcourt herself—when the sleek silver Porsche pulled up in front of Bonnie Little's restaurant.

Grober set aside the book (*Death Gets Knocked Up at Nine*) and watched. It was now six o'clock.

Hubbard Baylor stepped from the car. Wearing running shoes, tan slacks, and a white shirt with a little alligator over the heart, he moved smoothly on the balls of his feet, broad shoulders back, lean hips thrust forward, and Grober decided that he, personally, wouldn't want to go up against the man with anything less than a battle cruiser.

Baylor tried the restaurant's door, found it locked, and with no hesitation, reached into his pocket and pulled out a key.

Interesting, Grober thought.

Baylor walked across to the swinging doors, pushed his way through them. Five minutes passed. Then Baylor reappeared through the doors, recrossed the room, left the restaurant, and padded back to the Porsche. He started it and drove off, heading north.

Grober gave him a few seconds' head start, then followed. Hoping that Baylor kept the Porsche within the United States government's speed limit, which also happened to be the Pinto's.

Baylor did, and Grober followed him all the way into Santa Fe.

Baylor certainly wasn't acting like someone who had disappeared. First, he had a lavish dinner, alone, at the Sheraton on St. Francis Drive (Grober had salsa and chips and a couple of V.O. sodas at the bar). Then he drove to Victor's, on San Francisco, and savored one brandy, and then another (while Grober nursed two more V.O. sodas).

Grober was beginning to worry about the man's spotting him, so when Baylor drove to the Purple Hogan, Grober crept around to the empty alleyway in the back, and maintained surveillance through the small window that gave him a good view of the entire room. And it was here, at approximately one o'clock, that someone slammed him over the head with a locomotive.

"Well," said Danny, grudgingly, "your polygraph checks out." Because a police officer's brother was involved, the Department had used an outside polygraph expert, not their own, to verify Grober's story. "And Miss Gail should be here any minute."

"What about the Pinto and the gun?" Grober asked. "You lift any prints?" His head was pounding. He had just returned to Danny's office after spending two hours with Sergeant Munsen in the interrogation room.

Danny shook his head. "Both wiped clean."

"That makes sense. I shoot someone in my own car, with my own gun, and then wipe off the prints. The criminal mastermind at work."

Danny shook his head, sat back, stared up at the ceiling. "Jeez, Phil, how could you do this to me?"

"*You?*"

"Do you know how this is going to look on my record? My own brother, a suspect in a murder case. And not just any murder case. No. It turns out that we've been keeping an eye on this Baylor for the past two months. Hernandez, over in Narcotics, just spent ten minutes jumping on my tail."

"Yeah, my heart really bleeds for you and Hernandez. My troubles are zip compared to yours. I mean, hey, what's a little concussion, right? In another month or two I'll probably be able to eat solid food."

"The doctor that Munsen called in says you don't have a concussion."

"Yeah, well," said Grober, probing the lump on his skull with tentative fingers, "I'd like a second opinion."

"I've got a second opinion," Danny said. "You're a jerk."

Grober nodded. "For this, I used to stop the neighborhood bully from beating up on you when we were kids."

"Phil, when we were kids, you *were* the neighborhood bully."

Grober ignored that. "Narcotics, huh? What kind of drugs are we talking?"

"Coke."

"Yeah? So what was the deal?"

Danny made a sour face.

"Come on, Danny. I'm in this movie, too, remember."

Danny frowned. "The story was that Baylor had connections to some bigtime buyers down in Albuquerque. He was supposed to be there on a meet yesterday."

"If Narcotics was keeping an eye on him, then how come ..." Grober paused, and then suddenly he laughed. "They lost him, didn't they? They tailed him to Albuquerque and then they lost him."

"He pulled a U-turn at an intersection downtown. He must've spotted them."

Grober laughed again. "That restaurant down in Coreyville. Did they know about that?"

Danny nodded. "They had a man there. The cook. But no one thought of getting in touch with him, and he was under orders not to break cover."

"That's really terrific teamwork there, Danny."

Danny grunted. "It was Hernandez, not me."

"What about Baylor's car? The Porsche? You found that yet?"

"It was still in the lot at the Purple Hogan. A forensics crew just finished tearing it apart. Clean, no coke. Hernandez thinks whoever killed Baylor ripped it off. If it ever existed."

"Some dealer killed him?" Grober shook his head. "No. It was that woman down in Coreyville. Bonnie Little."

Danny looked at him.

"First of all," said Grober, "how would a dealer know that I had any connection to Baylor? Why would he sap me in the alley?"

"Why would Little?"

"She knew I was hanging around, looking for him, and she wanted to get to him without me seeing her."

"How'd she know you were in the alley?"

"She recognized my car in the lot. She must've made me when I was in the Pinto watching her restaurant. She saw the car, and knew I had to be hanging around somewhere. Maybe she looked inside for me first. Maybe she was coming into the alley to use that window, the way I did."

"Uh-huh. And how did she know that Baylor would be at the Purple Hogan?"

"Maybe they'd arranged to meet there, earlier. Besides, a guy like Baylor, rich, how many places would he go to in Santa Fe? Three, maybe? Four? All she had to do was drive around, check them out until she found the Porsche."

"Assuming she knew he was in Santa Fe at all."

"Obviously, she did."

"Oh yeah. Obviously. Tell me this, Phil. Why'd she steal the Pinto?"

"She went through my pockets, she found my gun. She decided to dust him. She drives a motorcycle, Danny. That's not the best thing to use if you want to blow someone away in private."

"Why'd she go through your pockets?"

"How do I know? You're the cop, you find out. Danny, she's the only person involved in this who could've known that the keys in my pocket fit the Pinto."

Danny shook his head in mock admiration. "Amazing, Phil. I really don't know how the Department gets along without your help. Have you worked out a motive yet? I'd be real honored if you'd share it with me."

"There's gotta be one."

Danny nodded. "Yeah, generally. So suppose you tell me why Bonnie Little shot Hubbard Baylor, when the two of them got married just a week ago."

"They got *what*?"

"Married."

As Grober was assimilating this, someone knocked at Danny's door.

"Come in," Danny called out.

A woman entered. She was somewhere between fifty and sixty years old, and somewhere between two hundred and three hundred pounds. She wore sandals, a lemon-yellow caftan, and a broad- brimmed flowered hat atop an explosion of bright red hair. She turned from Grober to Danny and said, "I'm supposed to see a Lieutenant Grober?"

Danny stood up. "Yes, ma'am?"

"I'm Winnifred Gail."

Danny looked at Grober. Grober closed his mouth, which had dropped open. He sighed and said, "It figures."

Winnifred Gail knocked back the shooter of fifteen-year-old bourbon in one gulp and then, sighing happily, plopped her heavy body back in her chair. "So you think it was Bonnie Little."

Sitting on the padded leather ottoman opposite her desk, a slab of three inch glass maybe eight feet wide, Grober sipped at his shot glass. "The police think so, too. Sergeant Munsen asked the sheriff's department to bring her in for questioning."

Winnifred Gail refilled her glass from the bottle standing on a copy of *Art Space* magazine. "Well," she said, "it doesn't really surprise me. She's an artist. Painter. She may run a restaurant, but she thinks of herself as an artist. And artists are all nuts." She turned slightly in the chair, indicated with her shot glass the painting that hung on the wall behind her; it looked, to Grober, like two whoopee cushions mating. "That thing. Man who did it nearly killed his girlfriend last year. She started to hum while he was working, and he went bonkers. Tried to strangle her with his jump rope." She shook her head. "Lunatics, the whole bunch."

"Yeah, but why would Little kill Baylor?"

She shrugged. "Bonnie was the jealous type, I'd heard. Maybe *she* heard he was playing around."

"Was he?"

She shook her head. "Don't think so. He used to. Used to be famous for it. Different sweetie every month, and usually a little something on the side. But the way I hear it, he straightened up after he got involved with Bonnie. Went real domestic. They took turns staying at each other's place, and they were building a house down in Cerillos, between here and Coreyville. Hubbard just put his own house up for sale last week."

"What did he do, Baylor?"

"Do? For a living? Nothing. He didn't have to. Wealthy family, trust fund. If you asked him, he'd tell you he was in investments. Which was true, in a way—but they were all his daddy's."

"The police think he was dealing coke."

"Nah. Oh, he sold some now and then, but he gave away most of what he had. He never did it for the money, that's for sure. Didn't have to. Born with a silver spoon in his nose." She laughed, a short quick bark.

"Sounds like you knew him pretty well."

She shrugged. "I sell Indian artifacts. We've done business together, Hubbard and I. He was a collector. So was Bonnie—sold her a few pieces when she first came to town, a year ago. Their collections, that's what first brought them together. That, and their money."

"Money?" said Grober, surprised. "You mean Little's got money, too?"

"Sure. Another trust fund baby."

"Then how come she runs a restaurant? How come she goes around dressed like Walter Brennan?"

"Some rich folks are just plain embarrassed by their cash. Bonnie paints, she runs the restaurant, she does charity work. The money's not supposed to matter." She grinned. "Course, when it came to marrying, you'll notice she didn't pick herself a busboy."

"And you say she was the jealous type?"

"Yep."

"Who'd know about that?"

"Here in Santa Fe? Anyone. Everyone. This is a small town. Greenwich Village in the desert. Santa Fe produces four things—good art, bad art, good Mexican food, and dandy gossip. Everybody knows who's sleeping with whom, and who isn't, and why. Don't get me wrong. I wouldn't have it any other way." She barked again. "A girl's got to have *some* fun."

"It'd be my guess," Grober grinned, "that you get more than some."

She grinned back. "Buttering me up, huh? Good. Good technique." She eyed him speculatively. "Shame you're not twenty years younger."

Grober shrugged. "I didn't look any better then."

She barked. "It's not the looks, honey, it's the stamina."

"I gave up stamina when I was twelve. It was wearing me out."

Another bark. "Here. Have some more of this good bourbon. Build up your strength."

"Is that a threat?" Grober asked her as she refilled his glass.

She barked again. "Take it any way you want."

Grober decided that the safest thing to do was to ignore it. He said, "This woman who came to my office and said she was you. She told me that Baylor had stolen some piece of Hopi art from her. A *talot*-something. Made out of cottonwood root."

"A *talaotsumsime?*" Still another bark. "Pulling your leg, honey. There are only four of them in the whole world, and they were all stolen last year from Shungopavi—that's the shrine on the Hopi second mesa, in Arizona. No dealer in his right mind—no reputable dealer, anyway—would touch one of those. The FBI's been tracking them since last December. And I know a Hopi or two, right here in town, who'd be happy to cut your throat if he thought you had one. Hopis are generally a real peaceful people, but those things were used in a couple of their most important rituals, and they're irreplaceable, the rituals can't be performed without them. The Hopis are pretty disturbed."

"Would she have to be an art dealer to know about them?"

"Not here in Santa Fe. We're all experts here."

"Why do you figure she used your name?"

She shrugged. "If she wanted to run this Hopi scam on you, I'm the only game in town. There are only two well-known dealers of ancient Indian artifacts in Santa Fe, and she would've had a real hard time impersonating Sam Taylor. He's five feet tall and bald as a honeydew melon. About as smart, too. What'd this bimbo look like, anyway?"

Grober described her.

"Skinny, huh," she said. "Well, some are built for speed." She leered over her shot glass. "And some are built for comfort."

Grober decided to ignore that, as well. "Do you know her?"

She shook her head. "Don't think so. No one around here dresses like that. Except at Halloween."

"She talked," Grober said, "like she went to one of those women's colleges back east. Vassar, Bryn Mawr. Like she had a mouth full of marbles."

"Nope ... Oh. Of course. Of *course*. That *witch*. Wait, I think I've even got a picture."

She got up, walked to a file cabinet, pulled out a drawer. "Back issue of *Southwest Art*," she said. "I think, let me see, I think it was last December. Big opening over on Canyon Road. Here." She slipped out a magazine, opened it, riffled through the pages. "Hah. Score one for the large lady."

She came over to Grober and laid the opened magazine on his lap. "That her?"

Grober nodded. "That's her."

She was wearing black slacks and a grey silk blouse when she opened the heavy hardwood door. Her hair was shoulder length now, but Grober, having seen her photograph, was expecting that; she had worn a wig when she came to his office.

The moment she saw him, her face tightened and she reached out for the door again. Grober rammed his foot against its bottom.

"Hi," he said. "You come here often?"

Her upper lip curled back. "I could call the police."

Grober grinned. "That'll be swell."

She glared at him.

"It won't take long," he said. "I only want to fill in a few details."

Abruptly, wordlessly, she spun around and stalked down the hallway, her heels clicking on the red tiling. Grober followed her, pushing the door shut behind him.

She crossed the living room and stopped before the broad expanse of window, her back to Grober. She folded her arms beneath her breasts and looked down at the city of Santa Fe, the mountains far beyond turning pink now as the sun set.

It was an enormous room. A twelve foot high ceiling, supported by carefully oiled *vigas*, beams of straight pine log. Persian carpets, a long white sectional couch, leather chairs, a huge fieldstone fireplace.

"Verritt," Grober said. "Monica Verritt. That right?"

She said nothing.

"Did you hear the news?" Grober asked. "It was on the radio a while ago. Bonnie Little just confessed to shooting Hubbard Baylor."

She turned to face him. "What do you want?"

"Just a talk. Why don't you sit down."

Her eyes narrowed. "Blackmail. Is that it?" Suddenly her face relaxed; she laughed. "You sad, deluded little man. You haven't a prayer of getting a dime from me."

Grober shook his head. "No blackmail."

"I've done nothing wrong. I have absolutely no moral responsibility for what happened."

"Moral responsibility," Grober nodded. "Nice."

"And even if I had, whose word do you think the police will accept? *Mine*, or that of some fat, sleazy private detective?"

Grober sighed. "Sit down, lady, and shut up, so I can get this over and get out of here."

She sucked in a breath, let it out, then walked to the couch and sat down, her back rigid. "You have ten minutes."

"Terrific." He sat down opposite her in a leather chair. He said, "Six months ago, you and Hubbard Baylor were an item. Lot of people thought the two of you were going to make it permanent. So did you. But he dumped you, and after a while he took up with Bonnie Little. You didn't like that. You've got a pretty large idea of who you are—rich widow, patron of the arts, very hot stuff here in Santa Fe—and the idea of Baylor and Little didn't sit too good with you."

She leaned forward, opened a small mahogany box on the coffee table, removed from it a thin brown cigarette. "You appear," she said, "to have become a mine of information about me."

"I had a talk with Winnifred Gail. The real one."

She lit the cigarette, blew a cone of blue smoke toward the floor. "That absurd old hag. She's pathetic. She buys young boys, did you know that?"

Grober shrugged. "Not much point in buying old ones.

"Anyway, it didn't sit any better with you when Baylor and Little got married. You decided to do something about it."

With thumb and ring finger she plucked a tobacco flake from her lower lip. She smiled blandly. "Did I?"

"You came up with a plan. You couldn't use a local—everyone here in Santa Fe knows everyone else. And you needed an airhead, someone who didn't know what the deal was, someone who'd take in all the smoke you put out about Hopis and missing art. So you found me. You gave me that picture of you and Baylor, told me it was taken a week ago, told me I should use it to prove I was Baylor's friend. There was maybe a fifty- fifty chance I'd have to show it, but you figured that if I did, Little would go off the beam. You knew she was goofy with jealousy."

"There's virtually no way I could have anticipated what happened."

"Yeah. When you toss a spanner into a diesel engine, you never know what's gonna go first. And here's some other stuff you couldn't know. I talked to the cops before I came here. Little clubbed me over the head outside the Purple Hogan. When she was looking for the picture you gave me—she wanted to throw it in his face, she says—she found my gun. She took it along. To scare him into telling the truth. She also took my car—she didn't want to talk to him in the Porsche. That was his territory, she says. Sounds loopy to me, but I don't think she had all her oars in the water right then."

Grober crossed his legs. "Anyway, Little picked him up and drove him a few blocks away, showed him the photograph, pulled out the gun. Baylor denied having anything to do with you. But here's the cute part. It turns out that he *was* playing around, with some cutie down in Albuquerque. He went down there yesterday for a couple of hours of slap and tickle."

"The cops were following him at the time—they were looking for a cocaine bust. Baylor spotted the tail and lost it—he thought it was Little, or someone hired by Little, checking up on him. Pretty funny, huh? Everybody was running around in circles yesterday. Slapstick city."

Monica Verritt didn't smile. She said, "So you see he *was* unfaithful. He deserved to die."

"Maybe. He probably had a different opinion. But he didn't have all his oars in the water either, it looks like, because he told all this to Little while she was holding a gun on him. And she shot him."

Monica Verritt raised her cigarette, inhaled on it, and blew a languid plume of smoke toward Grober. "She's thoroughly insane. I warned Hubbard about her."

"Yeah," he said. "I bet you did."

She flicked the cigarette lightly against the ashtray. "Are you quite finished now?"

"Almost."

"Good. This has all been rather tedious."

"Nah," Grober said, shaking his head. "The tedious part doesn't start till we get to court."

She raised an eyebrow. "To court?"

"Sure. The cops got a confession from Little, so her lawyer, whoever he is, even if he's some total doofus hot out of law school, he's bound to shoot for temporary insanity. Since I'm the guy who set things in motion, I'll be subpoenaed to testify. And naturally, being under oath and all, I'll have to tell them about you."

She smiled. "They'll never believe you, you know. I have a certain standing in this community."

"Not then you won't. Not after the lawsuits."

She laughed, lightly, musically. "*Lawsuits?*"

"Mine and Winnifred Gail's. She's suing you for punitive damages because you used her name. It's not illegal to impersonate an art dealer." As Winnifred Gail had said, and barked with laughter, a lot of people did that in Santa Fe. "But it is illegal to impersonate a *particular* art dealer, or any particular business owner, and sign his name to a contract. It also leaves you open to civil suit. Section 55 of the Criminal Code, Article 3, Paragraph 405. I looked it up."

"How enterprising of you." She smiled, clearly entertained. "And you're suing me as well, are you?"

"Right. It was me you signed the contract with. For one week, at a hundred and fifty per diem. You paid an advance of three hundred, but never paid the balance."

She sat back, her smile widening. "So it *is* blackmail. Or a pitiful attempt at it."

Grober shook his head. "No. I don't want your money. I'd rather sue. That way, I can collect punitive damages, just like Winnifred Gail."

"Ah, but you seem to be forgetting something. How are you going to prove that I did any of this?"

"You're the one forgetting things. Your handwriting is on the contract. Your prints are all over my office. And remember that picture you gave me, of you and Hubbard Baylor? The cops have it now. Your prints are on that, too, and so are mine. All of it will come out at your trial."

"*My* trial?" Surprised, and no longer smiling.

"Right. The one for fraud and forgery. Winnifred Gail and I already went to the cops with all this. They're drawing up a warrant right now."

Once again she laughed, but now the music had drained away, leaving the laughter hollow and brittle. "You can't be serious."

Grober nodded. "Sure I can."

She leaned forward, carefully put out her cigarette. She looked up at him. "It'll never get to court."

Grober shrugged. "Maybe not. But maybe it will. And it'll definitely get to the newspapers. With that, and with the civil suits, mine and Winnifred Gail's, by the time Bonnie Little comes to trial, your swell standing in the community will be lying down, flat on its back. You know, I wouldn't really be surprised if she got an acquittal. Young artist, just married, jerked around by a nasty older woman. That's the way I'd go, if I were her lawyer."

Monica Verritt sat back, crossed her arms beneath her breasts. "Why?" she said. "Why are you doing this?"

Grober said, "Winnifred Gail's doing it because she doesn't like you.

Come right down to it, I don't think very many people do. I know I don't. You used me. *I* was the spanner." He shrugged. "Like you said in my office. It's a matter of pride."

Her lip curled. "*Pride.*"

"Yeah," he said. "There's a lot of it going around." He stood up, turned, and walked away, across the Persian carpet.

He had almost reached the front door when, behind him, at the end of the hallway, she shouted, calling him a particularly unpleasant name. He wheeled around in time to see the cigarette box come spinning toward his head. He ducked; it shattered against the door, thin brown cigarettes flying everywhere. He looked back at her.

She stood there, breathing heavily, arms limp at her sides. Then her face screwed up and she spat the name again. But more softly now, and with spite rather than fury, and the spite hopeless and empty, like a wounded child's.

"Right," Grober said. "See you in court." He opened the door and stepped into the night.

A Greek Game

(*Alfred Hitchcock's Mystery Magazine*, May 1985)

Living on the Greek island of Kos, I soon discovered that the African novel was falling apart. I had been too long away from Kenya. In a short story, you can fake details, or you can at least successfully imply them. In a novel, you can't. Ultimately, to fulfill the St. Martin's contract, I ended up writing the first Joshua Croft/Rita Mondragon novel, Wall of Glass. *(And I ended up liking the characters so well that I wrote another four books about them.)*

While I was on Kos, trying to figure out what to do, I wrote this story. The house in which Fallon lives in a more elegant version of the house in which I was living at the time; but the hill upon which it sits, and the dirt track leading up to it, were as I climbed them.

I appropriated the name Fallon, by the way, for a much later book of mine called Perfection, *about a serial killer who selects his victims on the basis of the junk food in their grocery carts. (Too much of it and they're potential victims.) The two Fallon characters are completely different, but I've always liked the name.*

TODAY, as he climbed up the steep sun-splashed dirt road to the house hidden in the grove of fig trees, the wind was so strong that he could almost lean against it, like a wall. Grey clumps of thyme shuddered in the fields; ripples of silver raced through the green of the gnarled wild olive on the ridge. With his canvas duffel bag slung over his left shoulder, his speargun in his right hand, he pressed himself against the swell of air, thrust himself through it, digging his sandals, muscles clenching, into the dusty white gravel skittering beneath.

Today's spearfishing had hardly been worth this effort. Or any other effort, for that matter.

He was, he realized, still annoyed. For the first time in two weeks he had been offered a shot at a fish, and he had blown it. He had flippered out to the big rock that stood alone seventy yards from the shingle beach, sucked a deep breath in through the snorkle, and dived, planning to circle its broad base at bottom level, forty feet from the surface.

He was running out of air, ribs beginning to clutch at his lungs, when, skimming above the sand, he rounded a spur of rock and saw the fish. A plump mullet, suspended a foot above the bottom, nuzzling and poking at the dull grey weeds that furred the rock. Excited and yet completely sure of himself—so sure that he tendered the usual silent apology—he raised the speargun and pulled the trigger. The gun bucked against his hand; ahead, a metallic muscular flurry, a billow of smoky sea-dust. And then nothing: only the irrevocable spear lying on the sand. Mocking.

Now, trudging up the hill, he smiled. Not the fish's fault, after all. His alone: overeager, he had fired too soon. And so now, my friend, he told himself, you pay the price. No fried fresh mullet for lunch today.

He looked up at the massive shoulder of white rock, jagged, speckled with thyme and sage, that rose behind the fig trees, soaring a hundred feet toward the bright blue cloudless sky. Perched halfway up it he saw (how the *hell* did they do it?) two goats, a beige and a black, tiny at this distance, and indistinct.

And then he saw, below them, parked alongside his Land Rover just this side of the fig trees, the police car.

Any car would have surprised him. His infrequent guests never arrived unannounced; and the road had been graded, intentionally, in such a way that only a four-wheel-drive vehicle was likely to make it to the top. But a police car?

He glanced quickly around. Police cars invariably made him uneasy. No one was in sight.

The car, he learned when he reached it, was empty. The gate to the fence was open, its padlock hanging on one of the wooden struts of the frame. When he left, the gate had been shut, the padlock locked on the hasp. He entered, closed the gate, walked along the flagstones to the front of the whitewashed house. No one beneath the portico. He circled round to the back.

A man, immensely fat, wearing a policeman's uniform, was sitting in one of the chairs under the almond tree on the patio. It was a cheap wooden director's chair, and it looked very frail now as it supported the man's bulk: at least two hundred and fifty pounds of it, probably closer to three.

The man's head was tipped forward, the brim of his cap covering his eyes. His thick arms were folded together above the broad swell of belly. Asleep?

No. Abruptly the man raised his head and, beneath dark black sunglasses, grinned with what was, apparently, huge delight. "Ah," he said, and in Greek: *"O kýrios Fallon, then eísteh?"* Mr. Fallon, are you not?

Fallon nodded. Once; warily. In polite Greek he said, "Yes. How may I help you?"

The man uncrossed his arms and pushed himself from the chair. It squealed, protesting. Grinning, he stepped around the coffee table and offered his hand.

Fallon shifted the speargun, took the hand.

"I am Nikos Mikalis," the fat man announced cheerfully, "the new chief of police for the town. Forgive me for intruding, but I presumed upon your hospitality and waited for you here. Your gate was open."

Fallon smiled pleasantly. "I must have forgotten to lock it." He knew he hadn't. A chief of police who picks locks and then brazenly lies about it: what have we here? "But you are, of course, welcome. I didn't know that Chief Daskalos was no longer with us."

The fat man frowned sadly. "Oh yes, it was very sudden. Four days ago. A family tragedy. His aunt, I believe. Or his cousin." He moved his hand in small vague circles in the air. "Who can say? We have so many relatives here in Greece."

"Welcome to the island, then," said Fallon. "And, as I said, to my house. And is your visit today professional, or social?"

Mikalis grinned again. "Ah wonderful! You Americans. So direct, so forthright. It is a quality I very much admire."

Fallon nodded, waiting, wishing he could see the man's eyes behind the dark glasses.

"Well," said Mikalis, "to match your admirable directness with my own, it has occurred to me that it is my obligation, now that I am here, to make the acquaintance of the residents of the town."

Fallon, who noted that the man had not, in fact, answered his question, said, "Very conscientious of you."

"Yes," agreed Mikalis happily, "I believe it is."

"And I'm very flattered that you chose to make mine so soon after you arrived."

"Oh, but Mr. Fallon, you are one of the earliest foreign residents of the island. You are *famous*, of course."

Fallon smiled. "I doubt that. Look, would you mind if I put these things away? It won't take long. And could I get you something? An ouzo? A coffee? Both?"

"Splendid!" said Mikalis. Two enthusiastic bushy eyebrows jumped up from behind the sunglasses. "Both, yes, absolutely."

Fallon nodded. Then, as he turned to leave, Mikalis said, "Are you a lucky man, Mr. Fallon?"

Fallon turned back. The very blandness of the question had itself been suggestive. "Pardon me?"

"With the fish," said Mikalis, grinning again, ingenuous, as he pointed at the speargun. "Did you have good luck today?"

"No," Fallon said. "Not today."

"Ah well, it doesn't matter." He waved a hand. "They slip away from time to time, but sooner or later we nab them, eh?" He grinned.

Fallon looked at him for a moment, and then said, "If we're lucky." He smiled.

As he busied himself in the kitchen, Fallon wondered what it was the fat man wanted. A bribe? But Fallon's papers were in order, his record on the island spotless.

So why the games? The picking of the padlock, those generalissimo sunglasses, that deliberately ambiguous remark about nabbing fish? Fallon, who had a certain unhappy familiarity with police procedure, and knew that it was, in some respects, similar throughout the world, had the uncomfortable feeling that he was being Mutt-and-Jeffed. With the fat man playing both roles, trying to get him off balance and keep him there.

Well. We shall see.

Onto a large silver tray Fallon loaded everything—the ouzo bottle and two empty glasses, the two tiny cups of Greek coffee, two glasses of water, two forks, some paper napkins, a plate holding sardines, black olives, slices of tomato and cheese—then carried the tray out to the patio.

Chief Mikalis, sitting once again, raised both hands in a gesture of surprised pleasure. "And *mezedes* as well! *Wonderful!*" He leaned slightly forward, confiding: "But I really shouldn't eat anything, you know. I've already had lunch." He patted his round stomach. "Someone told me, just yesterday, that I begin to resemble Orson Welles in the movie *A Touch of Evil.*"

In English, Fallon said, "You arrested him, of course." He placed the tray on the table, sat down opposite Mikalis.

Mikalis was looking at him, puzzled. "I'm sorry. I speak no English."

Fallon thought that unlikely, but repeated himself in Greek.

"No, no," said Mikalis. "It was my wife."

Fallon smiled. He opened the bottle of ouzo, poured some into each empty glass, handed one to Mikalis, took one himself. He raised his glass and Mikalis clinked his own against it. "*Styn yeia mas,*" Mikalis said. To our health.

"*Yeia mas,*" said Fallon.

Mikalis downed his ouzo in one gulp, gave a blissful sigh, and sat back. The chair, once again, squealed beneath him; he ignored it. He looked around him. "*Beautiful* grounds," he said expansively. "And such a house! I understand you built it yourself."

Fallon refilled Mikalis's glass. "With quite a lot of help."

Mikalis took a fork, stabbed at a sardine, and popped it between his teeth. He chewed, swallowed.

"You did a *splendid* job." He lifted the ouzo, tossed it off, sighed again. "Truly quite splendid. But tell me, isn't it true that foreigners are not permitted to own land here in Greece?"

"Of course," said Fallon, and sipped at his ouzo. "I'm only leasing."

"Ah yes," said Mikalis. "Yes, I believe I heard something of this. You lease the land from Dimitri Kostakis, who is also your partner in the nightclub, eh?" With his fork, he impaled a slice of tomato.

Fallon nodded. "You're well informed."

Chewing the tomato, Mikalis shrugged. "Part of the job, merely. Nothing." He leaned forward, aiming the prongs of the fork thoughtfully at Fallon. "Help me, however, to become more well informed. There is a story that one day, out on your boat, you saved the life of this Dimitri Kostakis. Is this true?"

"An exaggeration," Fallon told him, pouring more ouzo into Mikalis's glass.

"Oh no," said Mikalis, frowning. "Surely not. A sudden storm, was it not? Very violent. And Kostakis's caïque had capsized, and the poor man couldn't swim. But you came along and plucked him, yes, *plucked* him—" he speared a sardine and held it up, grinning merrily, "—from a fierce and hungry sea."

"I happened to be nearby," Fallon said. "Luck."

Mikalis ate the sardine, nodding, smiling. He swallowed. "Luck, yes. Very good luck. Excellent luck." He frowned. "As a matter of fact, the luck of Kostakis has been excellent since that day, eh? Soon after this lucky accident at sea he begins to buy land—this piece of property first, and then the piece by the beach, where the two of you built the nightclub." The dark sunglasses peered at Fallon. "Curious, is it not? Where do you suppose a poor fisherman like this could find so much money?"

"The fishing was good that year."

Mikalis smiled. "Without a boat?"

"I sold him mine. Later, when he resold it, he made a profit."

Mikalis smacked his forehead. "This foolish memory of mine, it betrays me every time. Yes, I had forgotten. He made a *splendid* profit, if I've been properly informed. He sold it to that drunken Englishman, did he not? Another friend of yours, as it happens, eh?"

"I know him."

"Of course, yes, now I recall." He lifted his ouzo, swallowed it all. Sighing, he put his elbows on the table and leaned toward Fallon. "Tell me, Mr. Fallon, merely to satisfy my curiosity, how much are you paying for the lease on this property?"

Fallon was certain the man already knew; the information was on public record. "Thirty drachmas a year." He refilled the fat man's glass once again.

Mikalis nodded. "And how much is that, approximately, in your currency?"

"Approximately twenty-five cents."

Mikalis nodded. "Quite a bargain, it would seem."

"You underestimate Dimitri's cunning," said Fallon. "The lease is for ninety years, and he knows I'll be dead before then."

Mikalis looked at him for a moment, then sat back and grinned. "And so here you are, Mr. Fallon, living on a picturesque Greek island, running a popular and lucrative night-club. What a life you lead. I envy you. Like Humphrey Bogart, eh, in the movie *Casablanca?*"

"Exactly," Fallon smiled. "Exactly like Humphrey Bogart."

Mikalis smiled, speared a piece of cheese. "Tell me," he said, "are you familiar with Kostakis's sister?"

"Anna? Yes, of course." Anna? Where was all this leading?

Mikalis chewed on the cheese, swallowed it. "And with her husband? The Turk?"

"Ali once worked for us, at the bar."

"Once?" Spearing another sardine. "No longer?"

"We had a disagreement." The boy had broken one of Fallon's, and Dimitri's, cardinal rules, had been selling drugs to tourists. Hashish, in small amounts only, and discreetly. But to the Greek government, there was no such thing as a small amount of hashish; the prison sentences handed down for drug possession were always long ones.

What had Ali done now?

Mikalis swallowed the sardine. "He was found this morning. Stabbed to death. We discovered, in his pocket, a piece of paper with your telephone number on it."

Far off, up the mountainside, the faint tinkle of a goat bell; nearby, the intoxicated humming of a bee. The wind had died when Fallon came over the ridge, rounded a huge upthrust fist of rock, and padded down a narrow path between yellow thistles. The path ran for a while now along the rim of a ravine choked with ragged boulders and thickets of oleander, the flowers small explosions of pink against the polished green of the leaves. Across the gully, a magpie shrieked and launched itself from a wild olive tree, its white wingtips flickering like flames as it wheeled and banked.

Not Mutt-and-Jeffed, Fallon thought. *Sandbagged.*

For a moment, after Mikalis had told him about Ali, Fallon had very nearly let his anger overwhelm him. He wanted it, perhaps needed it: a cleansing cathartic rage, at Ali's death, at the fat man's stupid games. He realized, immediately, that it would be a mistake.

He took a sip of ouzo, set down his glass, and said, "I'm surprised you didn't bring someone along with you, to take down my confession."

After swallowing a mouthful of cheese, Mikalis smiled. "Why? Did you kill him, Mr. Fallon?"

Fallon kept his voice steady and even. "No."

"Did you see him last night, or speak to him?"

"No."

"When was the last time you did see him?"

"Two weeks ago, maybe three. We passed on the street. We said hello."

"The two of you got along?"

"Well enough."

"He harbored no resentment toward you for this ... disagreement at the nightclub?"

"No." Fallon remembered Ali's face when he had told him. No resentment there, only puzzlement and hurt. Fallon had explained that the drugs endangered not only Ali himself, but his wife, his brother-in-law, the business. And Ali had nodded sadly, eyes averted, and said in his broken English, "Yes, boss, understand. Sorry, boss."

"And he did not telephone you last night?" Mikalis asked.

"I told you. No."

"Where were you, Mr. Fallon, between three and six o'clock this morning?"

"Here. Asleep. The bar closes at two. I got home a little before three."

"Can anyone corroborate this?"

"Would you like a note from my mother?"

"Mr. Fallon—"

"He was killed sometime between three and six?"

Mikalis frowned, as though it were not his role to answer questions. Then, at last, he shrugged. "There is no proper pathologist on the island. The doctor who examined him is guessing, merely, but I suspect he is correct. All the bars, like yours, close at two o'clock. By six o'clock, there are people up and about. His body was lying not far from main street. If he had been killed before three, or after six, I believe someone would have seen it happen."

Fallon nodded. "Has the weapon been found?"

"No," Mikalis said. He considered Fallon for a moment. "You were a policeman once yourself, is that not true, Mr. Fallon?"

Fallon said nothing, wondering how Mikalis had known.

"For eight years, I believe, in New York City. Then, some difficulties. Testimony before an investigating committee, innocent yourself but the star witness. Corruption in the police department, bribes, payoffs. Your fellow officers never quite forgave you, eh? Like Al Pacino, yes, in the movie *Serpico?*"

"Daskalos," Fallon said, suddenly realizing. "Daskalos had a file on me." It surprised him.

Mikalis shrugged. "Of course. This is a frontier island, only thirty miles from Turkey. You are a foreigner. He felt he needed to know. He had an associate in the American government. It took only a letter to him."

Mikalis lifted the ouzo bottle, poured some into his glass, some into Fallon's. He set down the bottle, clicked his glass against Fallon's, and tossed back the ouzo. He put the glass on the table and leaned forward, elbows on the arms of the chair. "As a former policeman, perhaps you can understand something. Whoever killed that boy was someone who knew how to use a knife. He stabbed him once, just below the rib cage and up into the heart. And he did this in what is now *my* town, on *my* island. Whoever he is, wherever he is, I am going to find him."

He poured more ouzo into his glass, returned the bottle to the table. "Now," he said. "Can you tell me why he would have your phone number?"

"No," Fallon said. "Have you talked with Anna or Dimitri?"

Mikalis nodded. "The boy telephoned Kostakis at one o'clock last night, asking for your number. He wouldn't explain why he wanted it."

"He could have come to the bar. Or called me there. He knew I stayed there until three."

"Presumably, what he wished to discuss was private."

Fallon frowned. "Have you talked to the people he worked with? I heard that he got a job on one of the boats."

Mikalis nodded. "A Turkish boat, yes, the *Yesmin*. I spoke with the other hands. Ali left the boat, they said, at twelve o'clock last night. He never returned."

"You've searched the boat?"

Mikalis smiled blandly. "For what?"

"The obvious," Fallon said. "Drugs."

"Ah," said Mikalis. "Drugs." He nodded. "I know, you see, about the cause of your 'disagreement' with the boy. And here is a boat registered in Turkey, from where hashish comes, and opium. Drugs were the first thing I considered. I telephoned to Rhodes, and had the harbor police there send up, on this morning's hydrofoil, one of their trained dogs. We searched the boat, the dog searched the boat. No drugs.

"Besides," he said, "the *Yesmin* has been out of the harbor only once in the past few weeks, yesterday, and for only two hours. They are getting her ready to sail to Amsterdam, where the owner is waiting for her. A Mr. Hadji."

"Amsterdam," Fallon said. It was the point, he knew, at which most hard drugs entered Europe by ship.

Mikalis smiled. "There are no drugs on the boat."

"Perhaps they plan to load the boat after they leave, on their way to Holland. Perhaps Ali learned about it."

"The boat," said Mikalis, "will of course be watched after it leaves port."

"And when will that be?"

"A day or two." He shrugged. "I have neither the authority nor the desire to hold her. I can establish no connection between the boat and the boy's death."

"This Hadji," Fallon said, "who is he?"

"A financier. Whatever that is. All I know is that he is rich, and that he is influential. Why all these questions about the boat?"

"You said that the boat went out into the harbor yesterday. Ali was killed last night. You don't find that suggestive?"

"Mr. Fallon," Mikalis said, "I can, if I wish, find *anything* suggestive. But in terms of actual facts, I have only a dead Turkish boy and a slip of paper with a telephone number on it. *Your* telephone number." He raised the ouzo, drank it off. He stood, reached into his shirt pocket, took out a pen and a piece of paper, scribbled something. He handed the paper to Fallon. "*My* telephone number, at home. Call me if you remember anything else."

And, without offering his hand, he had turned and waddled off through the shade, toward the gate and his car.

A nice exit, Fallon had thought.

And now, an hour later, gravel crunched beneath Fallon's sandals as he approached the ruined Doric temple. Small, no more than twenty feet long, it stood in the midst of a grove of cypresses, overlooking the sea on a rise of land jutting out from the mountainside. Two of its columns had been reassembled atop its uneven marble floor; segments of others lay nearby among the weeds and grasses and brown pine needles.

The Italian archaeologists who had begun excavating it in the early 1920's had never finished their work, probably because larger and more important sites had been unearthed on the other, more easily accessible, side of the island. It was still mentioned by one of the tourist books (in a nicely-phrased aside: "small temple of undetermined god"), but the only road approaching it was rutted dirt, poorly maintained. Fallon had never seen anyone else there. It was his favorite place on the island.

He sat down at midpoint on the marble floor in the full lotus position, spine erect, his back to the deep, distracting blue of the sea, and began *zazen*. After his wife's death, he had slowly become involved in Zen Buddhism, trying, he realized later, to fill up the emptiness that the loss of Megan had left within him.

Years ago, that had been, before he sold the restaurant he and Megan had opened and once run together. Before the boat, before the island.

He sat now in the center of a stillness, attending only to his breath. Time passed. Twenty minutes. Forty. At last, taking in a final deep lungful of air, he stood. He knew, without having thought about it consciously, exactly what he was going to do.

No blame, the I Ching would say. In one sense, no one is responsible for the life of another. But guilts, nevertheless, sometimes still remain.

"Yes, boss, understand. Sorry, boss ..."

When he returned to the house, he called Anna, offered condolences and any help she might need. He called Dimitri, and from him learned that the *Yesmin* had been moored in the harbor for a year, having left it only for an occasional day trip.

Then, in the storeroom, he checked his scuba tanks. The air pressure was down slightly, so he topped them off with the compressor. He carried them, and the duffel bag containing his mask, flippers, and weight belt, out to the Rover and stashed them in the back. He drove into town.

The *Yesmin* was moored in a slip not far from his own former boat, the *Meltemi*. He had seen her before, over the past year, without really noticing her. As he drove past, he looked her over.

A ketch, standard configuration, maybe forty-five feet long, white fiberglass hull, teak decking. Good lines, probably Swedish built. No one was topside.

He parked before the *Meltemi*, went aboard, asked Brian Leonard, the Englishman who eight years ago had bought her from him, via Dimitri, if he could have the use of the boat later that night. Brian, who preferred to sleep at the house of his mistress, a widow who owned a local taverna and kept him supplied with free Greek brandy, agreed.

Fallon drove to Le Cirque. It was a long night, tourists crowding the room until closing time, and he couldn't get away until two thirty.

A full moon hung overhead. On the deserted street fronting the harbor, the cafes and tavernas were locked; all the sidewalk tables and chairs, arranged in neat geometrical rows, were empty. From the bowline of the *Meltemi*, Fallon lowered himself into the water.

It was dark and not particularly clean. Diesel fuel filmed the surface, bits of refuse—an orange peel, a limp scrap of paper—bobbed and drifted. Still holding onto the line, he tested the regulator with two quick breaths. Then, letting go of the line, he dived.

Slowly, blindly, he went to the bottom, twenty-five feet down; his fingers jerked back instinctively as they sank into the ooze. He righted himself, then waited there, blinking behind the mask, letting his eyes adjust to the faint moonlight sifting down through the darkness. At last he could make out, directly overhead, the black silhouette of the *Meltemi's* hull against the silvered surface. Twelve hulls down lay the *Yesmin*.

He paddled off toward her, into the murk, his regulator hissing and gurgling as he inhaled and exhaled. Although it sounded preternaturally loud in the blackness, he knew it was inaudible above the water. More dangerous was the trail of bubbles in his wake. Anyone up there, awake and watching, could spot it.

He had paused beneath the fourth dark hull when, in the cloudy water off to his left, something moved. Something large, a ponderous, predatory shadow. He froze, and suddenly his heart was thumping against his ears.

Not a shark, he told himself. How many sharks have you seen in eight years? No, a grouper, or maybe a big mullet, magnified by the water, by the mask.

He waited, suspended in the water. He saw nothing. Whatever it had been, it was gone now.

He let out his breath and began swimming again.

Not a shark, he told himself. But the water seemed colder, more alien, than it had before.

Ten hulls ... eleven ... twelve.

He rose very slowly, keeping his breathing shallow to minimize the bubbles. Flippering up along the keel, he reached out and let his fingers trail against the cool, slick fiberglass. Now, in the filtered moonlight, he could see the white glow of the underhull.

And then a powerful hand clamped around his left ankle.

Without thinking, without even looking back, Fallon made a great twisting lunge, thrusting out with his right foot. He wrenched free, his left flipper gone.

Later he realized what had happened. One of the Turks, on guard topside, had seen the water roiling where Fallon's bubbles emerged, had at once known what they meant. Had quietly slipped into the water and come after him. Even without tanks, without a mask, he would have had no fear of the sea: Fallon knew of Turks and Greeks alike who could free-dive to a hundred feet, and stay there for a full minute.

Fallon raced headlong into the gloom, still not looking back. He thought he had made it, that he was clear, when suddenly the hand clutched at him again.

He whirled, bubbles boiling around him. *Knife*, he thought. *There has to be a knife.*

The Turk was only a vague dark shape against the grey, an impossible sea creature. Fallon kicked his left foot out toward the shadowy face. The Turk jerked back. Fallon ripped free the weight belt at his waist and, holding one end in his right hand, let it swing before him. Watching the Turk, he backed away.

The advantage was still Fallon's. His mask provided visibility, his tanks provided mobility. The other man couldn't stay under much longer.

When the Turk darted forward, right arm swinging toward him, Fallon saw the moonlit gleam of the knife blade as it slashed for his stomach. He whipped the weight belt at the knife hand, furious at how slowly he moved against the resistance of the water.

The Turk's move had been a feint; the blade slipped away from the belt, tore up toward Fallon's face, sliced past it. And sheared his air hose.

All at once Fallon's mouth was filled with water.

The Turk shot toward the surface to snatch another breath before he returned and finished Fallon off.

Quickly, knowing he had little time, Fallon unbuckled the scuba harness, shrugged out of it, then, holding the tanks above him like a weapon, kicked himself upward.

The Turk was still at the surface, and Fallon's tanks caught him just below the sternum. He doubled up around them, as though trying to fold them in an embrace. And then Fallon was up himself, face free of the water, lungs lurching for air as his left hand went for the knife and his right arm coiled around the Turk's neck, going for the chokehold. ...

"Neh?" Yes? The voice of Chief Mikalis.

"This is Fallon."

"Ah, Mr. Fallon! What a pleasure! I was just thinking of you."

"You sound very cheerful for five o'clock in the morning."

"Thank you. But you, I am afraid, do not."

"I'm using the public phone here in the square, and I can't stop this stupid shaking."

"Shaking? Whatever for?"

"Never mind. Listen, I have a gift for you."

"Indeed?"

"A Turkish deck hand."

"Yes?"

"Yes. Tied up, unconscious, on the *Meltemi.*"

"Ah."

"And I have a knife. It may be the same knife that killed Ali."

"Ah."

"He tried to use it on me. I swam out to the *Yesmin* tonight, to see if I could find something you people missed."

"Ah."

"*Ah?* Is that all you can say?"

"Well, to be perfectly frank, Mr. Fallon, I already knew about the Turk."

"You—wait a minute. You had someone watching the boat."

"Yes. I just finished speaking with him. He is stationed in a room above one of the cafes."

"... So he saw everything."

"Oh yes. Everything. Saw you arrive at the Englishman's boat with your underwater equipment, saw you enter the water. He was quite concerned there, for a moment, when the Turk went into the water after you, with the knife."

"Concerned."

"Quite, yes. But by the time he got down to the water, you were towing the man to the other boat."

In English, Fallon said, "You suckered me. You set me up."

"*Signómeh?*" Excuse me?

"You used me," Fallon said in Greek.

"Yes. Yes, I am afraid I did. The relationship between Greece and Turkey is, as you know, at the moment rather delicate. I could afford to bring only so much pressure to bear on the crew of that boat—we need no diplomatic incidents here. But it occurred to me that you, as an American, would have no such restraints. From what I had learned of you, you appeared the sort of person who would seek things out for himself. Yes, my friend, I confess that I did use you as a sort of, what is the word?, yes, *catalyst.*"

"The word is *pawn.* You realize that I nearly got myself killed?"

"Ah, yes, that is most regrettable. I am truly sorry. And truly surprised. I had not expected them to react with so much ... enthusiasm. They must be very frightened. I thought that if you ... ah ... *prodded* them in some way, they would merely make an attempt to frighten you off."

"They frightened me, all right."

"But even that, you see, would have been enough pretext for me to hold the boat while I continued the investigation. Now, of course, things have worked out splendidly. I have already dispatched a car to pick up the Turk. If you are willing to testify against him, we can bring a charge of attempted murder. The knife will be sent to Athens for examination. I have learned from the doctor that the blood of the boy, Ali, is of an unusual type. Perhaps we can establish that the knife was the murder weapon. Perhaps not. The important thing is that I can keep the boat here until I learn more."

"Keeping the boat is a very good idea."

"*Signómeh?*"

"That boat isn't the *Yesmin.*"

"I do not understand."

"The *Yesmin* has been here, in the water, for over a year. She would be ready for cleaning, in drydock. That boat in the harbor has been in the water no longer than a week. Her hull is brand new. No fouling, no barnacles, nothing. It's a duplicate. A copy. They switched boats when they took the *Yesmin* out the other day."

"... So you are telling me—"

"The keel. The drugs are built into the keel. That's why the dog couldn't smell them. And there are probably a lot of them, judging by all the time and effort required."

"Ah. Good. *Good.* Excellent, Mr. Fallon."

"I doubt that you'll be able to prove anything against the owner, Hadji. He can always claim he knew nothing about it. But you should be able to send the crewmen away for quite a while. And they're the ones responsible for Ali's death. Ali must have had second thoughts about being involved in something like this. The others suspected, and they killed him." Killed him before he could call Fallon and ask for his advice.

"Mr. Fallon," said Mikalis, "I am most grateful."

"Fine," said Fallon. "I'm going home."

Then, in a demonstration not only of fluent English, but also of considerable skill as a mimic, Mikalis said, "You know, Louis, this could be the beginning of a beautiful friendship." Bogart, to Claude Rains.

Despite himself, Fallon laughed. He said, "That's supposed to be *my* line." But Mikalis, with a mimic's sense of timing, had already hung up.

Connection Terminated

(*Alfred Hitchcock's Mystery Magazine*, January 1994)

So far as I know, this is the first story that ever used a "chat room" as the setting for a mystery. Rereading it, I get a huge kick out of the way technology has advanced. Back then, no one had heard of the Internet, or of broadband. A 900 baud modem was considered blindingly fast.

His tobacco and papers in his lap, Lizard rolled the wheelchair up to the computer console and stabbed his thumb at the power switch. As the monitor screen flickered to life and the computer snapped awake, disks clicking and whirring, he sat back and tugged open the sack of Bull Durham. Carefully, methodically, he built his three cigarettes of the evening: tapping the brown flakes along the crease in the delicate white paper, twirling the paper with practiced fingers, lightly dancing the tip of his tongue down the dainty strip of gum, gently twisting shut the ends. His hands, the skin rough and freckled with age, the ligaments ropy, were still strong and steady; he spilled no tobacco at all. With a sense of satisfaction that he knew was foolish, given the triviality of the achievement, but was nonetheless real, he placed each cigarette, one beside the other, next to the heavy crystal ashtray.

Finished, he leaned toward the keyboard and tapped out the word "com." He hit the ENTER key. The computer, clever little devil that it was, snared his communications program from the hard disk, slapped it into memory, dialed the database, logged on with his password and I.D. number. On the screen, a message announced: "Welcome, Lizard! You have E-Mail waiting. Go E-Mail? Y/N?"

He tapped at the Y key, hit ENTER.

There were two messages. He saw that one of them was from FANCY PANTS, and he smiled. The other was from someone who called himself GrungeBoy, a handle that Lizard had never seen before. Saving the best for last, he called up the message from GrungeBoy.

On the screen he saw:

MESSAGE TO: Lizard
FROM: GrungeBoy
They say around here you know everything there is to know about military history and stuff. Maybe you could help me? I'm doing a paper for my history class about the battle of Agincourt, in France. What's a good book you could recommend about this battle? Thanks for your trouble.

Reply to message? Y/N?

Lizard tapped Y, hit ENTER, composed his reply:
MESSAGE TO: GrungeBoy
FROM: Lizard
Nobody knows everything there is to know about anything, but many thanks for the fulsome flattery. Almost all the famous books about military history discuss Agincourt—you could try anything by Creasey or Liddle-Hart. But the best account, in my not-so-humble opinion, is given by John Keegan in "The Face of Battle." I hope that helps. Good luck with your paper. Let me know if I can do anything more.

He sent the message and then called up the electronic mail from FANCY PANTS. Reading it through, he smiled again, at the familiar upper-case characters, the familiar quirky punctuation, the familiar quirky exuberance. But by the time he reached the end, his smile had faded.

MESSAGE TO: LIZARD
FROM: FANCY PANTS
HEY THERE DOCTOR LIZARDO YOU NASTY OLD MAN!!! HOW YOU DOIN? HAVENT BEEN AROUND FOR AWHILE MYSELF BUT YOU NEVER NOTICED PROBABLY. WORK WORK WORK!!! JEEZE NO REST FOR THE WICKED HUH? YOU STILL HANGIN OUT IN ALBUQUERQUE??? WHEN YOU GONNA ROLL YOUR ANCIENT OLD BONES ONTO A AIRPLANE AND COME OUT AND VISIT ME IN LOST ANGELES LIKE YOU PROMISED??? OR MAYBE I CAN COME VISIT YOU!!! LOOKS LIKE THIS GIRLS GONNA COME INTO SOME SERIOUS MONEY SOON!!! WERE TALKIN BIG TIME!!! FOUND OUT THAT SOMEONE AT THE OFFICE WAS PULLING A REALLY TRICKY LITTLE SCAM AND THE TWO OF US HAD A TALK. WE DECIDED HE SHOULD SHARE THE WEALTH IF YOU KNOW WHAT I MEAN. MAYBE ILL GIT MYSELF A NEW MACHINE—A BIG 486 WITH A SUPERFAST 9600 MODEM!!!
WANNA TALK? BE ON TONIGHT—THIS IS TUESDAY—AROUND SEVEN YOUR TIME.

Frowning now, Lizard looked at his watch. Seven fifteen. He picked up a cigarette, stuck it between his lips. From the shotglass beside the ashtray he plucked a kitchen match. He scratched its head with his thumbnail and the match flared immediately—something that, normally, would have provided another small private satisfaction. But just now he was too distracted for private satisfactions.

He sucked smoke into his lungs, typed "Go CB," hit ENTER, and waited impatiently as the database shuttled him to the CB simulation. As soon as the screen prompt appeared, he typed in: "Locate FANCY PANTS."

"FANCY PANTS," the screen informed him "is in Living Room #9."

He typed: "Go LR9."

An instant later the screen was crowded with lines of dialogue scrolling upward, computer users all over the United States communicating with each other by modem along millions of miles of telephone lines:

Cosmic Cal:	I know Clint deserved SOME kind of award, I just don't think it should've been the Oscar. "Crying Game" was a 100% better movie.
StorminNorm:	"Howard's End" shoulda got it.
Esthete:	Who on earth watches movies anyway?
Zorro45:	Clint DID deserve it! He's been underestimated for years! "Josey Wales" was one of the best westerns ever, until "Unforgiven."
Irene Adler:	If you win for Best Director, you should win for Best Film—it only makes sense, no?
FANCY PANTS:	ESTHETE ARE YOU GONNA SIT THERE AND CLAIM YOU NEVER GO TO THE MOVIES?
Snoopy:	How come Rob Reiner didn't get a nomination?
Dylan:	I agree with Norman—"Howard's End" was the best film.
Esthete:	Never, FANCY PANTS. Movies are common.
Cosmic Cal:	Best western ever was "The Wild Bunch."
Irene Adler:	Maybe because people can't take a Meathead seriously, Snoopy.
Stormin Norm:	Yeah, Esthete sits at home and admires his wallpaper.
FANCY PANTS:	ESTHETE I THINK YOURE NOT LEVELING WITH US.
Zorro45:	Right on, Cal. "The Wild Bunch" was terrific.

Lizard typed in "Hello, folks," tapped the ENTER key, and watched his own handle, electronically provided by the database, appear at the bottom of the screen, followed by his message:

Lizard:	Hello, folks.
Irene Adler:	The best western ever was "High Noon."
Esthete:	I confess that I do like my wallpaper.
Irene Adler:	Hi there, Lizard! Hugs and kisses!
Cosmic Cal:	Hi, Lizard.
Snoopy:	But he's a dynamite director, Irene. I think "Princess Bride" was awesome. Yo, Lizard!
FANCY PANTS:	LIZARDO!!! HOW YOU DOIN SWEET THING?
StorminNorm:	Hey, Lizard.
Esthete:	"High Noon" was pretentious drivel.
Lizard:	FANCY PANTS, go private?
Dylan:	Hello, Lizard!
Zorro45:	'Lo, Lizard.
StorminNorm:	Esthete, I thought you never went to the movies.
FANCY PANTS:	SURE THING LIZARD. SEE YOU THERE. BYE ALL.
Cosmic Cal:	What do you suppose Lizard and FANCY do when they go private?
Irene Adler:	Bye, Lizard. Bye, FANCY. Esthete, how can ANYONE call Gary Cooper pretentious?
Esthete:	Years ago that was, before I knew better.

Lizard tapped some keys. The screen went momentarily blank and then, at its top, showed only the phrase FANCY PANTS:. Lizard watched as her message appeared.

FANCY PANTS:	LIZARD BABY LONG TIME NO SEE. YOURE WELL?
Lizard:	I'm fine, FANCY. But I'm a little concerned about you.
FANCY PANTS:	HOW SO LIZ?
Lizard:	Just what is it you're up to?
FANCY PANTS:	UP TO?
Lizard:	Don't go coy on me, woman.
FANCY PANTS:	OH YOU MEAN WHAT I SAID IN THE EMAIL MESSAGE.
Lizard:	What you said in the E-Mail message, yes. What's going on?
FANCY PANTS:	LIZARD YOURE NOT GONNA GO AND GET ALL MORALISTIC ON ME?

Lizard: Probably. Tell me about it.

FANCY PANTS: I CANT TELL YOU. I PROMISED.

Lizard: Promised whom?

FANCY PANTS: I LOVE IT WHEN YOU TALK CORRECT.

Lizard: Promised whom?

FANCY PANTS: THE GUY I TOLD YOU ABOUT.

Lizard: The guy running the scam?

FANCY PANTS: UH HUH.

Lizard: Look, woman, you wouldn't have sent me the message if you hadn't wanted to talk about this. Maybe you have a few moral qualms yourself, hmm?

FANCY PANTS: NO ONE LIKES A SMARTASS LIZARD.

Lizard: Talk to Daddy.

FANCY PANTS: YOURE NOT MY DADDY AND ITS NO BIG DEAL LIZARD. REALLY.

Lizard: Then why leave me the message? What kind of scam is this guy running?

FANCY PANTS: I PROMISED I WOULDN'T TALK.

Lizard: And what do you get in exchange for not talking?

FANCY PANTS: FREEDOM.

Lizard: Freedom?

FANCY PANTS: REAL FREEDOM. FOR THE FIRST TIME IN MY LIFE LIZARD ILL BE ABLE TO DO ALL THE THINGS IVE EVER DREAMED OF. TRAVEL. I CAN SEE ROME. IVE ALWAYS WANTED TO SEE ROME. I CAN BUY NICE CLOTHES. ILL BE ABLE TO STOP WORRYING ABOUT MY BILLS. ILL BE A WOMAN OF LEISURE. WERE TALKING ABOUT LIBERATION.

Lizard: From what you tell me, kiddo, it sounds like we're talking about blackmail.

FANCY PANTS: THATS A REALLY NASTY WORD LIZARD.

Lizard: Blackmail's a really nasty thing, FANCY.

FANCY PANTS: ITS NOT REALLY BLACKMAIL THOUGH. I MEAN I DIDNT ASK HIM FOR THE MONEY OR ANYTHING. I WENT TO HIM TO DISCUSS SOME DISCREPANCIES IN THE ACCOUNTS. HE INVITED ME TO LUNCH AND WE TALKED ABOUT IT. HES A CREEPY GUY—ONE OF THOSE JERKS WHO ALWAYS KNOW MORE THAN ANYONE ELSE. HE TRIED TO BE COOL ABOUT IT BUT I THINK HE WAS FURIOUS. BUT HE DID OFFER ME THE MONEY.

Lizard: I'll bet he did. How much money are we

FANCY PANTS: LIZARD WHAT DO YOU KNOW ABOUT ME?

Lizard: talking about? I only know what you've told me, FANCY.

FANCY PANTS: MOSTLY WHAT IVE TOLD YOU IS LIES. IM NOT 28—IM 38. I DONT LIVE IN A CUTE LITTLE ONE BEDROOM—I LIVE IN A FOURTH FLOOR WALK-UP STUDIO THAT HARDLY GIVES ME ROOM TO BREATHE. AND IM NOT PRETTY LIZARD—IM FAT. AND MOST OF ALL

Lizard: FANCY, you

FANCY PANTS: MOST OF ALL LIZARD IM NOT HAPPY AND IT SEEMS TO ME SOMETIMES THAT IVE NEVER BEEN HAPPY. NEVER ONCE IN MY LIFE. EVEN WHEN I WAS A CHILD I WAS ALWAYS FAT AND ALONE AND MISERABLE. ALWAYS ALONE AND WATCHING EVERYONE ELSE BE HAPPY. THE ONLY REAL FRIENDS

Lizard: Maybe other people aren't as happy as you think they are.

FANCY PANTS: IVE EVER HAD—EVER EVER EVER—ARE THE PEOPLE HERE ON THE DATABASE AND THATS BECAUSE THEY DONT REALLY KNOW ME. THEY CANT SEE WHAT A PIG I AM.

Lizard: Stop it, FANCY.

FANCY PANTS: SPEAKING OF PIGS. BOY YOU SHOULD SEE ME NOW. IM REALLY GORGEOUS. MASCARA ALL OVER THE PLACE. SOB SOB SOB. WHAT A PAIN I AM. SORRY LIZARD.

Lizard: FANCY?

Lizard: FANCY?

Lizard: FANCY?

Lizard abruptly realized that he had, without thinking, finished one cigarette, stubbed it away, and started another. Two cigarettes in less than an hour—way over the limit he permitted himself. He ground out the cigarette, then tapped at the keyboard.

Lizard: FANCY? Are you there?

FANCY PANTS: IM HERE.

Lizard: Good. I was afraid I'd lost you.

FANCY PANTS: NOT MUCH OF A LOSS.

Lizard: Would you stop that? Listen, kiddo, just from talking to you on the computer like this I can tell you're an all right person. More than all right. You're smart and funny and

FANCY PANTS: FAT.

Lizard: a whole lot better than you think you are. Most people are a whole lot better than they think they are. Except for the ones who are a whole lot worse, and you're not one of those.

FANCY PANTS: YEAH BECAUSE I COULDNT POSSIBLY BE ANY WORSE THAN I THINK I AM.

Lizard: Well, I'm pretty sure you couldn't be any more annoying.

FANCY PANTS: HAH HAH.

Lizard: Now, FANCY, listen to me. I honestly think that

FANCY PANTS: LIZARD YOU KNOW YOU REALLY ARE A WONDERFUL MAN. I REALLY MEAN IT. HERE I AM ROLLING AROUND IN SELF PITY AND YOURE STUCK IN THAT CRAPPY WHEELCHAIR ALL BY YOURSELF AND YOU STILL TAKE TIME TO HELP OUT A SLOPPY OLD FAT WOMAN. I THINK YOURE REALLY TERRIFIC.

Lizard: Yeah, yeah. I'm a prince. Listen to me. I think that, deep down, you don't want to be involved in this business. This blackmail. I think the idea bothers you, bothers some fundamental, important part of you. I think that if it didn't you wouldn't have left me that message. I think, kiddo, that you wanted me to talk you out of doing it.

Lizard: FANCY?

FANCY PANTS: IM HERE.

Lizard: What are you thinking?

FANCY PANTS: IM THINKING YOURE TOO DAMN SMART FOR YOUR OWN GOOD.

Lizard: One of the advantages of getting older. If you're lucky, you also get smarter.

FANCY PANTS: YOURE NOT ALL THAT OLD LIZARD. UNLESS YOUVE BEEN LYING TO ME LIKE IVE BEEN LYING TO YOU.

Lizard: No lies. I'm sixty-four. An old crippled psycho war vet.

FANCY PANTS: BUT A PRINCE.

Lizard: Well, there's that. FANCY, when did all this happen? Your lunch with this guy?

FANCY PANTS: TODAY.

Lizard: Is he running this scam all by himself or is there someone else involved?

FANCY PANTS: IM NOT SURE. I THINK MAYBE THERES SOMEONE ELSE.

Lizard: Is there anyone at the office you can go to with this? Someone you trust?

FANCY PANTS:	YEAH. PETER ALLBRIGHT. HES ONE OF THE GOOD GUYS I THINK.
Lizard:	And will you be going to him?
Lizard:	FANCY?
Lizard:	Oh, FANCY ... ?
FANCY PANTS:	DAMMIT. THERE GOES ROME.
Lizard:	We'll always have Paris, kid.
FANCY PANTS:	HAH HAH. WHOOPS. SOMEONE KNOCKING AT THE DOOR. WEIRD. HOLD ON LIZARD. BACK IN A FLASH.

Lizard sat back and discovered that he was exhausted. A droplet of sweat was tickling its way down his ribs. He felt as though he had been wrestling with the woman not figuratively but physically, flesh battling flesh, sinew struggling against sinew. But he felt relieved, too, and pleased with her for having made the right decision. And—let's face it, he told himself—he felt fairly pleased with the old Lizard as well. The gnarly White Knight rides to the rescue on his valiant two- wheeled steed.

Silly old man.

Still, a White Knight, gnarly or not, should get a reward now and then.

He lifted his last cigarette from the table, took it between his lips, struck the kitchen match against the table's underside, lit the cigarette.

Exhaling smoke, he looked up at the screen.

It looked back at him, the cursor blinking with a moronic metronomic relentlessness below her last message.

He glanced at his watch. Eight o'clock. An hour's difference in Los Angeles, so seven o'clock there.

Dinnertime. Strange time for a guest to call.

But maybe the guest had been invited?

No. The monitor screen still displayed the dialogue between the two of them, the last twenty-two lines of it. WEIRD, she'd said when she heard the knocking. She hadn't been expecting a guest.

Lizard sucked on the cigarette, set it in the ashtray, and, exhaling, leaned forward and tapped at the keyboard.

Lizard:	FANCY?

He waited.

No response.

She wouldn't be able to see the screen, of course, if she were away from the computer, talking to someone.

Someone who'd just stopped by to ask directions?
A fourth floor walk-up, she'd said. No one climbed up four flights of stairs to ask directions.
He tapped at the keyboard.

Lizard: FANCY? Are you there?
Lizard: FANCY?

He didn't want to think about it, didn't want to grant it recognition, but he knew that the awareness lurked somewhere back in a dim gray corner of his mind: there was one person, there was one man who might have come to see the woman. One man who might want to see her for a particular reason of his own.

HE TRIED TO BE COOL ABOUT IT BUT I THINK HE WAS FURIOUS.

Lizard could feel his heart knocking against his ribs. An old man's heart, thin and frail as it pounded in an old man's thin, frail chest. Lizard heart, Lizard chest.

Calm down.

His cigarette had burned away to ash.

He picked up the rolling papers, tore a sheet from the sheath, flipped the sheath to the table, fumbled open the pouch of Bull Durham. He shook tobacco onto the paper, spilling a few brown flakes along his lap. He slapped them away and then, quickly, he rolled the cigarette, scraped a match alight. Puffing, he squinted at the screen.

Lizard: FANCY?

It could be a neighbor. Stopping by to borrow something. A cup of sugar. A stick of butter.

He looked at his watch.

Seven minutes after eight. Seven minutes after seven, L.A. time.

And then:

FANCY PANTS: HELLO.

The message appeared so suddenly, lunging across the screen, that it startled him. Relief hissed between his teeth as he bent over the keyboard.

Lizard: Good Lord, woman, where were you? You had me worried there.

FANCY PANTS: SOMEONE AT THE DOOR. SHE HAD THE WRONG APARTMENT. IT'S ALL RIGHT.

Lizard stopped breathing.

IT'S ALL RIGHT.

IT'S.

Such a small thing, that apostrophe was. Smaller than a flea. An insignificant speck on a cathode ray tube, a few pixels, a tiny, fragile fleck of phosphor electronically illuminated, destined to disappear, forever vanish into the ether, as soon as the power drained away.

In all the time they had talked together on the database, all the hours they'd spent tapping away at each other late into the night, FANCY had never used an apostrophe. Never once.

Make certain, he told himself.

Lizard: You're sure?
FANCY PANTS: I'M SURE.

And so was Lizard. A chill emptiness settled in his chest.

FANCY was gone.

And miles away, in that small apartment somewhere in Los Angeles, a stranger was sitting at her keyboard.

A stranger who'd seen the dialogue on her monitor screen, and who'd known what it meant. Known that she'd been connected to Lizard.

What had he done to FANCY? Hurt her?

Something worse?

And what should Lizard do? What *could* he do?

All at once his mind seemed as ineffectual as his shrunken, shriveled legs. Immobilized, tangled in cobwebs, useless.

Think, you old fool.

FANCY PANTS: LIZARD?

Lizard took a deep breath, leaned toward the keyboard.

Lizard: Yes?
FANCY PANTS: CAT GOT YOUR TONGUE, LIZARD?

All at once Lizard was filled with a swift, shivering rage—at himself, at his own impotence, at this smug, self- possessed bastard sitting at FANCY'S computer, using FANCY'S name.

Lizard:	Put her on.
FANCY PANTS:	COME AGAIN?
Lizard:	Put her on. Now.
FANCY PANTS:	WHY, LIZARD, I HAVE NO IDEA WHAT YOU'RE TALKING ABOUT.

Mocking. *The sonofabitch was enjoying this.*

Lizard:	I know who you are.
FANCY PANTS:	WELL, OF COURSE YOU DO. I'M YOUR OLD FRIEND, FANCY PANTS.
Lizard:	Put her on, you schmuck.
FANCY PANTS:	MY, MY. SUCH LANGUAGE, LIZARD. YOU REALLY SHOULD BE ASHAMED OF YOURSELF.
Lizard:	I'll make a deal with you. Put her on and I won't go to the cops with what I know.
FANCY PANTS:	AND WHAT MIGHT THAT BE?
Lizard:	Everything. She told me everything.
FANCY PANTS:	I RATHER DOUBT THAT.
Lizard:	Put her on.
FANCY PANTS:	WELL, WE'VE GOT A BIT OF A PROBLEM THERE, LIZARD. SHE'S UNAVAILABLE AT THE MOMENT, YOU SEE. A TOUCH INDISPOSED.
Lizard:	Put her
FANCY PANTS:	SHE REALLY DOES WEAR FANCY PANTS, YOU KNOW. PINK, WITH A SORT OF FRILLY LACE ALONG THE HEM. PATHETIC, REALLY, UNDER THE CIRCUMSTANCES. YOU AGREE?

Lizard rapped at the EXIT key.

Exit Private Talk? Y/N?
Y
Exit CB simulation? Y/N?
N
Command?
Go User Index.
USER INDEX
Search by:

1. Handle
2. Last Name
3. City
4. State
5. Computer
6. Interests
Please enter a number.
1
1. Search by Handle. Handle?
FANCY PANTS

Handle:	FANCY PANTS
Name:	LESLIE D'AMICI
St. Address:	405 MACALLISTER, 4B
City:	LOS ANGELES
State:	CALIFORNIA
Zip:	90069
Hm. Phone:	1-310-555-7825
Age:	28
Sex:	FEMALE
Computer:	IBM/286
Interests:	COMPUTERS, FOOD, TRAVEL, FOOD, MOVIES, FOOD

Her name was Leslie.

He hadn't known that. He had never looked her up in the Index, never learned her real name. Without ever consciously thinking about it, he had believed that somehow this would be an intrusion, a violation of her privacy.

Leslie D'Amici.

And she was not twenty-eight, but thirty-eight.

If Lizard was right—and he knew that he was, and he hated the knowledge, almost hated himself for possessing it—she would never be thirty-nine.

Lizard tapped a key, and his printer briefly clattered as it copied, onto paper, the contents of the monitor screen. He tore free the sheet, hit the power switch. The screen went black. He scooped up the telephone receiver, dialed the number for Los Angeles information. The operator came on, her voice listless and bored, the voice of someone cocooned within the tedium of safety, untouched by danger or death. Lizard asked for the number of the L.A. police. The operator clicked off, and a recorded voice came on and gave him the number. He broke the connection, dialed it.

"Los Angeles Police Department." A male voice, as bored and listless as the operator's, but grown weary, this one, of danger and death, become inured to them.

Lie, cheat, steal, but get someone there. "I want to report a murder." Lizard realized that he was panting, as though he'd been running a marathon. Lizard hadn't run, hadn't walked, in over forty years.

"Sir, we show that you're calling long distance. Are you sure it's the Los Angeles police department you want?"

Caller I.D. Of course. An LCD display on the telephone itself, one that revealed the phone number of the person calling in. The police would want that new technology, would find it useful.

"I'm sure," Lizard snapped. "I want to report a murder in Los Angeles."

"Yes, sir. And your name, sir?" Bored, and plainly disbelieving. An idiot.

Lizard gave his name.

"And your address, sir?"

Lizard gave it.

"And who was murdered, sir?"

"A Miss Leslie D'Amici. Apartment 4B, 405 MacAllister. Phone number 555-7825."

"Yes, sir. And how do you know she was murdered, sir?" A dull, mechanical politeness. The typed messages on the computer's screen had seemed more alive.

"I was talking to her on the telephone. Five minutes ago."

"Yes, sir," said the voice. "And what happened, sir?"

"She was murdered is what happened, dammit."

"Yes, sir. Calm down now, sir. Did you hear gunfire, sir?"

"Yes, I did. Gunfire. Now would you please send someone over there?"

"Are you sure it wasn't the television, sir? Sometimes people make that mistake."

"I know what I heard, dammit."

"Yes, sir. Please calm down, sir. You were talking to her on the telephone and you heard gunfire. And then what happened, sir?"

"I hung up the phone. I called you."

"We have no reports of gunfire in that area, sir."

"I'm reporting it, right now."

"Yes, sir. From Albuquerque. Have you tried to call her back, sir?"

"I called *you*. Look, a woman's been murdered out there. Doesn't that mean anything to you?"

"We'll send a unit to investigate. Don't worry, sir. Thank you for calling." From the sound of his voice, the unit wouldn't be sent until sometime tomorrow. If then.

Lizard hung up, trembling once again with anger.

Moron. Imbecile.

But calling her on the telephone. He should at least try. Maybe it *was* all a mistake. Or maybe it was some elaborate, silly joke she was playing. And when he called, FANCY PANTS—Leslie—would answer. And he would bitch at her, testy for teasing an old man, and the two of them would have a fine great laugh about it.

He knew he was deluding himself, or trying to.

SHE REALLY DOES WEAR FANCY PANTS, YOU KNOW. PINK, WITH A SORT OF FRILLY LACE ALONG THE HEM. PATHETIC, REALLY, UNDER THE CIRCUMSTANCES.

It was no joke.

He dialed her number.

Busy.

The bastard was still on the phone, still hooked up to the database.

Or else he'd taken the phone off the hook.

Either way, if that idiot cop called her number, if he *bothered* to call her number, he'd hear the busy signal and assume that she was on the phone, alive.

What now?

Lizard switched the computer on, watched as it connected him once again to the database. Once again he moved to the CB simulator and, within it, to the User Index. He requested the names of all users in Los Angeles who were currently connected to the simulator.

Five Los Angeles users currently online:
Romeo 12
BroncoBilly
Catwoman
FourWheel
CapnKosmos
Command?
1. Send online message.
2. Send E-Mail.

Please enter a number.
1
Send online message to?
All.
Send online message to all. Message?

MESSAGE TO:	Romeo 12, BroncoBilly, Catwoman, FourWheel, CapnKosmos
FROM:	Lizard

This is an emergency. A database user in Los Angeles is in serious trouble. I need help. Please join me in private talk immediately.

Send as is? Y/N?
Y
Message sent.

Lizard tapped the keys that would send him to the Private Talk section of the database.

Lizard:	Hello.
Catwoman:	Hello, Lizard. What's the problem?
Romeo12:	Hi.
CapnKosmos:	Hi.
BroncoBilly:	What's up?
Lizard:	I was just online with a user named FANCY PANTS. I think she's been hurt. I've tried calling the police, but they won't buy
Romeo 12:	This some kind of joke?
Lizard:	my story. This isn't a joke—I'm absolutely serious. I need help. Someone in Los Angeles has to call them, or they won't do anything. Can one of you help me? FANCY'S real name is Leslie D'Amici. Her address is 405 MacAllister, apartment 4B. If one or more of you call and report hearing gunshots there, maybe the police'll move.
CapnKosmos:	It's against the law to report something like this to the cops if it isn't true. How could you hear gunshots if you were online with her?
BroncoBilly:	L.A.P.D. has caller I.D. They can identify anyone who calls.

Lizard:	CapnKosmos, I didn't actually hear gunshots. But someone's got to report SOMETHING.
FourWheel:	Sorry I'm late. I know about you, Lizard. Lizard is okay, folks. If he says it happened, it happened. I'll call right now.
Catwoman:	You're really serious, Lizard?
Lizard:	Completely serious. Thank you, FourWheel.
FourWheel:	Signing off.
BroncoBilly:	Too weird. You people are nuts. I'm outa here.
Catwoman:	Okay. I'll make a call.
Lizard:	Thank you.
Romeo 12:	I'll call too, Lizard.
Lizard:	Thank you, Romeo.
CapnKosmos:	This is my parents' phone, Lizard. Okay if I call from a booth somewhere?
Lizard:	Fine, Capn, thank you. I'm signing off now. The police may call me back. Leave E-Mail or call me on voice phone. My number's in the User Index.

He thought for a moment, then tapped some keys.

Exit CB simulator? Y/N?
N
Command?
Locate FANCY PANTS.
FANCY PANTS is currently off line. Command?

So the bastard had disconnected from the database and taken the phone from the hook.

Lizard exited from the simulator, logged off from the database, then switched off the machine.

The telephone rang, for the first time, half an hour later.

Lizard had rolled the wheelchair into the kitchen, lifted a bottle of Calvados from the cabinet, poured himself a balloon glass of the apple brandy, replaced the bottle, and rolled himself back into the living room, to the computer desk. Once again he had dialed the phone number of Leslie D'Amici. The line had still been busy.

He had sat there, drinking Calvados faster than Calvados should ever be drunk, barely tasting it, and he had waited. He had never been good at waiting. He tapped his fingers along the wheel of his chair, sipped the Calvados, and stared at the phone, willing it to ring.

When it did, sharp and sudden, it startled him.

He slapped the balloon glass to the desk. A dollop of pale brown liquid sloshed over the lip, spattered onto the desktop. He grabbed the phone.

"Hello?"

Nothing. No voice, no breathing, not even a faint crackle of static.

Again he said, "Hello."

Nothing.

As though no one were there.

But Lizard knew that someone *was* there, and he knew who that someone was.

He waited, hearing only the sound of his own breath. Distant, as though from another body, in another room.

And at last he heard, very faintly, a chuckle, low and slow and rattling. And then, in a whispered hiss that sent frost slithering down his spine: *"Cat got your tongue, Lizard?"*

Lizard used, emphatically, a word he never used.

The faint, low chuckle came again. And then: *"She's dead meat, old man. And so are you."*

"Come and get me," Lizard snarled.

Another chuckle, and then a click, and then a dial tone.

Lizard hung up the phone. Or tried to: it bounced from its cradle and off the desk, swinging like a hanged man on its tangled cord. Cursing, he snatched at the cord, yanked it in, slammed the phone onto the cradle.

His hands were shaking. He looked at them with mild surprise and a remote curiosity, as though those forlorn freckled lumps with their quivering fingers belonged to someone else. To some poor pitiable wretch, decrepit and feeble and terrified.

It wasn't anger now that caused the tremor. It was fear.

He had thought he had forgotten fear, battled it down, left it forever behind him. For a while it had been his entire world. During those endless hours he had spent lying in the freezing muck at the Reservoir, his spine and his life shattered, his mind gibbering away in the darkness and pain. During those endless nights in the hospital when he came screeching out of sleep, hurling himself away from the vile, faceless, slathering monsters who stalked his dreams, hunting him across a blasted landscape, through an eternity of night. In the dreams, he could still run. ...

He thought he had left it behind. And now here it was. An old acquaintance, despised in the past and only vaguely remembered now, yet looking after all those years exactly the same.

How had the bastard gotten his phone number?

The User Index.

His phone number, his address, his real name: they were all there, on the Index.

The bastard knew who he was. Knew *where* he was.

She's dead meat, old man.

Old man. Lizard's age was listed on the Index as well.

Come and get me.

Brave words, coming from an old man. A crippled, frightened, worthless old man.

And what if he did come?

The phone rang.

Lizard stared at it.

It rang and it rang, peremptory, its buzzer as shrill and sinister as a dentist's drill, and Lizard stared at it.

It's only a telephone. Pick it up, you stupid, gutless old man.

He reached forward, lifted the phone.

"Hello." His voice was thin and strained, as though a stranger's cold fingers were coiled around his neck. He coughed, clearing his throat.

"Is this Lizard?" A woman's voice, unfamiliar, and he felt a sudden rush of hope. FANCY?

"Yes," he said, deliberately keeping the hope from his voice, deliberately suppressing it. Magical thinking: hopes could be crushed.

"This is Karen Bartholomew. Catwoman—from the database? I, uh, I called the police, Lizard, and I gave them my number. They just called me back. They went there, some patrolmen did, to her apartment."

"Yes?" Not actually phrasing the question. More magic: as though by not asking it, he could alter the answer.

"She's dead, Lizard. I'm sorry."

Lizard took in a deep, shuddery breath. Let it slowly out.

"Lizard?"

And as easily as that, as easily as the breath left his lungs, she had left the world.

"Lizard?"

"Yes. Sorry."

"This is—nothing like this has ever happened to me before. Was she—did you know her?"

"Only from the database." Words scrolling up the face of a cathode ray tube. Words that over the long nights had created, had disclosed, a set of attitudes, a sensibility. A unique individual. A human being. Gone now, eternally, like the words that had revealed her.

"I should get off the phone. They're going to call you, Lizard. The police. I gave them your number. I got it off the database—I hope that was all right?"

"Yes, of course. They had it already—I gave it to them."

"But I wanted to let you know."

"I appreciate that, Karen. I do. Thank you."

"Call me if I can do anything. Or leave me a message on the database."

"I will. Thank you."

"Goodbye."

"Goodbye."

He hung up the phone, sat back.

He looked at the balloon glass. It was as empty as his heart.

More Calvados? No. He needed to stay alert. It would be a long night.

"Okay," said the brusque voice of Sergeant Bradley, "let me see if I get this. You were like talking to Miss D'Amici on this database thing. Fancy Pants, she called herself, you said. Why Fancy Pants? What's the idea there?"

"I don't really know, sergeant. It was the handle she chose."

"Handle? Like on a CB radio?"

"Exactly. The people on the simulator pick a handle. I couldn't tell you why she picked Fancy Pants."

"And your nickname was what?"

"Lizard." It sounded silly, childish in his ears. "I'm an old man, sergeant. One of my few pleasures is lying out in the back yard, in the sunshine. Hence the name."

"And what kind of work do you do? I need it for the report, see."

"I'm a freelance researcher."

"Uh-huh." Dismissive, perhaps even slightly contemptuous, as though Lizard had admitted to being a gigolo. If Lizard was to get information from the sergeant, he needed the man's respect.

"It's more a hobby than a career. Before I retired, I taught history at the University of New Mexico."

"A professor, like?"

"Precisely like." *Precisely* pronounced in his most professorial tone.

"And you go onto this database for what, exactly?"

"The database itself I use in my work, for information searches. The CB simulator I use as a form of relaxation, a way to talk to people all over the country. I'm not able to leave the house as often as I'd like."

"Why's that?"

"I'm handicapped, sergeant. I'm in a wheelchair." Pedally impaired, as he had mockingly described it to FANCY.

"Oh." And once again Lizard thought he heard in the man's voice that hint of dismissiveness.

A gimp. A crip.

And possibly the sergeant had heard it as well, for he added gruffly, "That's too bad."

Forget your pride. Give away another small piece of your soul. You need this man and his knowledge.

"It happened a long time ago, sergeant. In Korea."

"The war there, you mean?"

"Yes."

There was a pause as the sergeant digested this. Then: "Had an uncle got killed in Korea. Place called the Chosin Reservoir."

"Yes. I was there."

"It was rough, they say."

"It was rough, yes."

Another pause. Then, the voice warmer now: "Okay, look, professor. You say you talked to this guy. The guy that killed her."

"That's right. Twice, in fact. Once while we were on the CB simulator and again, later, over the telephone."

"Anything special about his voice?"

"Not really. He spoke in a whisper."

"So you can't tell me anything about him, is that right?"

"Well, yes, I believe I can. I can tell you that he knows how to use a computer. He recognized a dialogue from a database when he saw it onscreen. He realized that Miss D'Amici was connected to someone. And he knew how to maintain the connection, knew how to talk to me. And he was cool enough, collected enough, to do that."

"Lot of people know how to use a computer."

"I realize that, sergeant."

"Anything else?"

"Well, I think it's safe to say that this is an arrogant man, a man who believes himself to be above the law. And who feels he can flout it with impunity."

"You got that from what he told you on the database?"

"Yes, and from what Miss D'Amici said about him."

"Yeah, well, like I say, professor, I sure wish you'd of kept some kind of record of what she said."

"So do I, sergeant." And he could have, had he possessed the presence of mind: he could have pressed a single function key, at any time, and his communication software would have saved his entire conversation with FANCY on the computer's hard disk. But, useless old man that he was, scattered and muddled, he had neglected to do so. "But we also know, from what she said, that the man was someone with whom she worked."

"Yeah, but see, professor, we only got your word for that. I mean about the scam and the blackmail, what we talked about before. I'm not saying you're lying, naturally. I'm positive you're not, in fact. A guy like you. But see, that's what they call in a court of law your basic hearsay evidence, and it doesn't help us. And also it doesn't mean that this was the same guy, the one who killed her."

"But it couldn't have been anyone else."

"But we don't know that, see. Not for a fact. I mean, this could of been exactly what it looks like, this killing."

"And what does it look like?"

"Like she went to the door and opened it and the guy rushed in and took her out. Killed her. And then he looked around for money. Her purse is on the floor. Wallet's missing."

"Window dressing, sergeant. He's trying to throw you off the track. Is there a peephole in the doorway?"

"Nope. So it *could* of gone down the way it looks. Some freak, revved up on angel dust."

"Someone on angel dust wouldn't have talked to me on the computer. He wouldn't have called me back, later, to threaten me."

"Sure. Right. But like I say, we only got your word for that, professor. We got to convince a jury, and we need more."

"How was she killed, sergeant?"

The sergeant paused, as though coming to a decision. Finally he reached it. "He used a knife. He cut her up pretty bad. I don't think you want the details, professor."

"A knife."

"Yeah." And the official side of the sergeant felt obliged to add: "Not a gun, like you told everyone to report to us."

"Yes. I'm sorry about that, sergeant. It seemed important to get someone to her apartment."

"Sure. I understand that." Gracious once again, now that he'd delivered his veiled reprimand.

"Was she sexually assaulted?" Lizard asked him.

"Doesn't look like it. The medical report will let us know for sure. Anything else you can tell me about this guy, the one at the office?"

"He's ruthless, sergeant. And I believe that, in a way, he's enjoying himself. He thinks he's smarter than everyone else, and this is giving him a chance to prove it. It's a game to him."

"How d'you figure that?"

"From the way he sounded on the phone. The way he threatened me."

"Yeah, well, I wouldn't pay that any mind, I were you. Out there, Albuquerque, you're a long ways away."

"Yes. You're right, of course."

"You want, I can call up the Albuquerque P.D. Have them send a cruiser around, keep an eye out." A tempting offer. The sergeant added: "But, you ask me, it'd be a waste of time. He's not going out there. He leaves town, right away he points a finger at himself."

"Of course. No, I don't think you need to call them, sergeant. I'll be fine."

"What I figured." Clearly, the sergeant could expect no less from the Hero of Chosin Reservoir.

"What happens next?"

"We talk to the people in her office. We try to find this guy. You don't know where she worked, you said."

"No. She never told me."

"We'll find out. I'll get back to you later today, professor. Let you know what's going on."

"Thank you, sergeant. I'd appreciate that."

"One thing, if you don't mind me asking."

"What's that?"

"You say you taught history and all, at the university out there."

"That's right."

"You were a teacher before you went to Korea?"

"No. I attended U.N.M. afterward, and got my degree."

"In a wheelchair?"

"Well, sergeant, at the time, I couldn't afford an automobile."

The sergeant laughed. "Right. Right. Okay, professor. Thanks. Talk to you later."

Catwoman:	So now what?
Lizard:	I wait until I hear from Sgt. Bradley again.
FourWheel:	What was your hit on Bradley? He seem okay to you?
Lizard:	Yes. He's a good cop, I think.
Romeo12:	I wish we could do something besides sit around like this.
FourWheel:	Do something like what?
Romeo12:	Anything.

Lizard, too, was restless.

After talking to Sergeant Bradley, Lizard had known he wouldn't be able to sleep. He had rolled the chair out into the back yard, where, hidden by the redwood fence that circled the small lot, he had undressed and lowered himself into the lap pool. Slowly, steadily, working the adrenaline and the tension free from his body, he had swum the length of the pool, up and down, up and down, again and again until his arms ached and his breath rasped. Then, muscles straining, he had pulled himself from the water and positioned himself back into the chair.

The night was clear but growing cool, and to keep off the chill, he had turned on the portable heater he kept by poolside. For nearly an hour he had sat there in the heater's pale orange glow, beneath the cold snickering stars. Sat there remembering FANCY, and remembering, too, the others in his life who had slipped off the edge of the world and disappeared. His parents. His brother.

Live long enough and death acquires a certain familiarity. A familiarity that breeds not contempt but weariness, gray and barren and bone-deep. He was tired, finally, of losing people. Live long enough and you lose them all.

He had thought his days of losing them were over. His friends were gone, his family was gone. Except for the users on the database, there was no one in his life, no one close. And he had somehow persuaded himself, unconsciously, that the users, masquerading behind their gaudy, often silly nicknames, were in a sense unreal. He had never seen them, never met them: they were merely words on a screen.

He was in his seventh decade, and his capacity for self- deception remained undiminished.

FANCY had been real. Leslie D'Amici. And now, like the rest, she was gone.

Foolish old man.

In the end he had dressed and returned to the computer. When he connected to the database, he found that over twenty messages awaited him. News of FANCY'S death had flashed through the system; users from all over the country had tried to contact him. Some of the messages were irritating, tainted by that prurient, slightly feverish curiosity often spawned by catastrophe, phosphorescence glowing in a ghost ship's wake. But he knew that turning death into a circus, roadside carnage into an entertainment, was one way to diminish its awesomeness. And most of the messages were simple, unadorned expressions of sorrow: condolences. Lizard had been moved.

Romeo 12, FourWheel, and Catwoman had been online again, and Lizard had gathered them together in private talk to thank them and to relate his conversation with Sergeant Bradley.

Romeo12:	If we knew where she worked, we could maybe break into their system and get to their records. I know a hacker who could do it. Then maybe we could find out who this guy was.
FourWheel:	Maybe their system can't be accessed remotely.
Catwoman:	Besides, it's illegal.
FourWheel:	So is murder.
Catwoman:	The police are doing what they can.
FourWheel:	But maybe that's not enough.
Lizard:	I think Catwoman's right. I believe we should wait to see what Sergeant Bradley learns.
Romeo12:	It's just that sitting around and waiting for someone else to do something drives me crazy.
Lizard:	I sympathize, but I still think we should

CONNECTION TERMINATED

Lizard stared, disbelieving, at the screen.

His software was telling him that somehow he had lost contact with the database.

Impossible.

He picked up the telephone.

No dial tone.

He tapped the button once, twice, three times.

Nothing. The line was dead.

A storm had knocked down the telephone wires?

But even as he considered the possibility, Lizard knew that it was absurd. There was no storm. No wind, no rain. The air was still.

He knew what had happened.

The line had been cut. Outside his house.

He looked at his watch.

Eleven o'clock.

Impossible. The man couldn't have gotten here so quickly.

Yes, he could. Work it out. He kills FANCY at eight, New Mexico time. He calls Lizard at eight thirty. Possibly he's even on his way to the airport by then. He buys a seat on a nine o'clock flight to Albuquerque. How long would the flight take? An hour, an hour and a half. He's in town by ten, ten thirty. He rents a car, he buys a local map—he already knows the address, he's gotten it off the database. He drives here, he gets rid of Lizard, he drives back to the airport, catches a plane back to L.A. By tomorrow morning, when the police arrive at the office, he's waiting for them, bright-eyed and bushy-tailed.

Wonderful. And why not sit here for another half an hour, working it out.

While the killer, whoever he is, sneaks around the house until he finds a way in.

No. Not sneaking around the house. Probably he was watching Lizard right now. Peering in through one of the windows. Waiting to see what Lizard would do.

Probably he was enjoying this.

Slowly, without looking around the room, trying to appear as calm as possible, Lizard reached forward and turned off the computer. Slowly he rolled the wheelchair back from the desk, turned it, rolled across the hardwood floor of the living room and onto the red Mexican tiles of the kitchen. The circuit breakers were in a small metal box attached to the wall on the right, beside the extension telephone. Lizard opened the box, flipped breakers off until the kitchen, the entire house, vanished into darkness.

He would realize now that Lizard knew he was here.

But in the darkness, in familiar territory, Lizard was at less of a disadvantage.

Silently he rolled the chair up to the counter next to the sink, silently he slid open a drawer, reached in, and, cautiously, slowly, he moved his hand over the kitchen tools inside. His fingers found the wide, sharp blade of the carving knife. Carefully he slid them down the blade, grasped the handle, eased the knife from the drawer. Setting it on his lap, he rolled across the room, toward the back door.

A mistake, he realized as soon as he got there. Outside the door there was only the pool and the back yard, fenced in, hidden from the neighbors. No way out. If he shouted for help, FANCY'S killer would come for him, silence him. Watching their televisions, wrapped within their own lives, Lizard's neighbors would never hear. Out there, in the starlight, Lizard would be visible, vulnerable. Out there, Lizard would be trapped.

Move.

No. Wait. Listen.

He sat there, listening. Waiting.

He suddenly thought: the car.

FANCY'S killer wouldn't want to leave any traces of his presence here. How could he rent a car without giving his name?

He gives them cash? A big cash deposit? But then they'd be sure to remember him. Everyone uses credit cards.

And so does he. He uses FANCY'S credit card. Leslie's credit card. Her wallet was missing. The name Leslie fits a man or a woman.

He uses the card to buy the plane ticket, rent the car ...

But the police. They'd check on her card, they'd notify the credit card company, someone would discover that he'd used it to purchase a ticket. A round trip ticket. The police would be waiting for him at the airport when he returned.

No, they wouldn't. They couldn't know that she owned a credit card, precisely because her wallet was missing.

Receipts. Credit card receipts. They'd search her house, they'd find them. But when? Tomorrow? By then it would be too late. Too late for them, too late for Lizard.

The darkness was complete. Not a sound came from anywhere in the house. Lizard could hear only the faint rasp of his own breath. He could feel, against his chest, against his ears, the thumping of his heart.

Catwoman, Romeo 12, FourWheel. They'd been speaking to Lizard on the database. Lizard's abrupt disappearance must have told them that something was wrong. They'd call the police. They *had* to call the police.

Lizard strained his ears, hoping for the sound of sirens.

Nothing. Utter silence.

Even if they called the police, the police wouldn't get here in time. Lizard suddenly found himself feeling absurdly petulant: Why me? Why is this maniac bothering with me?

Because he thinks you know who he is.

But I don't.

You told him you did.

He didn't believe me.

He's changed his mind.

Lizard shook his head, as much to clear it as to deny the logic of the argument. Petulance won't help. Self-pity won't help. *Think.*

What time was it?

He looked at his watch. In the darkness, he couldn't see its face.

But surely a great deal of time had passed? Ten minutes? Fifteen minutes?

Maybe there was no one out there at all. Maybe some freak accident *had* severed the phone lines. A car hitting the pole, a tree collapsing onto the lines. And Lizard was sitting here, cowering in the kitchen, for no good reason, making a complete fool of himself—

He heard it then. A faint tinkling of glass. From the bedroom, it sounded like. The bedroom window.

Lizard wheeled around in the chair, reached out for the back door, found the doorknob, twisted it, tore open the door. Quickly he rolled away from it, until he and the chair were hidden beside the refrigerator.

The killer comes in, sees the open door, goes out there to investigate. Lizard races around the refrigerator, escapes out through the kitchen, out through the living room, out the front door to safety.

It could work. It had to work.

And once outside? What then?

A neighbor's house, a passerby, anything. It *had* to work. He had no other option.

He waited.

Nothing.

He listened, his heart hammering.

Nothing.

And then, abruptly, a voice, hushed and amused, the same voice he had heard over the telephone: "*Lizard?*"

Lizard didn't move, didn't breathe.

A white light wobbled across the ceiling of the kitchen, then was gone.

Flashlight. He's got one of those pocket flashlights.

It was over. Impossible for him not to see Lizard.

"I know you're here, old man."

The light trembled at the ceiling once again, splashed across the white walls, brought the Mexican tiles up from darkness, the color now of blood.

Clutching at the knife, Lizard hid his right hand down along the side of the wheelchair.

The light moved closer, sweeping back and forth across the small room. And then, inescapable, inevitable, the beam swung toward Lizard, and then it was on him, full in his face, the lens of the flashlight only three or four feet away. He squinted, blinking, but he could see nothing beyond the light.

He heard then, once again, the low and rattling chuckle. *"Cat got your tongue, Lizard?"*

Whipping his arm up from the wheelchair, Lizard hurled the knife toward that bright, blinding light.

The light jumped and he heard a wounded squeal and then a wild, savage curse, and Lizard rammed his hands against the arm of the chair and thrust himself from it, flailing his arms, throwing himself at the flashlight and the man who held it.

He collided with a body, small and compact and powerful, heard a grunt, and the beam from the flashlight wheeled madly around the room, shadows leaping, twisting, and then Lizard heard the flashlight smash against the tiles and shatter as he and the other slammed to the floor, Lizard's hands groping for the other's arms. In the blackness, he felt a cold swift pain arc along his ribs—some strangely detached portion of his mind recognized it as a knife, opening his flesh—and then he had each wrist caught within his clenched hands and he was pounding them, as hard as he could, at the tiles.

The man squirmed beneath him, lashing out his legs, ramming his knees at Lizard, but that was useless, Lizard had felt no pain there since Korea.

And then a wrist broke free and fingers clawed at Lizard's eyes and a red brilliance exploded through his brain and, terrified of blindness, a blindness that would shatter the fragile balance he had created in his life, the balance that *was* his life, he struck out with all his force at the man's head and felt the impact through his entire body and he rolled away and began scrambling toward the door, his hands and forearms slapping at the tiles, frantic, desperate to get away.

And then he was through the door, dragging his dead legs behind him, snaking forward with a kind of back-and-forth shuffle, frenzied, pathetic, ignominious, but at least, thank God, he was *out*. And then he understood that it was the wrong door, the door to the pool, to the enclosed back yard, to a cul-de-sac, to the end of all this.

A mountain landed on his back, air erupted from his lungs. The man was atop him, and his fingers were wrapped around Lizard's neck and they were squeezing. Lizard's heart was about to rupture, and that oddly detached portion of his mind wanted to explain to the man that this was all unnecessary, all this violence, so unnecessary, for in a few moments the heart would burst into fragments and the man's job would be done for him.

Perhaps it was this eerie pocket of detachment that told Lizard what it was he must do. His hands, hands that had lifted him into and out of the wheelchair for forty years, hands that had grown stronger through the years as his legs had grown more wasted and withered, those hands fumbled at the stranger's hands around his throat until they worked a finger free, and then Lizard bent the finger down and out and heard it snap. Above him, the man whinnied, and Lizard propelled himself up with his left hand, pitching the man off him, to the side. While the man was still unbalanced, Lizard rolled over and struck out at him, and the man lurched off the cement deck and toppled into the pool. Water spattered Lizard as he wormed forward, found the electric heater atop its insulating mats of wicker and rubber, pounded a fist at its power switch, and then, with a swing of his hand, sent it flying off the mats into the pool.

A single quick flash, nothing dramatic. A rapid splattering in the pool, as though a child were clapping small giddy hands at its surface. No other sound. And, after a moment, not even that.

Lizard, panting, lay back against the damp cement. A minute passed, and then another, and then he could hear the sirens, off in the distance, coming closer.

Lizard: His name was Steven Peckingham. He was a vice president where FANCY worked, according to Bradley. He and another V.P., a guy named Peter Allbright, were ripping off the company. Allbright confessed this morning. Stealing was apparently okay, but it seems that he drew the line at murder. It's ironic, because FANCY was planning to go to Allbright to tell him about the scam.

Catwoman: So even if Peckingham had shut you up, Allbright would've given him away.

Lizard: Yes. Unless Peckingham was planning to take care of Allbright, too. Which is a possibility.

Catwoman: But if FANCY found some records showing that Peckingham was stealing, wouldn't the police find them also, when they checked?

Lizard: Maybe Peckingham planned to destroy the records. Maybe, if he planned to kill Allbright, he planned to make it look like a suicide. Maybe he planned to plant FANCY'S credit card, the one he used to get out here, on Allbright. It would've looked like Allbright was responsible for FANCY'S death, and for mine, and for scamming the company. And then, according to that scenario, Allbright killed himself, tortured by guilt.

Catwoman: But you can't know any of that for sure. You can't really know what Peckingham was thinking.

Lizard: No. I imagine we'll never know.

Catwoman: And why did Peckingham come after you? If you really HAD known his name, you could've given it to the cops already.

Lizard: Something else I don't know. Maybe he thought I'd be trying to blackmail him, like FANCY had.

Catwoman: Maybe he flipped out, after he killed FANCY.

Lizard: Maybe.

Catwoman: And what about you? You're sure you're okay?

Lizard: I'm fine.

Catwoman: When you went off-line like that, last night, I nearly died. I KNEW he was there. FourWheel and Romeo and I logged off and called the cops.

Lizard: I know. I appreciate that.

Catwoman: I still don't think you're telling me everything. You're really okay?

Lizard: I'm really okay.

Catwoman: Lizard, the newspapers this morning had a story about FANCY and they gave her mother's name, in Sacramento. I called her. There's going to be a service for her on Friday, here in L.A. I talked to Romeo and FourWheel and some other people on the database, and they'd all like to go. Would you like to come with us? I could meet you at the airport and take you into town. I have a van, so it wouldn't be any problem. And there's a spare room here; it's not elegant or anything, but it's okay. If you want to spend the night, I mean.

Catwoman: Lizard?

Catwoman: Hey, Lizard, I'm not talking about marriage or a one-night stand or anything. I wasn't coming on to you. I just wondered if you'd like to come with the rest of us to FANCY'S service. And I thought maybe you'd like to stay in town for a day or two.

Lizard took a drag from his cigarette, exhaled. He leaned over the keyboard. His back was stiff, muscles and ligaments bruised and torn.

Yes, he typed. *I'd like that.*

Lee Ann

(*Sleight of Hand*, Buffalo Medicine Books, 1983)

By the mid-80s, I'd established a good working relationship with Cathleen Jordan, the editor of Alfred Hitchcock's Mystery Magazine. *When I visited New York, I usually had lunch with her; and, generally, she published everything I sent to her. Except for this.*

I wrote "Lee Ann" as a kind of homage to the old E.C. Comics, which had been my prime reading material as a young kid, and which had been blown off the map by the congressional investigations of the '50s. The comics, our government decided, were a menace, a Bad Influence. Only one member of the old E.C. brand, Mad Magazine, *survived the purge.*

Cathleen felt that the story "wasn't for us." Ernie Bulow, who put together Sleight of Hand, *a kind of biographical/critical study of my stuff, liked it, and included it in that book. I can understand Cathleen's reluctance, but I do like the story's ending.*

And so I go in real quiet to check is everything okay. The lamp on the coffee table is on as per usual and the fire is lit in the woodstove we bought last winter. It's got a glass window in the front and inside there the flames are flapping like little arms back and forth.

I can hear the radio far off, so I know she's back in the bedroom listening to one of her dumb talk shows. As per usual.

I call out, "Hey, Lee Ann."

And she yells back in that scratchy whiny voice of hers, "*What?*"

"I'm home."

Nothing from her.

Hello Jim welcome home how you doing?

Yeah, sure.

I take off my jacket and lay it on the dinette table and I start pulling the stuff out of the pockets. I unfold the plastic poncho, it's thin and you can see through it, like Glad Wrap only thicker, and I slip it on. It's got these strings at the cuffs and I pull them tight. I get out the rubber gloves and I slip them on and make sure they're over the cuffs of the poncho. I bought the gloves and the poncho at K-Mart, different departments, different days. This was like three months ago.

I take out the knife. They call it a CIA letter opener. It's made of this amazing superstrong plastic so spies can carry it onto an airplane without getting caught, and it's real sharp, like a razor. You could shave with it, almost. I ordered it by mail from this place in California sells military stuff, and I had it sent to old man Mears's address, down the road. Old man Mears, he doesn't get home till after seven at night, and the mail comes by usually around four, so I just wait and check his box every day for three weeks until it comes. I paid for it, before, with a money order from the Seven-Eleven that I scribbled his name on. This was about three months ago also. I ordered two of them and I used one for practice. It worked fine.

We got one of these electronic cordless phones now in the kitchen. Lee Ann likes her gadgets, we got phones all over the place. We got a processor for food turns anything into a liquid, steak even. I pick up the phone and I walk around the corner to the living room where she can't hear me and I push the zero button for the operator.

The operator comes on and she says, "How may I help you." Very polite. I like that. Sometimes you get them, they're real snooty.

I tell her, "Please, miss, you gotta help me. I need an ambulance right away." My voice is all quakey and shakey.

"Is this an emergency, sir?" she says, and her voice is getting a little shakey also. I figure she's new at this. Well, me too. "Is this an emergency call?"

"Yes, please, you've gotta *help* me, she's lying here and there's blood all over, I don't know what to do." I should have been an actor, really.

"The address? What's the address, sir?" And I swear she makes a swallowing sound. New at this.

I give her the address, and I say, "You gotta *hurry*. The blood. It's awful. You *gotta*." I'm really falling apart now, is the idea.

"I will, sir, they'll be there as soon as they can," and by this time I swear she's almost crying. "I'm sorry. I'm sorry, sir, but I need your name."

"Jim Stoner," I tell her, and I hang up. She'll call the police up too, it's the law when someone wants an ambulance, police got to come along at the same time.

I go back into the kitchen, put the phone back on its recharger thing, and look at the clock on the wall. Ten thirty exactly. All systems go.

"Lee Ann," I holler.

No answer.

"Lee Ann!"

"*What*, for godsakes?" She's got a voice could cut through steel.

"Could you come out here a minute?" I call.

"I'm *busy*," she hollers. Like nothing in the world is important except what *she's* doing.

"Lee Ann," I shout, "come on *out* here."

"What *is* it?"

"I gotta show you something. It's important."

Okay. Finally. Action. I hear her big feet slam against the floor when she swings herself out of bed, *timber*, and the *thump thump thump* as she comes marching up the hall in her socks. She always wears socks to bed, which I think is sort of a disgusting habit, personally.

I put the knife between my teeth like a pirate and I pull the plug from the microwave out of the wall, and then I pick the microwave up off the counter and I move back behind the door and hold it up over my head, and then soon as she comes through the door and starts looking around, saying, "*Well*," in that nasty way she has, right then I smash it down on her head as hard as I can.

It's not as noisy as I thought it would be, and she hits the floor like a sack of potatoes. I dump the microwave, fling it away, and then I grab the cordless phone and get down on my knees next to her, real careful to tuck the poncho in under me so the blood won't get to my pants, and I turn her over, face up, and I start in on her with the knife.

They ever make a movie out of this, they should do this part in slow motion, with the knife rising and falling like it was underwater, because that's the way it happens, sort of. Up and down, up and down, slow and cloudy-like, with the blood spraying everywhere. I use the knife a lot because the idea I want to get across here, see, when they find her, is that it's some kind of crazy psycho person did this.

There's a lot of blood spreading across the floor, and I got to move her, tug her by her fat ankles across the linoleum, before it gets to my pants.

I stop for a while and turn on the cordless phone and dial Dr. Moore's phone number, which I committed to memory earlier. Dr. Moore comes on and I tell him, "Doctor, this is Jim Stoner and you gotta get over here right away! Sombody hurt Lee Ann!" I'm out of breath because of hauling Lee Ann around, so this sounds like genuine Oscar material here.

"Jim?" he says. "Jim Stoner?" Dr. Moore, he never was too swift on the uptake.

"You gotta get over here, Doctor! *Please!*" And I kind of gasp and I hang up.

I do a few more things with the knife, better safe than sorry, and then I quit. I stand up and look at the phone in my hand. No blood there, so I hook it back on the recharger.

The poncho is awful messy, like you might expect, so I slip it off me slow and easy and I put the knife inside there and fold the thing partway up. I strip off the gloves and stick them in the poncho and fold it up some more and I carry it over to the woodstove. I open up the stove door and shove the poncho in. Right away, *whoosh*, like I knew it would, it snaps up into flames, bright blue and yellow.

I close the door. The knife will go too. I tried this out with the first knife and it burned down to nothing in no time flat.

They could maybe find *something* in there, sure. I remember "Quincy." They got electronic stuff, lasers and all, can do wonders these days. But they got no way to prove it was me, see. Reasonable doubt. They got to prove it was me beyond a reasonable doubt. I rest my case, your honor.

I look around the room quick to see if I forgot anything. Looks good to me. Looks fine.

I go into the bathroom and check myself out in the mirror. Got a spot of blood, one tiny little spot, on my cheek. I rinse it off, run a towel over my face, and leave the water running in the sink to clean it out while I head back out to the kitchen.

Clock says ten thirty-seven, so seven minutes, which is pretty much what I figured, but it seems like a whole lot more time than that. That's why I say the slow motion thing if they do a movie.

Four months ago when this idea first came to me, I did an experiment where I called in and reported a fire at the Healeys' place, about two hundred yards down the road. Took the fire department and the state cops twenty minutes to get there, which meant the Healeys would have all been roast beef by then. Naturally I didn't use our phone to do the call. I used the one at the Seven-Eleven. My convenience store.

Okay. So I figure to myself I got at least another five minutes, conservative, before they show. I go into the bathroom and shut off the faucet, come back out and look around some more.

What about the door from the garage? Shouldn't it be open? I mean, I come in, I see Lee Ann lying there on the kitchen floor, and naturally I'm all horrified and everything, so wouldn't I leave the door hanging open and run over to her? I'm thinking this all out in my mind, see.

Cold outside. What I'll do, I'll tell them I left it open and then later I closed it because I was afraid the cold would get to Lee Ann. Naturally, the truth is that nothing at all could get to Lee Ann at this point in time.

Wait a minute, I think. Wouldn't I go over and check her out? Wouldn't I want to see if she was alive or not? Course I would. It's only natural.

So I walk over to Lee Ann. In order to reach her, I got to step in some of the stuff on the floor. Can't be helped, you take the bad with the good in this life. What I'd do if all this were real, I figure, is feel for her pulse. So I do. I pick up her fat arm and put my fingers against her wrist and hold them there ... and *Holy God* it's not *possible*, not looking the way she does, not after all my *work*, but there it *is*, I can feel it move against the tips of my fingers real weak and slow and trembly like a tiny little wounded animal, but it's there, her pulse is there, and Holy God she's still *alive*.

I look around quick for something to bash her with, smash out that wicked little throb of life she's got, the *microwave*, a hammer, an ax, *anything*, but it's too late now, I can hear the siren, how'd they get here so damn *fast*, and I'm thinking, "Lee Ann if you ever loved me for one day in your whole fat rotten life do this for me now, please, please, please *die*," and then their car is in the driveway and I'm running out to meet them.

* * * *

And so the cop says to me, "All right, Jim. Let's go over it one more time."

"I already *told* you everything, Lieutenant," I say. A hundred times at least. We been going round and round with this forever.

He nods. He's a big guy, they're all big guys, but he's wearing regular type clothes, a suit and tie and not a uniform like the others. He's maybe forty years old. We're in his office at the station in town.

"I know," he says. "Just one more time. When was it you last saw her?"

"Around six thirty."

"You left the house at six thirty?"

"I told you all this before."

"Where'd you go at six thirty, Jim?"

"Over to the mall. I met Jack Reuter there and we went to a movie."

"Which movie?"

"I told you. The Rambo movie. That Rambo Three."

"Good movie?"

"It was okay."

"What time did the movie start?"

"Quarter of eight."

"What time did it get out?"

"Quarter of ten, about."

"What'd you do then?"

"I hung around with Jack a while. And then I went home."

"What time was that?"

"Little after ten. Ten minutes after."

"How come Lee Ann didn't go to the movie?"

"She doesn't like movies. Lieutenant, can we call the hospital? Can we find out how she is?"

This is the hard part, see, trying to act like I'm all shook up about how Lee Ann is doing at the hospital. I *am* all shook up, sure, but not for exactly the reason I'm supposed to be.

It was weird, back at the house. Cops everywhere, and then the paramedic guys hooking tubes up to Lee Ann and carting her out to the ambulance like a bunch of Indians lugging a buffalo. I must have looked pretty nervous when they drove her away, because one of the cops puts his hand on my arm and he tells me, "Don't worry, Jim."

Yeah, I think. Easy for you to say. She can't send *you* to the Crisper.

But I discovered something about myself from doing what I did to Lee Ann. I discovered that even if I was nervous and worried, there was a part of me, way deep down, that I could move into and use as a hideout. It was kind of a place inside me that was strong, a fort, Fort Defiance, where no one could bother me, no one could hurt me. And so even if I wasn't too thrilled answering the same old questions again and again from the cops, I knew that no matter what happened I was going to be safe. I could escape when I wanted, at my ease.

So he says to me, the lieutenant, "They're doing everything they can, Jim. If there's any change they'll let us know. Now. You left the mall a little after ten."

"Right, yeah."

"You drove straight home?"

"Yeah."

"What time did you get there?"

"I told you," I tell him, "I don't know for sure. I didn't look at my watch. Ten thirty. I guess around ten thirty."

"Did you see anyone outside? Any cars parked along the road?"

"No."

He nods. "All right," he says. "You go inside. And then what?"

"Then I saw her *lying* there. Jeeze, do we got to *do* this again? I saw her lying there and for a minute I couldn't believe what I saw, and then I went over to her and I saw how bad she was hurt, and I was sick, and then I called up to get an ambulance."

"When did you call Dr. Moore?"

"A couple minutes later. The ambulance didn't get there right away, so I called him up."

"All right, now–"

A cop in uniform is knocking on the glass door of the lieutenant's office. The same cop who patted me on the arm back at the house. He's got one of those clipboards in his hand like a basketball coach and he's signaling with his finger for the lieutenant. The lieutenant gets up from behind his desk and tells me, "Hold on, Jim. Right back." And he goes outside and the two of them walk down the hallway out of sight.

I wonder is it about Lee Ann. *Lee Ann*, I think, *don't let me down now.*

I look around the lieutenant's office. On one wall there's a picture of the lieutenant and what I guess is his family. A gray-haired lady and a young kid and a girl wearing a high school jacket. Cute girl, blonde hair and blue eyes. Maybe I could get me something like that.

And it comes to me. Since Lee Ann's gone now, I can get me anything I want. I can do anything I want. I can do *anything* I want.

Except that Lee Ann's not gone, not yet ...

I start getting nervous again, but then I slip down into my new center for a minute, maybe longer, down into my fort, and I get my strength together, they can't touch me, and then the lieutenant's coming back and I'm ready for him.

"Jim," he says, and he puts his hand on my shoulder. "I'm sorry. They lost her."

God bless you, Lee Ann. I got the strength now. Goddamn, I got the strength and I can do anything. I let my shoulders go loose and I lower my head and I put my hand up to it.

He sits on the edge of the desk and I can feel him looking down at me, I can feel his eyes through the bones of my hand. "It was just too much," he tells me. "What happened to her."

I nod into my hand. Laurence Olivier we're talking here.

"Jim," he says.

I look up and the amazing thing is I'm really crying. I can feel the tears moving down my face like little snails. From relief, I figure.

"Jim," he says. "It's never easy. I'm sorry we had to put you through it. But we had to make sure." He takes a big deep breath. "That's our job, Jim. We have to look into everything. And we did. And your story checks out. I just want—"

There's another knock on the glass door and I look up and a new cop is standing out there, no clipboard. This one uses his whole hand, not just his finger, to signal the lieutenant. The lieutenant says, "Hold on, Jim," and he pats me on the shoulder again and he goes outside. They like patting you on the shoulder, cops.

I think for a second that maybe Lee Ann, maybe she's come back from the dead, be just like her to rain on my parade, but then I figure that's crazy. Not even Lee Ann could pull that off.

So I'm staring at the picture of the lieutenant's daughter when he comes back in, and what I'm doing, I'm mapping out all these new freedoms I got. Wine and women and song. It's all there for me now.

Two other guys come in with the lieutenant, the cop he left with and another guy, little guy in a raincoat with fidgety eyes. The lieutenant, he's carrying a tape recorder.

He says to me, and there's something strange in the way he talks, "I think you better listen to this, Jim." And then he sets the machine on his desk and he hits one of the buttons with his finger. His hand is shaking now like he's got a bad case of flu.

"Hello, caller?" the machine says. *"Are you there?"*

"Hello?" It's Lee Ann's whiny voice, which I never thought I'd ever hear again, naturally. *"Dr. Bob?"* I get this prickly feeling on my skin, like the hair there is starting to grow backwards, towards the bone.

Machine says, *"Go ahead, caller, you're on the air. What's your name?"*

"Lee Ann."

"How are you tonight, Lee Ann?"

"Okay I guess."

"And what would you like to share with us, Lee Ann?"

And Lee Ann, I can't believe this, Lee Ann starts whining and moaning about *us*, about *me*, telling the whole world what a terrible hard time she's having with *me*. Blaming *me* for everything, as per usual.

The lieutenant nods to the little guy and says to me, "This is Dr. Freeman," and his voice rides higher over Lee Ann's creepy whining. "He's a psychologist. He's got a call-in program here in town. He was still down at the radio station when he heard about Lee Ann's death, and he brought us the tape."

He turns to the little guy. "What time was the tape made, Doctor?"

"What?" The little guy can't take his weaselly eyes off of me, it's like he's hypnotized. "Oh. She called at twenty after ten tonight."

"I can't ask him to do anything, Dr. Bob," says the mechanical Lee Ann. *"He won't help me do anything around the house at all."*

The lieutenant's smiling a funny smile. "This is the part, coming up," he says. "Listen to it, Jim."

Lee Ann complains some more, and then–

"Hey, Lee Ann." I recognize my own voice even though it's small and all muffled up like it's coming through cloth.

"What?" she hollers back, and then she's whispering, louder than her holler, hissing like a snake from the machine, *"That's him, Dr. Bob, that's Jimmy. I gotta go."* And then I hear, *click.*

The lieutenant pushes the button on the tape machine and he crosses his arms and stands there looking down at me.

They're all looking down at me, leaning the weight of their eyes on me, all three of them standing there in that white florescent light that makes dark shadows like black paint on their faces.

The machine's off now, but I can still hear Lee Ann whining ... *"I know I'm only his stepmother and all but listen, Dr. Bob, since his crazy father died I been father and mother both to him, and I swear he's gonna be the death of me."*

And the lieutenant says, "You're through, kid. You're history."

And I smile up at him and a part of me slips back into my center, my core, where they can never get to me, never touch me, never come close in a million years. And the light gets whiter all of a sudden and their faces get strange, the paint is darker, the paint is blacker, and colors are curling at the edge of the picture, brown and red and orange like it's starting to burn, like there's a fire hungry behind it and the fire's going to eat it all away. And then suddenly it does, a bright flame bursts blue and yellow across everything, *whoosh*, and then it's gone, it's gone, everything is gone.

Gone.

Everything is.

Okay. Everything is okay. Everything is okay.

And so I go in real quiet to check is everything okay. The lamp on the coffee table is on as per usual and the fire is lit in the woodstove we bought last winter. It's got a glass window in the front and inside there the flames are flapping like little arms back and forth. ...

THE CASSOULET

(*Alfred Hitchcock's Mystery Magazine*, December 1996)

Of all the stories I've written, this is possibly my favorite. You love all your children, but sometimes, secretly, you give a little more attention to one of them. When I wrote it, I had just come back from Paris, and I was still infatuated with things French, including the food. While I'd been living there, I met several times for lunch with a bunch of friends, among them the amazing Sarah Caudwell.

Over the years, Sarah was a great friend and a brilliant and helpful critic. I gave her a manuscript copy of my book, Masquerade, *to vet, and she sent me an 18 page, single-spaced letter detailing her "suggestions," which read considerably more like commands. She was, however, right about every one of them, and the book is a better book as a result of her help.*

In a sense, this particular story, with its Parisian background and its elitist characters, was written for Sarah, to make her laugh. She had a wonderful laugh.

"I MUST speak with you," says Pascal, "regarding a matter of great importance."

"And which matter," I ask him, "might that be?"

Thoughtfully, using forefinger and thumb, he strokes his mustache. "The cassoulet," he says.

"Ah," I say, and within my chest my heart dips a few melancholy millimeters.

We are drinking Pascal's passable filtered coffee in his somewhat too elaborate dining room. The room is situated in a corner of his apartment, and the apartment itself on the top floor of a portly old building along the Quai de Gesvres. A pair of wide windows, running from ceiling to floor, afford us an uninterrupted view of the Île de la Cité and of Notre Dame with its many fine and graceful buttresses. The view no doubt is often charming; but today a gaudy sun is shining, and the river is perfectly reflecting the flawless blue of sky, as though posing for a tourist postcard; and I cannot help but find it all, as I find Pascal's dining room, a trifle overdone.

"You know, of course," says Pascal, "that I have always experienced a certain difficulty with the cassoulet."

"Yes, of course," I say. Pascal's failure with the cassoulet is renowned.

"I have never understood it," he says. As usual, Pascal is wearing black—a silk shirt, a pair of linen slacks—on the mistaken assumption that black makes him appear at once more intellectual and less corpulent.

"I believe," he says, "that I am in all other respects a tolerable cook. The cassoulet, however ..." he shakes his head "... invariably the cassoulet has eluded me. At the market I have purchased the most delectable of beans, the most savory of sausages, the most succulent of pork. When I used fresh duck, I obtained the plumpest of these, and I plucked their feathers myself, with the utmost care. Always, before the final cooking, I rubbed the casserole scrupulously with garlic, like a painter preparing a canvas. Always, as the dish bubbled in the oven, I broke the gratin crust many times—"

"Seven times," I ask him, curious, "as they do in Castelnaudary?"

"On occasion. And on occasion eight times, as they do in Toulouse."

He sits back in his chair and shrugs. "Yet no matter what I assayed, always my cassoulet lacked ..." Frowning, he holds up his hand and delicately moves his fingers, as though attempting to pluck a thought, like a feather, carefully from the air.

"That certain something?" I offer.

"Exactly, yes," he nods. "That certain something." He smiles sadly. "You recall the party last year, on Bastille Day."

"Only with reluctance," I say. For a moment that evening, after each guest had taken a small tentative taste of the cassoulet, no one could look at anyone else. Silence fell across the table like the blade of a guillotine. Poor Pascal, who had been so embarrassingly hopeful before the presentation, suddenly became quite embarrassingly, quite volubly, apologetic.

"Yes," he nods ruefully. "A disaster."

"I have always," I say, "accounted it rather intrepid of you, this endless combat with the cassoulet."

He wags a finger at me. "Intrepid, yes, perhaps—but confess it, my friend, also rather foolish."

"Ah well," I say, and I shrug. "In this life we are all of us permitted a certain amount of foolishness, no?"

He inclines his head and smiles. "You are, as always, too kind." But then he frowns again. "You know," he says, "it was largely because of this Bastille cassoulet that Sylvie wandered out of my life."

"Come now, Pascal." I smile. "You know very well that Sylvie was wandering long before Bastille Day."

"Certainly. Sylvie was a free spirit and, I agree, a prodigious wanderer. Yet despite our many difficulties, after her wanderings it was to our life here that she invariably returned. Until the day of that fatal cassoulet. The embarrassment was too much for her. The cassoulet was the ultimate of straws."

Pascal's way with a cliche can best be described as unfortunate.

"Nonsense," I tell him. "By her very nature Sylvie was utterly incapable of fidelity."

He smiles sadly. "As you learned yourself, my friend, isn't it so?"

I return his smile, replacing its sadness with curiosity. "Surely, Pascal, you cannot hold that against me, my little incident with Sylvie?"

He lowers his eyebrows and raises his hand, showing me his pale scrubbed palm. "But of course not," he says. "It is inevitable, the attraction between one's friend and one's lover. It is, in a way, a confirmation of one's high regard for both." He shakes his head. "No, my friend, all that is history now. Water far beneath the bridge. But I speak of Sylvie. A few weeks ago, I saw her in the Café de la Paix. She was sitting with her American."

"The American is still in Paris, then?"

"Astounding, is it not? Almost ten months now, and the two of them are as inseparable as ever. You've met the man?"

"I've heard stories only. There are boots, I understand."

"The boots of the cowboy, yes. Constructed from the skin of some unfortunate bird. A turkey, I believe."

"Not a turkey, surely?"

He shrugs. "A bird of some sort. And with them, inevitably, a ridiculous pair of denim trousers. *Gray*. Sitting beside Sylvie he looked like a circus clown."

"What was Sylvie wearing?" I ask in passing.

"A lovely little sleeveless Versace, red silk, and around her neck a red Hermès scarf."

I smile. "Sylvie and her endless scarves."

"Yes. She saw me, from across the room, and waved to me to join them. I could hardly refuse, not without causing a scene. Not in the Café de la Paix. So I crossed the room, and the American stood to greet me. He's quite excessively tall, you know. He *looms*."

"It is something they all do, the Americans. Even the women. Even the short ones. They learn it from John Wayne films."

"Doubtless. In any event, we shook hands, the American and I, and naturally he squeezed mine as though it were a grapefruit."

"Naturally."

"His name is Zeke." Frowning, he cocks his head. "That cannot be a common name, can it, even among Americans?"

"I shouldn't think so." I glance at my watch. Eleven thirty now, and I have a one o'clock rendezvous at La Coupole. "So you joined them?" I say. "Sylvie and her Cowboy?"

"What choice had I? The American sat back and crossed his legs, perching his horizontal boot along his knee, so we might all admire the elegant stitchery in the dead turkey."

"I hardly think turkey, Pascal."

"Whatever. The point is the *flamboyance* of the gesture. Why not simply rip the thing from his foot and hurl it, *plonk*, to the center of the table?" Pascal shudders elaborately. "And then he hooked his thumbs over his belt, as they do, these American cowboys, and he said, '*Sylvie tells me you're in chemicals.*'

"I said, 'Not *in* them, exactly.' "

"*Touché*," I say. "In French, this was, or in English?"

Pascal smiles. "He believed himself to be speaking French. It was execrable, of course. In simple self-defense, I replied in English. 'I have an interest in a small pharmaceutical company,' I told him. 'But naturally I leave the running of it to others.'

"And here Sylvie leaned forward and she said, 'Pascal's primary interest is the kitchen.'

" '*Is that right?*' said the Cowboy. I cannot duplicate the accent. You recall Robert Duvall as Jesse James?"

"Vividly. *The Great Northfield Minnesota Raid*. A Philip Kaufman film."

"Something like Duvall. A combination of Duvall and Marlon Brando in Kazan's *Streetcar*. '*Is that right?*' he said. '*I purely do admire the way you French people cook up your food.*' "

"Pascal," I say. "You exaggerate."

Indignant, he raises his chins. "Indeed I do not."

"And what did you reply?"

"I said, 'We French people are filled with awe at your Big Mac.' "

I smile.

"And then he grinned at me, one of those lunatic American grins that reach around behind the ears, and he said, '*Ain't all that big on burgers myself–*' "

"Pascal!"

"I do *not* invent this. '*Me*,' he said, '*I like to chow down on a real fine homecooked meal.*'

" 'Perhaps,' I said, 'one day you will permit me to prepare something for you.'

" *'That'd tickle me,'* he said, *'like all get out.'"*

"Pascal–"

"Wait, wait! Sylvie had been sitting in silence, leaning forward, her elbows on the table, her arms upraised, her fingers locked to form a kind of saddle for her chin. You recall how she nestles her chin against the backs of her fingers? How she watches, with those shrewd blue eyes darting back and forth from beneath that glossy black fringe of hair?"

"I recall, yes," I tell him.

"Suddenly she spoke. Blinking sweetly, with a perfectly innocent expression, she said, 'Zeke's favorite dish is the cassoulet.'"

"Ah," I say. "I was wondering if we should ever return to the cassoulet."

"I was, of course, stunned," says Pascal. "I had believed us to be friends still, Sylvie and I."

"Possibly your comment about the Big Mac ...?"

"Possibly. I was stunned nonetheless. And then the Cowboy, this Zeke creature, said, *'I reckon there ain't no food I like better than a good cassoulet.'*

"And at that point Sylvie, still the picture of innocence, sat up and blinked again and said, 'Why, Pascal would love to prepare a cassoulet, wouldn't you, Pascal?' "

"Clearly," I say, "it was your comment about the Big Mac."

"Very likely. But what could I do?"

"You had no choice, obviously, but to accept."

"None. I invited them to dinner on the following Saturday. As I said goodbye to them both, I could not help but notice in Sylvie's eye that little twinkle she gets when she is anticipating some devilment. You recall that twinkle?"

"I recall it."

"Well. This occurred on a Thursday. That afternoon, and throughout most of Friday, I pored over the literature. Brillat- Savarin. Prosper Montagné. The Larousse. On Friday evening I bought the *lingot* beans, the finest, the most expensive in Paris, and I carried them home–in a taxi, on my lap, so as not to bruise them–and I set them to soak. Early on Saturday morning I purchased the rest of the ingredients. Again, all the finest and the most expensive. And then, when the beans had soaked for exactly twelve hours, I began."

He strokes his mustache, remembering. "First I drained the beans. Then I cooked them in just enough water for them to swim comfortably, along with some pork rinds, a carrot, a clove- studded onion, and a bouquet garni containing three cloves of garlic."

"So far," I say, "the method is unimpeachable."

"Using another pan," he goes on, "in some goose fat I browned a few pork spareribs and a small boned shoulder of mutton—"

"Mutton? Pascal, this sounds ominously like the cassoulet you prepared for Jean Claude's birthday."

"The very same recipe." He nods. "I know, I know. A catastrophe."

"You are a brave man, Pascal."

"A desperate man, my friend. But to continue. When the meats were nicely browned, I transferred them gently to a large skillet, and I cooked them, covered, with some chopped onion, another bouquet garni, and two *additional* cloves of garlic—"

"Bravo."

"—as well as three tomatoes, chopped, seeded, and crushed. Then, when the beans in their separate pan were just approaching tenderness, I removed all the vegetables from them and I added the pork, mutton, onions, and a fat garlic sausage. And the preserved goose. It was while I was adding the goose that the accident occurred."

"The accident?"

"Yes." He glances at my empty cup. "Some more coffee, my friend?"

I look at my watch. Twelve o'clock. "Only a bit," I tell him.

He pours the coffee and sits back, sighing, and then with a ruminative look he stares out the tall window at the buttresses of Notre Dame.

"The accident?" I say.

He turns back to me. He smiles. "The accident, yes. It was extraordinary. Really quite extraordinary, in light of what followed. As I was cutting the leg of preserved goose, my knife slipped, and the blade went sliding along my left hand. You see?"

He holds out his left hand. Along the base of the thumb is the clear mark of a recent scar, nearly two inches long, still pink against Pascal's plump pallor.

"Impressive," I say. "Was it painful?"

"I barely noticed it at the time," he says, "so intent was I upon the cassoulet. And then suddenly I realized that I was bleeding. *Into* the beans."

"Goodness."

"I had bled rather a lot into the beans, as it happens. As soon as I understood what had transpired, I wrapped my thumb in a dishtowel to staunch the flow, and with a spoon I attempted to remove the blood from the beans. This was impossible, of course. Already it had mixed with the liquid in the pot. I had no choice but to mix it in more thoroughly and continue. You understand?"

"Certainly. It was too late in the day for you to begin anew. But still, Pascal ..."

He raises his brows. "Yes?"

"It is ... a tad macabre, don't you think?"

"Not at all. Think of blood sausage. Think of civet of hare. Think of sanguette."

"Yes, but human blood. Your own blood."

Dismissively, he shrugs. "I could not afford to be squeamish. As you say, it was late in the day. So, after having mixed everything, I simmered it for another hour, then removed the meat from the beans. I cut the meat, and I arranged all the ingredients in the casserole. A layer of beans, a sprinkling of pepper, a layer of meat, a sprinkling of pepper, a layer of beans—"

"I am familiar with the procedure."

"—and so on. Over the top I sprinkled melted goose fat and breadcrumbs—"

"Naturally."

"—and then I placed it in the oven. During the next hour and a half, I broke the gratin crust eight times, at regular intervals. By the time Sylvie and her Cowboy arrived, it was ready."

"And?" I say.

He smiles slyly. "And what?"

"You toy with me, Pascal. The cassoulet. It was a success?"

"Not a success," he says. "A *triumph*. Sylvie took a single bite and closed her eyes—you recall how she closes her eyes when she savors the taste of something, how that little smile spreads across—"

"Yes, yes," I say. "I recall." I had been recalling Sylvie rather more often than I liked. "And the Cowboy?"

"In raptures. He consumed three enormous portions. It was, and I quote, '*the best goldarned cassoulet*' he ever ate."

I sit back and shake my head. "You astound me, Pascal. A remarkable story."

"But no, there is more. Over the weekend, Sylvie and her Cowboy mentioned the cassoulet to everyone they knew. It became a *cause célèbre*. You were gone from Paris at the time."

"In Provence," I say. "I returned, as I told you, only last week."

"I began to receive telephone calls from people—occasionally from people whom I myself had never met—importuning me to prepare for them a cassoulet, You can imagine how gratifying this was to me, after my long and notorious history of failure."

"Certainly. But, Pascal. You could hardly repeat the accident which brought about your one success. The *contretemps* with the knife."

"Ah, but I could, you see."

"Pardon?"

Smiling, he unbuttons the cuff of his left sleeve. With a magician's flourish, he pulls the sleeve up along his thick arm.

Stuck everywhere along the pallid flesh are pink adhesive bandages, eight or nine of them.

For a moment I do not comprehend. And then I do.

"Pascal!" I exclaim. "But this is madness!"

Lowering the arm, he nods sadly. "I agree. I cannot continue. In the morning, I can barely climb from the bed. And yet everyone in Paris, it seems, hungers for my cassoulet."

I pick up my coffee cup, and very much to my surprise I drop it. It falls to my lap, spattering me with warm coffee, then rolls off and tumbles to the floor, shattering against the polished parquet. I look up at Pascal. "How very odd," I say.

He smiles. "The drug begins to take effect." He looks at his watch. "Precisely on time. It requires an hour. It was in your first cup of coffee."

"The drug?" Strangely, this emerges from my throat as a croak.

"A rather interesting variant of curare. A chemist at my pharmaceutical company developed it. Unlike curare, which paralyzes the body's involuntary muscles, this one leaves certain muscles untouched. One can breathe, one can blink one's eyes, one can chew, one can swallow. But one cannot otherwise move."

I open my mouth, attempt to say, "You are joking," but only a shrill sibilant hiss escapes me.

"Nor can one speak," says Pascal, and smiles. Paternally. At me, or at the drug and its effects.

I attempt standing. None of my muscles responds. Suddenly, without my willing it, my body slumps back against the chair. My head topples forward as though it might snap off at the neck, roll down my legs, and go rattling across the floor. I can feel my heart pounding against my ribs like an animal trying, frantically, to escape a trap.

"Relax, my friend," says Pascal. "You will only excite yourself."

With my head lowered, I can see of Pascal only his feet. They move as he stands up. I feel him clap me in a friendly manner upon the shoulder. Then the feet and legs disappear off to my right.

My mind, like my heart, is racing. The rest of me is frozen.

A few moments later I feel myself being lifted into the air. My head flops to the side. Pascal, for all his corpulence, is surprisingly strong. I am placed in what I recognize as a wheelchair. My head lolls back, and I have a view of Pascal's ceiling, and then of Pascal's face as he leans into my line of vision.

"Believe me," he says with an upside-down smile, "this will all go better for you if you simply accept it."

His face vanishes, and the ceiling unscrolls above me as he wheels me from the dining room.

"Perhaps you are asking yourself," I hear him say, "why I should choose you as the source of my—well, let us call it my *special seasoning*.

"First of all," he says, "you commend yourself to this purpose by the sheer emptiness of your life. No one will miss you. No one will ever even suspect that you are gone. Oh, here and there, I imagine, some poor benighted secretary, some simpleminded shopgirl, may wonder why you never telephone. But she will survive this."

We are in another room now. I feel Pascal lift me once again. The ceiling lurches, sways, and then I am lying on a bed. I feel Pascal's hand on my head as he swivels it, gently, to face him.

He stands back, pursing his lips. "And second," he says, "I confess that I have never been terribly fond of you. Your condescension, your arrogance. That metabolism of yours that permits you to eat whatever you like without gaining a gram. Insufferable. And of course there is your seduction of Sylvie. Her relationship with me was never the same afterward. You are as much responsible for her leaving me as that cassoulet of Bastille Day."

I want to cry out that it had *not* been a seduction, that Sylvie had been as willing as I, which is very possibly true. But no sound comes.

Smiling again, Pascal leans forward and pats me on the shoulder once more. "Please," he says. "Relax. We shall have a splendid time together, you and I. Like two beans in a pod. We shall have enormous amounts of time to discuss Sylvie. We can analyze her reasons for leaving us both, endlessly. And during the day, before I set off to gather the other ingredients of the cassoulet, I shall prop you up against the pillows, and you can watch the television. Game shows, soap operas. Not your usual fare, I suspect, but it will be great fun, eh?"

He stands upright. "And you need have no fear. I will never take more from you than you can afford to give. A pint here, a pint there. I am not a barbarian. And naturally, to keep up your strength, I shall provide you with the most nutritious and the richest of foods. Tonight you will be enjoying a lovely duckling in orange sauce. With American wild rice and baby peas. A vinaigrette salad of lettuce and arugula. And, I think, a nice St. Emilion. Until then I bid you adieu."

I watch him walk from the room, pull the door shut behind him.

I stare at the door. I have no choice but to stare at the door. Inside me, horror boils.

Boils and boils and goes screaming through my brain like steam from a kettle. And then, finally, like that steam, it exhausts itself. I continue to stare at the door. And all at once it occurs to me that Pascal is, as he says, a tolerable cook. And that his duckling with orange sauce is famous. His wine cellar, of course, is legendary.

MURDER ONE

(*Crime Through Time II*, edited by Miriam Grace Monfredo and Sharan Newman, Berkley, 1998)

Several years before, Miriam and Sharan had asked me to do an historical mystery short story for the first Crime Through Time *anthology. Because I was busy with a novel just then, I was forced, reluctantly, to decline. Luckily, a couple of years later, they asked me again, and this time I was free to accept. Miriam told me that the stories would be arranged chronologically: they would be organized in the anthology according to the different historical periods in which they were set. I decided to use Neanderthals–unless someone came up with a story about primordial ooze, I was pretty much guaranteed the opening slot in the book. And so it happened. This is the first of two stories featuring Berthold the Mead Master, and his assistant, Doder, Watt's son.*

NOWADAYS, of course, murder is an everyday kind of thing. Lie in your bed, snoring peacefully in the privacy of your own home, and you'll likely get your lifeline severed by some sneak thief. Walk along the street, minding your own business, and you'll likely get it snipped by some itinerant psychopath.

What does this teach us? That things have basically gone to hell. And that itinerant psychopaths keep better hours than sneak thieves. I blame agriculture, myself. It wasn't like that back in the old days, back when we were mostly hunters and gatherers. Back then we'd never heard of murder. Didn't even have a word for it. Not that everything was peaches and cream. We had mastodons to deal with, and cave bears, and saber-tooth tigers. And we had the weather. You think it gets cold now, I suppose, when winter comes around and the snow starts to flake away from those low gray clouds. You don't really know what cold is, let me tell you, until you wake up and look outside the cave and you see a big old glacier in the garden, trampling the petunias under a couple hundred feet of dirty hissing ice and ragged groaning rocks. We moved around a lot, back then.

But you want to hear about the murder. The first murder. It would make for a better story, probably, if I could tell you that it happened on a dark and stormy night, with the rain hurtling down and the wind rattling through the trees. But it wasn't like that. That's the nature of nature, of course, and that's why we storytellers get paid so well to improve upon it.

Okay. Once upon a time. I was sitting on the cave floor, in the anteroom, pounding at the acorns, when my wife came sauntering in. This was my first wife, Ursula.

"Marta wants to see you," she said.

I lowered my mortar. "Marta?"

She nodded, a bit impatiently. She was like that, Ursula. Lovely, very lovely, with long brown hair down her back, and down her front, too; pretty much everywhere, in fact. She had a beautiful brow ridge, wide and steeply sloped, that she sometimes cracked walnuts on, absent-mindedly, late at night as we sat around the fire. These days you don't see very many brow ridges like hers; and I've got to confess that now and then, when I'm alone in bed watching the firelight flicker softly against the ceiling, I still dream about Ursula's.

She was lovely, yes, but she was also definitely impatient. She said, "Marta, yes."

"Wants to see *me*?"

She rolled her dark brown eyes. "That's what I said, isn't it?"

"But why?"

"How would I know? Klaus came and said she wanted you." Klaus was Marta's consort that year.

"But I haven't done anything," I told Ursula.

She smiled a sour smile. "I'll say." If it hadn't been for that brow ridge I would've run away, long before this.

I set down the mortar. "I guess I'd better go find out what she wants."

She snorted. "I guess you'd better."

I stood up, brushed the chips of acorn shell from my chest, turned to leave.

"Wait a minute," said Ursula. I turned back to her.

She frowned, impatient again. "You're not going like that?"

I looked down at myself. I was naked, but I was always naked then. All of us were.

I looked at her. "Like what?" I asked.

"You've got little bits of acorn all over your face." She moved closer, brushed at my beard—almost affectionately, I thought. I grinned and reached for her, and she stepped smartly away.

"Forget it," she said. "You haven't got time."

I grinned again, my best grin, the one that Ursula used to say made her legs go all wobbly. "How about later," I said, "when I get back?"

"I'll be at my sister's," she said. Ursula's legs hadn't wobbled for a long time, and neither had we. "I won't be back till late. Maybe tomorrow morning."

"Oh."

She flapped her hands at me, fingers loose. "Go, go. Marta's waiting."

I went. It was a beautiful spring morning, bright and warm and spectacularly sunny; no dark, no gloom at all. The blue sky was stretched taut over our narrow little valley, and the trees that draped the hillsides were blazing with green. Children were running along the footpaths that wound through the tall shiny grasses, giggling and hooting. Off in the distance, a dog yapped merrily. It should have cheered me, all of it; but the fact is, I was uneasy. A summons from Marta usually meant that something was seriously wrong somewhere, and during the walk to her cave I spent most of my time trying to figure out what it might be. Always a waste of time—trying to anticipate the Gods' little pranks.

Marta was in the ceremonial chamber, sitting on her ceremonial throne, wearing her ceremonial robe. This was the skin of a lioness, smudged with woodsmoke now, and slightly tattered. (It was supposed to provide Marta with wisdom. It hadn't done that for the lioness, obviously, or she'd still be wearing it; but religion, as history teaches us, isn't necessarily rational.)

Sitting in a desolate heap on the floor in front of Marta, her legs crossed, head lowered, shoulders hunched, long black hair streaming forward, was young Karla, Marta's niece. And sprawled back along a stone bench at one side of the chamber was Berthold the Meadmaster. His long legs were outstretched, and his hands were raised back behind his narrow head, both the hands and the head resting against the gray wall of rock. He was smiling faintly as he steadily gazed at me. Lying beside the bench was that infernal leather bag of his, large and bulging. My heart sank.

"Greetings, Doder, Son of Watt," Marta said to me. More ceremony.

"Greetings, Most Sage and Slender Queen," I said. I glanced at Berthold. Neither his gaze nor his faint smile wavered.

"We have a problem," Marta told me. As though the presence of Berthold hadn't already made that clear.

"Oh?" I said, pretending interest. "What might that be?"

"Gunter is dead."

"Ah," said I. Gunter was Karla's husband. I looked down at Karla, who still sat hunched forward, lost in grief. "Sorry about that, Karla." I looked back at Marta. "So what's the problem?"

I wasn't being callous. I'd actually been fairly fond of Gunter, a nice young man and a fine hunter. But back then, dying happened a lot more frequently than it does now—the mastodons, etc.; and also some very unpleasant diseases, all of them unattractive and most of them fatal—so we took it with a certain nonchalance.

Marta said, "We're not entirely sure how he died."

I frowned. "What do you mean?"

"We think he may have been—" As I said, there was no word for it, and Marta hesitated before she came up with: "—destroyed."

I looked from her to Karla, whose shoulders suddenly shook—she was sobbing. I looked to Berthold. His smile had gone, but he was still watching.

I looked back to Marta. "Destroyed? By what?"

"By one of the Outlanders, we think."

I frowned. "But why would an Outlander, um, destroy Gunter?"

"We don't know."

"And what makes you think it was an Outlander who did it?"

"This," said Marta, and she held up a narrow strip of cloth, gray and frayed, and offered it to me.

I took it. The strip had been torn from a larger piece, and each end of it was crumpled, as though the two ends had been tied together. It was Outlandish, all right. At the time, we didn't have cloth. Didn't make it, didn't use it.

And it carried the smell of Outlander, a smell not unlike cumin, but a cumin that had gone somehow rank; a dense stench that burned the nostrils and clawed at the throat. It was faint on the cloth, but it was unmistakable.

"Where was this found?" I asked Marta.

"Wrapped around Gunter's neck. It was what destroyed him. He was strangled."

Somehow I stopped myself from hurling the filthy thing to the ground. We were nonchalant about dying, as I said; but not about the dead themselves. The dead we buried as soon as they hit the ground. Whatever it was that killed them, it might be catching.

"Ah," I said, and I nodded sagely, and handed the strip back to Marta with a casualness that was maybe a tiny bit brisk. Off to the side, I noticed, Berthold was smiling again.

"And what would you like me to do?" I asked Marta, although by then I already knew.

"We have instructed Berthold to investigate. He has requested your assistance."

"Ah," I said again. "Well, of course, Your Slenderness, he does me great honor. But surely there are other people in the clan who might provide—"

"Berthold has requested you. And, if you'll remember, you were of great help to him in the matter of The Missing Vat of Tasty Soup."

"Yes, but—"

"And also in the matter of The Disappearing Necklace of Pretty Blue Stones."

"Yes," I said, "but those were all simple thefts. This is much more complicated, Your Suppleness. I—"

Marta raised a hand. "The Great Mother wishes it."

Well, that was that, of course. This was before your Lightning Gods and your Cattle Gods and all the rest. Back then, the Great Mother wasn't just the Supreme Being, she was basically the only Being. If she—or Marta, her representative—wanted something done, it got done.

I sighed—silently—and nodded. "Of course," I said.

Marta returned the nod. "The Great Mother thanks you," she said, and she turned to the Meadmaster. "Berthold?"

Berthold lowered his hands to his lap and raised his eyebrows attentively. "If I might be permitted to ask a few questions of Karla?"

"Certainly. Karla?"

The young woman raised her head. I saw that her eyes were puffy, her face blotched. Her lower lip was caught between her teeth, as though she were trying to stop it from trembling. She sniffled once, nodded, and then turned toward Berthold. She seemed to me very vulnerable then, and even younger than her fourteen years.

Berthold swung his long legs off the bench of stone and sat forward, resting his arms on his thighs, clasping his hands together between his outspread knees.

"Now," he said. "Karla. Please tell me what happened this morning."

Karla glanced at Marta, who nodded. Karla looked back to Berthold. "I was asleep," she said, "when suddenly I heard a sound. A cry. It woke me up. The fire had gone out, but dawn was coming and there was enough light for me to see. I looked around. The cave was empty. Gunter was gone."

She sniffled again. "And then, as I sat there, I heard the cry again—"

"This second cry," said Berthold. "Was it as loud as the first?"

Karla nodded. "Yes. Yes, I think so. I knew it was Gunter, and I rushed from the bed and out of the cave. At first, I saw no one. And then I saw Gunter. He was lying about thirty feet from the entrance. I thought that he'd slipped, fallen down and hurt himself. I ran to him."

She sniffled again, took a deep breath. "He was lying on his back, and *that*"—she nodded toward the strip of Outlander cloth, which Marta had draped along the arm of her throne—"*that* was wrapped around his neck."

"He was lying," said Berthold, "on his back?"

"Yes. His face was ... blue, almost black, and his tongue was sticking out. It was *terrible*. I untied that *thing* and I ripped it from his neck. I—"

"The piece of fabric," said Berthold. "It was tied in the front?"

She frowned, puzzled. "Yes ... Why do you ask?"

He smiled. "Simple curiosity. Please continue."

"Yes," she said. "It was tied in the front, below his chin. I ripped it off and I shook him, tried to awaken him. I tried and tried. But I couldn't." She lowered her head once again.

"And what then?" asked Berthold.

She looked up. "I ran to the cave of my sister, Heidi. She's ill, she's been with fever now for two days, but I needed help, I was desperate. Heidi was asleep, but Ulrich was awake, her husband, and he ran back with me to Gunter. He tried to revive him, too. But it was no use. Gunter was ... dead."

"And then?" asked Berthold.

Karla glanced again at Marta, then back at Berthold. "And then we came running here, and we told Marta, and she sent for you, and"—Karla nodded toward me—"for Doder."

Berthold nodded. "And where is Ulrich now?"

Marta spoke. "I sent him back, to stand guard over the body, and stop people from trying to bury it."

"Excellent," said Berthold. He turned to me. "Well, my friend," he said, "time for us to get to work, eh?" He bent down, grabbed the rope that was looped around the top of the bulging leather bag. He stood up and held the bag out to me.

I took it. It was as heavy as I remembered it being. It was filled with crocks, and the crocks were filled with mead. Sighing again, I swung it up over my shoulder.

"Careful," Berthold told me. He turned to Marta. "My queen?"

"Yes?"

"May I take that piece of fabric? It may prove useful."

"Certainly," she said. She lifted it from the arm of the throne and handed it to him. Leaning toward me, he tucked it into the narrow opening of the bag. Then he clapped me merrily on the shoulder. The other shoulder. "Off we go," he said. It was, of course, to carry his mead that Berthold needed an "assistant." For some reason, several years ago, he'd taken a fancy to me. Not in any physical way—I don't think that Berthold had ever taken a physical fancy to anything, except mead. But he had decided that, during these investigations of his, he would have no one else haul his supply from place to place.

He had already cracked open his first crock by the time we arrived at our destination. Gunter and Karla's cave was one of the smaller ones, at the edge of the valley, on the other side of the mastodon tracks. As we approached along the dusty path, through the trembling fields of grass, we saw Ulrich standing alone. When we were nearer, we saw the body. It lay in the middle of the path, five or six feet away from where Ulrich stood.

"Greetings, Ulrich," said Berthold, almost cheerfully.

Ulrich was short, dark brown, thin and sleek. His face was grim as he nodded. "Greetings, Berthold," he said. "Greetings, Doder."

"Terrible thing, isn't it?" said Berthold. He took another swig of mead.

Ulrich nodded sadly. "Terrible. Why would they do such a thing?"

Smiling, Berthold raised a single eyebrow. "Whom do you mean?"

Ulrich looked at him, frowning. "But wasn't it the Outlanders? That strip of cloth ...?"

Berthold smiled again. "Ah yes. The Outlanders. Why indeed?" He shrugged. "Well, that's precisely the sort of thing we're here to learn." He turned to me. "Oh, stop puffing, Doder. You can set it down now."

With a grunt, I swung the bag from my shoulder, set it down on the ground. Crocks clinked and clanked within.

Looking down at the body, Berthold sipped thoughtfully at his crock, then said, "He certainly does look dead, doesn't he?"

That he did. Gunter's eyes were shut. His pale, stiffened tongue poked obscenely from his open mouth. The patches of skin that showed through his beard and hair were mottled a bluish- black, like an enormous bruise. Gunter was—had been—a small man, about the same size as Ulrich. He seemed even smaller now, somehow shriveled, as he lay there silent and naked against the brown dust. Berthold glanced left and right. "No good tracks," he said, and turned to Ulrich. "You and Karla did a fine job of disturbing the ground."

Ulrich frowned, as though wounded. "But we were trying to revive Gunter. We weren't thinking about tracks."

"Clearly not," said Berthold. He sighed. "Very well. Suppose you tell me exactly what happened this morning."

What Ulrich told him was more or less what Karla had said. He had been tending to his wife, Heidi, when Karla came running into the cave, hysterical. After a moment, he had understood that something had happened to Gunter. He had followed Karla back here, attempted to revive Gunter, then run with Karla to Marta's cave.

Berthold nodded. "Your cave," he said, "yours and Heidi's, is another hundred yards into the forest? In that direction?" He nodded toward the south.

"Yes."

"Did anything unusual occur this morning, before Karla arrived?"

"No."

"You heard nothing, saw nothing?"

"No. I was inside the cave, Berthold. With Heidi."

Once again, Berthold nodded. "When you first came to the body with Karla, did you see anyone about?"

"No."

Berthold sipped again at his mead. "And after Marta sent you back here, was the body as you'd left it?"

"Yes."

"And no one has interfered with it since?"

"Some people came by and wanted to bury it. But I told them that Marta wanted to wait." He glanced toward the south for a moment, toward his cave, then looked back to Berthold. "May I go now? Marta asked me to return to her when you arrived. And I must find someone to stay with Heidi."

Berthold was staring down at Gunter. He nodded. "You run along."

For a moment, Ulrich, too, looked down at the body. He said, "He was a good man." He looked back up at Berthold. "He'll get buried soon, won't he?"

Berthold smiled. "Tell the queen that she can send the burial detail whenever she likes."

Ulrich nodded, and then, with another sad glance at the body, he shuffled off.

Berthold watched him for a moment, then turned to me. He sipped at his crock, then said, "Let's see what we have here."

He squatted down beside the body and silently studied it for a few moments. Finally he said, "He's very clean, wouldn't you say?"

I nodded. "Gunter always had excellent grooming skills."

He reached out, lifted one of Gunter's hands. "No marks on the hands," he said. "No marks anywhere, except around his neck." He looked up at me. "Help me turn him over, would you?"

"What for?" I asked.

"To get to the other side," he said, and he grinned, for this was the punch line to a very old joke. His sense of humor was one of the many reasons why Berthold spent so much time alone. "Please don't ask questions, Doder. Just help me turn him over."

Reluctantly, I did. Gunter's flesh was cold and slack. I stepped back, rubbing my hands on my thighs. My thighs didn't warm them; they chilled my thighs.

"Curious," said Berthold.

"What?"

"Here. This indentation in the skull." His slender finger dipped lightly into the injury, and my stomach dipped lightly into my knees.

Swallowing bile, I straightened up. "He hit his head when he fell?"

Berthold shook his head. "There are no rocks here, nothing that could make such an impression. No, he was struck with some sort of blunt instrument."

"A musical instrument?" I frowned. "A whistle?" At the time, the whistle was our only musical instrument. "How could a whistle do that?"

"Not a *musical* instrument."

"A great many whistles, maybe, dropped from a great height?"

"No, no," he said impatiently. "I mean a *thing*. A *blunt* thing."

"Ah." I nodded. I looked at him. "What blunt thing?"

His eyes narrowed. "When we discover this, perhaps we shall also discover who destroyed him."

He pulled himself upright and then stared off thoughtfully across the valley. Without looking at me, he handed me the empty crock.

I took it. "Another?" I asked.

He nodded, still looking off. I slipped the empty into the bag, pulled out a full crock, uncorked it.

Handing him the crock, I said, "Was it the Outlanders?"

He turned to me and smiled. "Let's ask them, shall we?"

The Outlanders lived to the south, a few miles beyond the cave of Ulrich and Heidi. We walked the distance in silence, Berthold sipping now and then at his mead. When we were still more than a few hundred yards away from the Outlander village, the dense, rank stench of them began to clot the air.

By then, Berthold had finished the second crock. He handed it to me and said, "Another, please."

I swung the bag from my shoulder, slipped in the empty, plucked out a fresh one. "You're going through those pretty quickly," I pointed out.

Taking the fresh crock, he nodded. "This is a three crock problem, my friend." He sipped at the crock. "Now, listen to me. When we're among the Outlanders, do me the kindness of keeping your thoughts, such as they are, to yourself."

"I—"

"Not a word."

"All right," I said. "Fine." His fine hand at diplomacy was another reason why Berthold spent a lot of time alone.

The smell got stronger and more suffocating as we approached. To my amazement, Berthold was well-known to the Outlanders. When we passed by the first of their frail wooden structures, some of them emerged from inside and waved merrily, calling out his name. The young of their breed ran toward us, laughing, cooing with pleasure, jabbering in their ridiculous Outlander language. The reek was so thick now that my eyes were watering.

They were a strange-looking race—they were all immensely tall, for one thing, and they all wore clothes, trousers of leather, blouses of cloth. They wore them, I guess, because they were mostly hairless, except for some thin, flimsy, yellowish stuff sprouting at the tops of their round little heads. All of them, young and adult alike, looked like infants who had somehow grown to a preposterous size. I was coughing badly, nearly gagging, when an Outlander male suddenly came toward us.

"Hey, Berthold," he cried. "Fantastic! You're looking great!" He spoke The Language surprising well. Grinning widely, he held out his enormous hand and snatched up Berthold's smaller one and pumped it furiously.

"Thank you, Bob," Berthold said. "This is my assistant, Doder."

"Hey!" said Bob. He held out his hand and a wave of stench blasted me. Swallowing, I took the hand and let it crush my own for a moment. "Fantastic!" said Bob. "Any friend of Berthold's is a friend of mine!" He released me finally, then turned to Berthold. "So what's happening? What brings you here?"

"Nothing good, I'm afraid," Berthold told him gravely. "One of our people has been destroyed."

"Oh, no," said Bob. He shook his head sadly. "Bad one."

Berthold said, "The piece of fabric, please, Doder."

I set down the bag, rummaged through the crocks inside, found the strip, handed it to Berthold.

"And this was found," he said, "wrapped around the man's neck." He held the strip out to Bob, who took it and examined it for a moment.

"Hey," said Bob, and looked up. "This is ours!" He frowned. "Looks like some of Tammy's stuff." He glanced around at the crowd of wide-eyed Outlanders who now surrounded us, then called out, "Tammy?"

A female stepped forward. Bob jabbered at her for a moment, handed her the cloth, then jabbered some more.

The female nodded, jabbered back at Bob, then returned the strip.

Bob looked at Berthold. "She says it's part of a blouse she made. The blouse was stolen. It was hanging out on the line, and someone walked off with it."

"When was this?" asked Bertold.

"Last week."

Berthold nodded. "Tell me, Bob. Has anything else gone missing from your village lately?"

Bob cocked his round little head. "Funny you should ask," he said. "There *was* something."

"And what was that?"

"Some thorn apple seeds. Someone took them from Pete's house. That was about a week ago, too."

"Pete the Priest?" said Berthold.

"Right." Bob seemed concerned. "I've been pretty worried. I wouldn't want the wrong person to get his hands on those."

Berthold nodded, then took a sip of mead. "I suspect, Bob," he said, "that the wrong person already has."

Before nightfall, we were all back in Marta's cave–Marta, Karla, Ulrich, Berthold and me. We were sitting around on the stone benches, except for Marta, who sat on her ceremonial throne, and Berthold, who stood in the center of the room.

"Clearly," he said, "it was not an Outlander who destroyed Gunter." He upended his crock, took a swallow of mead.

"But what," said Marta, "of the strip of cloth?"

"Their leader, Bob, informed me that the strip came from a blouse stolen last week from one of the Outlander women."

Marta sat back, crossed her legs. "And how do you know that this Bob"—her sarcasm curled around the strange-sounding syllable—"spoke the truth?"

"One has merely to smell the thing," said Berthold. "It smells of Outlander, yes, but the smell is faint. Had an Outlander been in contact with it recently, it would fairly reek of their distinctive odor."

He sipped again at his crock. "And even assuming that some Outlander possessed a motive for killing Gunter—obviously an unwarranted assumption—why would this mythical Outlander bother to strangle him? Even the smallest of their women is larger and stronger than Gunter was. Any Outlander could have killed him with a simple blow to the head."

"But there *was* a blow to the head," I said. "You told me so yourself."

"There was indeed. But could an Outlander, stinking as he would, approach close enough to strike Gunter without Gunter being aware of it?"

"The Outlander could've thrown a rock," I said.

He smiled. "Perhaps. But the blow that struck Gunter was powerful enough to render him unconscious immediately. And yet—" he swigged some mead, turned to Karla "—Gunter's wife tells us that Gunter cried out *twice*."

Karla blinked. "But perhaps he saw the Outlander, and cried out. And then he turned and ran, and the Outlander, as Doder says, threw a rock. And he cried out again when he was hit."

"Gunter would then have fallen forward. But there was no dust on his face or chest."

Karla frowned. "Maybe I made a mistake. About the second cry."

"Oh, you made a mistake," said Berthold, and smiled cheerfully. He turned to Marta. "Karla, of course, stole the blouse from the Outlander village. And she also stole some thorn apple seeds. Now, very few people know that the effects of these seeds, when eaten, is to mimic serious illness—fever, night sweats, prolonged sleep, and ultimately death. But Karla would have known. As your niece, she is of the royal line."

Scorn flashed across Karla's face. "Ridiculous! Why would I steal thorn apple seeds?"

Berthold smiled once more. "To give them to Ulrich, of course. So he could feed them to his wife. So she would be quite unconscious while he helped you destroy Gunter."

Ulrich was very quick. He leaped from the bench, dashed across the room, hurtled out the door. Only to be dragged back through it, an instant later, by two of Marta's guards, Wolfgang and Friedrich. Berthold had posted them there before the meeting. Two other guards, Leopold and Loeb, followed close behind.

For a moment, Ulrich squirmed against two pairs of strong hands. Then he turned to Berthold and shouted, "It was her! It was her idea! I hit him, yes, with a rock, but it was she who strangled him!"

"Idiot!" snarled Karla. "*Coward!*"

Marta looked at Leopold and Loeb. "Take her," she said.

And that's the true tale of the first murder. Karla and Ulrich confessed—not with any great eagerness, naturally; but we had ways of making them talk. They were in love, and poor Gunter and Heidi, Ulrich's wife, stood in their way—so they decided to remove them. Back then it was strange, unheard of; now, of course, it's an old story.

The funny thing is, even after they were stoned to death, and Gunter's relatives (and Heidi) had been appeased, the village was never quite the same. A kind of closeness was gone from among us. People began to eye each other warily. It was as though Karla and Ulrich had let loose some sort of demon. By doing what they'd done, by demonstrating a capacity for evil, they had also demonstrated that all of us, any of us, might share in it.

Some of the people actually left the clan, wandered off in pairs or on their own. Among them was Berthold. He just disappeared one day, vanished, six months later. It was said that he'd gone to join the Outlanders; but no one really knew.

As for me, after Berthold left I stayed with the clan for another few months. And then my wife, Ursula, took sick—a terrible fever, with night sweats and prolonged sleep—and at last the poor woman passed away. And I decided that it was time for me to move on, as well.

And so I came here, to this valley. And along the way ...

But that's another story.

Beneath the Sighs

('*Tis the Season for Murder*, Worldwide Books, 1998)

Feroze Mohammed, the executive editor at Worldwide, which published the Joshua Croft stories in paperback, asked me for a "Christmas" story to include in an anthology. At that point, I had essentially finished the Joshua Croft series, but I'd left the ending somewhat open, so I could pick the series up again, if I chose to do so. I decided to pick up Joshua in this case, even if only briefly. I suspect that Feroze was hoping for some jolly, tinsel and tinkling bells kind of story. Which isn't, of course, what he got.

When I got to Vanessie's on Monday night, around eight, the place was nearly empty. Not too many years ago, at that hour on any night of the week, you wouldn't have been able to find a seat at the broad rectangular bar.

But there was a new owner now, and there was a new piano player behind the big black Steinway, and there were new cocktail waitresses wearing the familiar black skirts and white tuxedo shirts. Gordon, the literary bartender, was off in Europe somewhere—writing a novel, I'd heard—and I didn't know the man who was pouring drinks these days. He was younger than Gordon had been, and he was certainly younger than I was. He looked about twelve.

And the few customers who were there, sitting around the piano, or huddling at the small tables near the two big fireplaces at opposite ends of the enormous room, were all younger than the people I remembered. It seemed that every day there were more and more of these young strangers in town, jostling and bustling, pushing the rest of us farther and farther away from the center of things, and closer and closer to the edge of the ledge. They probably thought that we belonged at the edge of the ledge. Or over it. And maybe they were right.

But Jim was at the bar, as Jim usually was, sitting in one corner, hunched over his snifter of Rémy Martin. He was wearing an opened shearling coat and a black Western shirt with mother- of-pearl buttons. On his head was a black Stetson. Jim was originally from New York, but he'd been here for twenty years and he took his Western wear seriously.

When I unzipped my leather jacket and sat down next to him, he smiled at me wearily and raised his glass. "Merry Christmas, Joshua."

"Merry Christmas," I said. It was the twenty-second of December. Two more shopping days until the Big Event. We hadn't had any snow for nearly a month, but the new piano player was softly singing "Winter Wonderland."

Jim took a drag from his cigarette and said to the bartender, "Give my father here whatever he wants."

The young man looked at me and I said, "Jack Daniel's on the rocks, a water on the side." I turned to Jim. "How's it going?"

"Same old same old." In his late fifties, overweight, Jim didn't look well, and he hadn't looked well for a long time. His loose jowls were gray, his cheekbones were flushed with the exploded capillaries of the heavy drinker. "My lungs are shot," he said, "my stomach's going, and I've got a pancreas the size of a football."

My drink arrived. I held it out and Jim clicked the snifter against it. "To good health," he said.

His hand was shaking slightly. It would shake less and less as the evening wore on, and by the end of the night, when he could barely walk, it would be rock steady.

"How about you?" he asked me.

It was a good drink, fire and silk, my first of the day and as welcome as a ticket home. "Hanging in there," I said.

"You heard from Rita?" Exhaling smoke, he stubbed his cigarette out in the ashtray.

"No," I said.

"She's on the Navajo reservation, right? Doing something with kids?"

"What I hear."

"You know where, exactly?"

"No."

"But you could find out, right? I mean, you're a detective. That's what you do."

"She asked me not to. She wants some space."

He nodded. "Plenty of space on the Navajo reservation."

"Yeah."

"Must be hard," he said, "losing a partner like that."

I didn't say anything. Rita had been more than a partner.

Jim took another sip from his Rémy. "You keeping up with the work?"

"What there is of it."

Jim frowned suddenly. "Hey. I got an idea."
"Got to be careful with those, Jim."
"No, I'm serious. You want a job?"
I looked at him. "Doing what?"
"Finding someone."
"Who?"
"You know Phillip? The homeless guy with the beard, hangs out at the library? Wears the monk's robe?"
"The one who makes those signs?"
"Yeah. It's poetry. You ever read any of it?"
"No."
"It's pretty good. I mean, some of it's a little loopy. UFOs and aliens. "X-Files" stuff. But some of it's about the sky and the trees, the arroyos. Nature. I like it." He took another sip of brandy. "At least it scans, which is more than you can say for most poetry these days."
"He's missing?"
"Yeah. I asked at the library today. They said they hadn't seen him for three or four days."
"It's winter," I said. "And it's cold." The temperature hadn't climbed above freezing for a week. "Maybe he left town."
"Yeah, right. He chartered a Learjet and he flew to the Caymans. He's homeless, Joshua. He hasn't got dime one. And he's been here for six or seven winters that I know of."
"Why the interest in him?"
"What? Oh. You remember that last wedding? Mine, I mean?"
"To Sophia?"
"Sophia was the one before. This was Evelyn, the cocktail waitress." He tapped a cigarette from a pack of Camel Lights, stuck it in the corner of his mouth.
"Right," I said. "Whatever happened to Evelyn?"
With a gold Dunhill lighter he lit the cigarette. He inhaled deeply, exhaled a cone of blue smoke. "Took the divorce settlement," he said, "and went off to Phoenix. Opened a bar of her own. Doing pretty well, I hear. All of them are. All five of them. I'm like that MacArthur guy, with the Genius Grants. Except that none of my wives needs to be a genius. All she needs is a lawyer. And he doesn't need to be a genius, either."
He sipped at the brandy. "Anyway, I didn't really know Phillip. Saw him in the library for years, working away at those signs with his Magic Marker, but I never said a word to him. Or vice versa. And I don't know how he

found out about the wedding—don't know how he knew who I was, even—but I'm over there one day, in the library, and he comes up to me and hands me one of the signs. A big sheet of white cardboard, about two feet by three. It was a poem. About the wedding. My wedding. And it was a pretty nice poem, too. I still have it somewhere." He frowned. "Unless Evelyn walked with it."

He drank some more brandy, inhaled some smoke, exhaled. "I thought it was damn sweet of him. I offered him money, but he said he never took money for his work. He's not much of an entrepreneur, Phillip. So what I did, a few months later, when I saw him at Christmastime, I gave him a twenty. A Christmas gift, right? Had nothing to do with his work. And I've been dropping a twenty on him every Christmas, last couple of years. I don't know what he does with it. Doesn't use it to get that damned robe dry-cleaned, that's for sure. Maybe he spends it on Magic Markers."

I smiled. "You're a soft touch, Jim."

"That's what Gonzales says. My divorce lawyer. Anyway, no one's seen Phillip for three or four days, and Christmas is coming up. Look." He reached back, tugged out his wallet, brought it around in front of him. He opened it, slipped out two fifties and laid them on the bar. "How much of your time will that buy?"

"Put it back. I'll check around, see what I can find out."

He lifted the fifties, folded them and slipped them into my shirt pocket. "Don't be a jerk. Take the money. I'll only waste it on this poison, anyway." Lightly he waved his glass. He noticed that it was empty. He looked up at me. "Speaking of which, you ready for another?"

"Sure. But this one's on me."

It became a long night. We talked about the people we knew who had left Santa Fe for other towns, or other worlds. There were a lot of people. By the time I got out into the parking lot, it was nearly one in the morning. Fat gray flakes of snow were slowly spinning down through the yellow lights of the street lamps. Maybe we'd be having a white Christmas after all.

By the time I woke up, the snow had stopped falling and the sun was shining. Outside the window, everything beneath the blinding blue of the sky was blinding white. I was feeling a little rocky, and I poured myself a beer. It tasted better than it should have tasted at eight o'clock in the morning. There was some leftover pizza in the refrigerator and I tore off a chunk and nuked it in the microwave.

While I ate, I turned on the weather channel. Lately I hadn't been using the television for much of anything else. A large part of my living room was taken up by a twenty-one-inch thermometer with stereo sound.

According to the experts, the local temperature was twenty degrees, and the high today would be twenty-eight. I felt a bit better after the beer and the pizza—a well-balanced meal will do that for you—but after seeing the forecast, I wanted to crawl back into bed.

I had promised Jim, though, so I showered, dressed, slipped on my sunglasses and stepped out into the cold.

In town, the four inches of snow had already turned to gray slush in the streets. Land Rovers and Ford Broncos and Chevy Blazers all took turns splashing it at each other as they whizzed by.

The main library is on Washington Street, in the same building that once held the police department, before the P.D. moved out toward Airport Road. It was in this building, years ago, that I'd first met Sergeant Hector Ramirez, who had introduced me to Rita. Normally when I went to the library I didn't think about that, but I did today. This would be my first Christmas in a long time without her.

Janice was working behind the desk. She was a trim, handsome woman in her fifties, wearing Levi's and, over a white blouse, a red crew-neck sweater with a white band at the chest, where reindeer pranced. Like a lot of women in Santa Fe, she had let her hair grow naturally gray, and she wore it wrapped atop her head, attractively careless in a thick loose bun.

"Merry Christmas, Joshua."

"Merry Christmas, Janice. How's the book business?"

"People still read, amazingly enough. How's Rita? Have you heard?"

"No. Listen, Janice, I'm trying to locate Phillip. The guy who hangs out here. With the robe?"

Her face went concerned. "Is he in trouble?"

"Why do you ask?"

"Well, if you're looking for him ..." The sentence trailed off into a question.

"A friend of mine knows him," I said. "He wanted to give him something for Christmas, but he hasn't seen him around."

"No one has. Not since last week. I saw him—when was it? Thursday, when I gave him a sort of early Christmas present."

"What'd you give him?" I was curious what sort of gift you gave a homeless man who wore a monk's robe while he painted poetry on cardboard signs.

"Just an old watch. Like this one." She held up her wrist and showed me an electronic timepiece. "I just bought this for myself. I had an earlier version, and it seemed silly to throw it out, so I gave it to Phillip. It holds phone numbers."

"Phillip makes a lot of phone calls, does he?"

She smiled. "You don't have to use it for phone numbers. You can use it for whatever you like. Phillip put poetry in it. I showed him how to do it with the computer."

"The computer."

"The watch downloads from a computer monitor. You type in the information, then hold the watch up to the monitor."

"Black magic."

She smiled again. "More like a bar code reader."

"Like I said. Black magic."

"You really are a Luddite, aren't you, Joshua?"

"Want to see my membership card? It's hand-printed."

Another smile. "Anyway," she said, "I put the software onto one of our computers, and then I helped him to get started. He was very excited. It was fun to watch him. He likes the computer, likes using it for his poetry. And now, he said, he could carry it around with him wherever he went."

"And where would he go, Janice? Do you know where he lives? Where he stays?"

She shook her head. "Up in the hills, I think. I think he has a shack somewhere, up behind St. John's College. But I couldn't tell you where, exactly."

There were thousands of acres of forest land in the hills behind St. John's.

"Does he have any friends?" I asked her. "Does he hang out with anyone?"

She frowned, thinking for a moment, and then said, "I've seen him with Brent. Another homeless person, an older man. He's usually here—most of them come here in the winter, during the day, for the warmth. But he hasn't been in today. Thank goodness."

"Why thank goodness?"

She frowned. "Well, I don't like to say anything unkind about these people. The homeless. Some of them obviously don't have any choice. And some of them, like Phillip, are really very sweet. But Brent—there's something...unpleasant about him."

"Unpleasant how?"

"Furtive. Sneaky. We've had a couple of people lose things here—purses, book bags. No one could prove it was Brent, but I'm fairly certain it was."

I asked for a description and she gave me one—in his fifties, bearded, bald, thin, usually wore a long black overcoat.

"Anyone else?" I asked her.

"There's a Native American man named John. He's a panhandler. I always see him asking people for money, just outside the library. I've asked him to stop, but he only goes across the street, in front of the bank, and does it there."

"Big guy, long black hair? Usually drunk?"

"Yes. Do you know him?"

"I've seen him over there. Okay, Janice. Thanks."

"Will you get back to me?" she said. "Will you let me know if Phillip's all right? I've been a little worried. He's usually here every day."

"Sure," I said.

John, the panhandler, wasn't across the street. I went through town on foot, looking for him and Brent.

John I found on the Plaza, hitting up the tourists in their color-coordinated ski costumes.

He was a big, bulky man wearing an old red parka, greasy Levi's, battered cowboy boots. Leaning against one of the elm trees along San Francisco Street, I watched him for a while. His approach to panhandling walked that fine line between begging and extortion. He would come looming up to a tourist, all broad shoulders and long black hair and bleary red eyes, the stereotypical Drunken Indian, and he would say, in a gruff and whiskey-scarred voice, "Got some spare change, bro?" Almost all the tourists found some cash for him, happy to get away alive, and with their scalps intact.

After a few minutes of watching, I wandered over to him. "Hey, John," I said.

The red-rimmed eyes squinted at me. "I know you, bro?"

"Joshua Croft." I put out my hand and he took it. Neither of us was wearing gloves. He might have been drunk, but his hand was still strong. It was also damp.

I let go of his hand, and I was careful not to wipe mine against my pants. "John," I said, "I'm looking for Phillip."

He looked at me blankly. "Who?"

"Phillip. The guy who writes those signs in the library."

His big body was wavering slightly, forward and back, as he stood there. He was an inch or so taller than I, with a broad Indio face and slack, thick lips and that dull, blank expression. I didn't like him much, but not because of his face. I didn't like him because he was a drunk, and he reminded me of that beer I'd finished off at breakfast.

"Oh," he said. "Yeah. Phillip." He squinted again. "How come?"

"His family is trying to find him."

He shook his head. "Phillip don't have no family, bro."

"Not in Santa Fe. Back East. An uncle. There's some money involved."

The eyes narrowed again. "For Phillip?"

"Yeah. And for anyone who helps me. I hear he's got a place up in the hills. You know where it is?"

The eyes darted briefly to the right and then his glance found mine again. "What're you? Like a cop?"

"Private detective."

"Like Magnum P.I.? The guy on television?"

"Yeah." Apparently John hadn't been watching his television for a while, either.

He put his big head slightly back. "So what's it worth to you?"

I pulled out my wallet, opened it, slipped out a ten.

He reached for it and I jerked it back. "Hold on." I slid the wallet back into my pocket, tore the ten in half.

"Hey!" he said.

"Here." I handed him one half of the bill, put the other in my pocket.

"This is no good," he said, looking up from the torn banknote.

"You tell me how to find the place. When I find it, I'll come back and give you the other half."

He mulled that over. Then, squinting once more, he said, "How do I know you'll give it to me?"

"What am I going to do with half of a ten-dollar bill?"

"Yeah, but how you gonna find me?"

"I found you this time."

"Yeah, but maybe I'll be out of town."

On another chartered flight to the Caymans, maybe.

I took out a pen. "Here, give me that."

He pulled his hand away. The thing had been worthless until I reached for it.

"Don't worry," I said. "I'll give it back."

Reluctantly he handed over the note. I took out a pen, wrote my office address on it, handed it back. "If I don't find you, you come find me."

He looked down at what I'd written as though it were Sanskrit.

"Okay," I said. "How do I get to Phillip's place?"
He told me.

I PARKED THE CHEROKEE along the side of Camino Cabra, the road that led up to St. John's College. Through the narrow clearing on the east, its grasses bowed beneath the snow, a narrow white unmarked pathway led up toward the nearby hills, among the juniper and piñon. I got out of the car and I started walking.

I walked for over a mile, the snow crunching beneath my work boots, the path wandering higher and higher, above the scrub pines and up into the dark ponderosas. I was panting and my heart was thudding against my ribs. I was out of shape. Not enough swimming in the municipal pool lately, and too many Jack Daniel's in the local bars. Too many beers for breakfast.

I kept walking, and I missed a turnoff I was supposed to take, and I had to backtrack to find it, nearly sliding down the slippery slope, and then I kept walking again, through the dimness beneath the big solemn trees. In some places the branches overhead were so thick the snow hadn't reached the layer of pale brown pine needles covering the ground.

After almost an hour I found it, tucked at the rear of a small flat clearing, half-hidden beneath the slumping, snow-draped boughs of a ponderosa.

Shack was optimistic. It was about four feet high and about seven feet long. It had been hammered together with bits of plywood and scrap lumber. Its roof was a sagging sheet of rusted corrugated iron. There was a rough wooden door with a loop of rawhide for a handle. I pulled on it.

Tumbling out of the shack came the reek of unwashed human. I took off my sunglasses, stuck them into my jacket pocket. I was still panting from the climb, but I turned my head, took a breath, squatted down into a duck walk and went inside.

No Phillip, and not much of anything else. A cheap thin mattress on the hard-packed dirt floor. Carefully folded into a neat pile at its foot, three or four old woolen blankets. Beside the mattress, a Mickey Mouse coffee cup that held three Magic Markers. Beside that, a plastic designer-water bottle, its sides scratched and dented as though it had been refilled many times. It had been half-filled with water, but now the water was ice.

I was breathing in there, but not happily. I looked around some more. In one corner of the tiny room there was a small pile of ash and, next to it, an old aluminum saucepan. Stacked neatly against the wall there were three or four of Phillip's white cardboard signs. I lifted one, held it so I could read it by the light from the open door.

Two lines in thick block letters.

and beneath the sighs,
only the perfect Silence

I put back the sign and scuttled out the door. I stood up and sucked in a deep lungful of sweet fresh air, edged with the spiky scent of pine. I walked away from the shack, into the clearing, and I stopped to look out toward the west.

The sun was shining and the cloudless sky was that cobalt blue you sometimes find on old Chinese porcelain. The ground dropped off at the far end of the clearing, and I could see past the tops of the ponderosas, wrapped in snow like old men in shawls, down to the brown adobe clutter of Santa Fe, all the tiny roofs frosted over now, here and there a thin gray streamer of smoke curling upward from a tiny chimney. Farther out, beyond the thin brown line of trees that marked the Rio Grande, I could see the distant white slopes of the Jemez Mountains. Everything looked clearer and cleaner and sharper than it had any right to look.

Something happened then, and I'm not sure why. Maybe it happened because I was seeing all this after being trapped inside the cramped, tidy misery of that little shack.

My heart was still thumping in my chest. I could hear it. I could hear my own breathing. Somewhere nearby, a raven cawed. Closer, somewhere, a small clump of snow slipped from a branch and made a faint puffing sound when it landed.

And then, suddenly, as I stood there below that sleek blue bowl of sky, in that dazzle of white, in the center of that fierce bright beauty, I could hear the sound that lay beneath all the others, the sound that Phillip had written about. The perfect Silence.

It didn't last for long, for a moment or two, maybe for only a second or two. But while it lasted, I was a part of it. Everything else fell away. Rita, the failures, the triumphs, the griefs, the joys, the sorrows, the hopes. Everything. If I had died just then, it would have been okay. It would have been perfectly acceptable.

And then two more things happened. They seemed to happen simultaneously, but one of them may have caused the other. I don't know.

Somehow, abruptly, the Silence changed its pitch, became higher; and I noticed a narrow mound of snow near the north side of the clearing.

The Silence disappeared as I walked toward the mound. I squatted down at one end of it, brushed away the snow. Phillip had blue eyes, clouded over now as they stared up at the cloudless blue sky.

"You should've stayed there," Hector Ramirez said.

"How was I supposed to call you from up there?" I said. I was back at the library, using one of the pay phones outside the building.

"Why don't you break down and buy a cell phone?"

"Listen, Hector. It won't be hard for your people to find him. My footprints go right up to the body. But you're going to need a good-sized crew to get him down from there."

"You didn't fool around with the scene any?"

"I told you. I went inside the shack. I touched one of those signs. I touched the body. I cleared the snow away from his face and away from his wrist. That's it."

"I want you in here, making a statement."

"Soon. I've got to do a few things first."

"It's always got to be *your* way, right?"

"If I hadn't found him, you wouldn't know he was there."

"Two hours. And then I want you in here."

"Right. See you later."

He hung up.

I went into the library, to tell Janice.

There aren't a lot of pawn shops in Santa Fe, and it didn't take me long to find the one that had what I wanted.

"That watch there," I said, and pointed.

The fat man opened the door at the back of the display case and took out the watch. He wiped it off with a gray cotton rag. I didn't bother trying to stop him. If it was the right watch, fingerprints wouldn't matter.

"This is very high-tech," he said. "Stores your phone numbers, your addresses, what have you. You download everything right from your computer. Right off the monitor."

The air inside the shop was stale and stifling. Under my leather jacket I was sweating.

He wasn't wearing a jacket, only a black T-shirt, but he was sweating, too. He handed me the watch. "You need the right software," he said, "but the company, they've got a web site you can download it from. You're on the web, right?"

"No," I said. I pushed one of the buttons on the watch. The liquid crystal face lit up. Wrong button. I pushed another. Some letters went scrawling across the face and they became words. *and beneath the sighs.*

I put the watch down on the countertop. It made a small clicking sound as the metal met the glass.

"Who brought it in?" I asked him.

"Sorry, buddy. I can't divulge my clients' names."

I nodded. "Mind if I use your phone?"

"Local call?"

"Yeah," I said. "The cops."

I talked to Hector, and then the fat man talked to Hector, and he told Hector who had brought in the watch, and then I talked to Hector again and told him I'd come by to make my statement as soon as I checked the mail at the office.

Fifteen minutes later I was about to unlock the office door when I heard a sound behind me.

The office was on the second floor of a three-story building. John had been sitting on the flight that led up to the third floor, waiting.

He lumbered toward me in his red parka, his bulk filling the narrow corridor. "You found it, right?" he said.

"I found it."

"So can I have my money now?"

"The guy at the pawn shop said he gave you a ten for the watch, John. That's the last ten dollars you'll be making for a while."

He was big but he was slow and he was drunk. Six months ago he wouldn't have been able to touch me. But I was out of shape and I was still exhausted from climbing through the mountains.

His big right fist came up from the floor, it seemed like, and I dropped my keys and almost managed to block the punch with my left arm. But the fist slammed into the side of my head and scraped back along my ear, and for a second I was stunned. He threw another punch, a left, and it caught me on the shoulder. My right arm went numb.

I needed some room. I smashed the toe of my boot against his shin and he grunted, and I straight-armed him in the chest, ramming him away from me. I backed up. My right was beginning to work again.

He didn't stay away for long. He was finished with the fancy stuff. No more punching. He moved toward me, hands out, fingers open, wanting to tear me apart. But his expression hadn't changed. It was still the same dull, blank expression it had been when I first met him. It probably hadn't changed when he clubbed Phillip, or when he stripped the watch from his wrist. It probably changed only once in every day, when he had that first drink of the morning, the one that promised to wipe away all the pain.

He lunged for me, head and shoulders down. There wasn't room in the corridor for me to play bullfighter, so I braced myself and let him come, and when he hit me, shoving me back, I slammed both my hands, fingers locked, at his neck. He grunted again and I brought my knee up into his face, as hard as I could. His arms dropped and I smashed him with the other knee. He made a huge crashing sound when he met the floor, and then, immediately, as though he'd just rolled over in bed, he started to snore.

I found my keys. It took me a while to locate the right one, and then it took me a while to get it into the lock. The lock kept jumping around. But finally, I managed it, and I went inside and called Hector.

Afterward, after Hector and the others had left, taking John with them, I called Jim and told him.

"Ten dollars?" he said. "He killed Phillip for ten dollars?"

"Yeah."

For a few moments he was silent on the line. Then he let out his breath in a long slow sibilant sigh. "Sometimes," he said, "I don't think there's any hope for any of us."

"Yeah," I said. "I know the feeling."

When I hung up, I noticed that the mail was waiting in the brass box beneath the slot in the door. It had probably been there the entire time. I got up from the desk, went across the room, pulled out the envelopes. I carried them back to the desk, sat down and started to go through them. Three or four Christmas cards from friends, a brochure from some "security equipment consultants," a few bills.

And an envelope that had my name written on it in a neat, familiar script, and a postmark from Chinle, Arizona. Chinle was on the Navajo reservation.

It was a simple card with a simple, almost childish print of a Christmas tree on the front. Inside, she had written, "Merry Christmas, Joshua. Soon, I think." And then her name.

Soon, I thought. And what then?

I opened the drawer of the desk and took out the bottle of Jack Daniel's and a water glass. I opened the bottle, poured myself a drink. I swiveled the chair around and sat back and put the heels of my boots up on the windowsill. I took a sip of the drink and I stared up at the white mountains shouldering into the clear blue sky.

I sat there for a long time, slowly drinking, in the silence.

But it wasn't a perfect Silence. I couldn't remember what that had sounded like.

A MISHAP AT THE MANOR

(*Malice Domestic #9*, edited by Joan Hess, Avon Books, 2000)

When Joan Hess asked me to write a story for the ninth Malice Domestic *book, an anthology dedicated to Agatha Christie, I decided to have a bit of fun with two of Ms. Christie's well-known characters, and with the whole idea of the amateur sleuth. I don't know if all the readers shared in the fun, but I know that Sarah Caudwell did. She read it in manuscript, in the fall of 1999. We were going to meet the next summer in Washington, at the Malice Domestic Conference. Unfortunately, Sarah didn't make it. She died in January of 2000.*

*Lulubelle Courage, by the way, is the name of a character in a remarkable trilogy written in the 1960s by Frank McAuliffe—*Of all the Bloody Cheek, Rather a Vicious Gentleman, *and* For Murder I Charge More. *These dark, clever, very funny books feature a professional assassin named Augustus Mandrell, and I'm pleased to say that they will shortly be re-issued by PointBlank Press.*

A HUNDRED yards away, their long necks stretched taut, two giraffes elegantly nibbled at the leaves of an elm tree.

"A nasty business, sir," said Sergeant Meadows.

"Nasty enough, Sergeant," said Inspector Marsh. His hands behind his back, he stood staring out at the library's casement window. Hard to believe, with giraffes lolling about outside, that he was still in Devon. "Some sort of an explorer, wasn't he? This lord fellow?"

"Not an explorer, not as such," said Meadows. "More of—well, sir, what you'd call him, I suppose, would be a kind of wild man. He lost his parents in an airplane crash in 1902, and nearly died himself. He was adopted by a tribe of great apes, they tell me. In Africa, this was."

"Africa, eh? Extraordinary. And when did he return to England?"

"Just after the war. From all accounts, he got along well with the old lord, his grandfather. He went into the family business, and took it over when the old man died."

"Publishing, isn't it?"

"That's right. Greystoke Press. Thrillers, crime novels. Trash, basically.

But he did very well with it."

"Curious."

"How so, sir?"

"Fellow like that. Raised by apes—"

"Great apes, sir."

"Yes, but still. One wouldn't really expect him to shine at the business side of things. Even a thing like publishing."

"He claimed, so I heard, that the jungle taught him everything he needed to know."

"Not everything, it would appear."

"Excuse me, sir?"

"It didn't teach him how to avoid a bullet, did it?" Marsh's eyes narrowed slightly. A chimpanzee had just capered, screeching, across the formal garden and disappeared behind the chrysanthemums. Remarkable.

"You don't believe it was suicide, then?"

Marsh smiled grimly. "I believe that someone would very much like me to believe that it was suicide."

The sergeant nodded. "You reckon one of the guests did him in."

"Oh, I think so, Sergeant. In a situation like this, a manor house, a weekend party, a dead lord, you can almost always count upon your guests. And didn't you tell me that at night, tigers were set free to roam the grounds?"

"Lions, sir."

"Ah, lions. They're the ones with the manes?"

"That's right, sir. Tigers have stripes, I believe."

"Well, your lion is a largish sort of beast, isn't he? And a carnivore, too, eh? I suspect that they'd prove something of a deterrent to any smash-and-grab passerby. No, Sergeant, I think we can safely focus on the guests."

"They're waiting in the conservatory. Shall we talk to them all at once?"

"No. Individually, I think. Ask Constable Hill to trot one of them in here, and we'll have a go."

The first guest, a Miss Eudora Fields, was a woman in her fifties. She wore a flowered hat atop her curly grey hair, a belted black dress elaborately printed with red fleurs-delys, and a pair of sensible black walking shoes. Hanging from her shoulder was a large rectangular handbag. She sat down on the leather- covered divan and carefully arranged the handbag on her lap. Marsh sat down opposite her in a padded club chair. Off to the right,

Sergeant Meadows lowered himself to another club chair, his notebook ready.

"First, Miss Fields," said Marsh, "I'd like to thank you for cooperating with us. I know that this must be a trying time for you."

"Oh, dear me, no," said Miss Fields. "No, I'm quite used to this sort of thing."

Taken a bit aback, Marsh said, "Which sort of thing?"

"Murder," she said cheerfully.

"Used to it?"

"Yes. I'm something of a sleuth myself, you see. Only an amateur, of course." She smiled comfortably. "But you've heard, no doubt, of the Lower Wopping Horror."

"I can't say," said Marsh, "that I have."

Miss Fields's smile faltered. "Really? It was one of my most celebrated cases."

"Cases?"

"So I like to refer to them."

"And how many of these 'cases' have there been?"

"Oh, for a time, while I was living in Lower Wopping, there were literally dozens of them. It sometimes seemed that I couldn't leave the house without stumbling upon a corpse. There was Colonel Bedford—bludgeoned in the hydrangea bushes. There was Lady Windham—pecked to death in the aviary. There was Father Elliot, the parish priest—impaled."

"Impaled?"

"On the peak of the church tower. It took me forever to determine exactly how he had got there."

"I shouldn't wonder. And how had he, exactly?"

"A Crane."

"A builder's crane?"

"No, no. Lester Crane. One of the Middle Wopping Cranes. He'd learned, you see, that Father Elliot was in fact Willoughby Rutledge, his nemesis from Eton."

"Ah. But how had he actually contrived to impale this Rutledge fellow upon the church tower?"

"Derek."

"A builder's derrick?"

"No, Derek Crane, his cousin. The two of them used ropes. Hempen ropes. It was a thread of hemp, actually, that did them in."

"Ah."

"And then there was poor Mr. Todd, the barber. And Mr. Norman, the greengrocer. And Mr. Prebbles, the postman—"

"I must say," said Marsh, "that this Lower Wopping of yours sounds a most unpleasant place to live."

"It was dreadful," said Miss Fields. "No proper vegetables. No mail service. No Mass on Sunday. And people are so strange, aren't they, Inspector? Everyone in town—the few who were left—had stopped having me over for tea. As though it were *my* fault that these corpses kept popping up."

"That must have been very difficult for you."

"Unbearable, in the end. I finally gave up and moved."

"To where, might I ask?"

"Upper Wopping."

"And have you been troubled there by this ... problem?"

"No, thank goodness. This is my first murder in ages. But it's a bit like getting back on a bicycle, isn't it? It all comes back to one." She smiled happily. "I'm very much looking forward to working with you on this, Inspector."

"Yes," he said, and glanced at Sergeant Meadows, who rolled his eyes elaborately. "Now, Miss Fields, I understand that it was you who found Lord Greystoke's body this morning."

"That's correct. At precisely eight-oh-five."

"And how can you be so certain of the time?"

"Oh, I'm always certain of the time. One never knows, after all, when one might stumble upon a corpse. And when one does, precision is of the utmost importance. Consequently, I never open a door or go down a stairway without referring to my pocket watch." She reached into the pocket of her dress, plucked out a gold watch, and held it up for Marsh's admiration. "I synchronize it, on the hour, with the BBC broadcast."

"But I understood you to say that you hadn't been troubled by corpses of late."

"Yes, but old habits die hard, don't they?"

"Of course. But what was it, Miss Fields, that brought you to Lord Greystoke's rooms at eight-oh-five this morning?"

"He had suggested I come round at that time, so that we might discuss my book."

"Your book?"

"An account of one of my cases. The Curious Affair at Middle Wopping."

There was a faint interrogatory note at the end of the sentence, as though Miss Fields were discreetly wondering whether Marsh possessed a familiarity with this adventure.

Marsh, who did not, chose to proceed with his own. "And what was it," he said, "that you found in Lord Greystoke's rooms?"

"May I consult my notes?"

"Your notes?"

"I always take notes when I stumble upon a corpse."

Marsh nodded. "Yes, by all means, consult your notes."

Miss Fields opened her handbag, rummaged through it, and at last produced a notebook identical to Sergeant Meadows's. She flipped through it for a moment. "Yes. I knocked on Lord Greystoke's door at eight-oh-five. Receiving no answer, I tried the doorknob. The door was unlocked. I opened it and proceeded into the room and immediately discovered the body of Lord Greystoke. He was naked except for a bolt of brightly colored material, a loincloth, covering his lower torso."

She looked up. "It passes between the legs and is bound around the waist, so that a piece of the material falls in front and in back. It's an article of clothing sometimes worn by aboriginal peoples. And sometimes, it would seem, by Lord Greystoke as well."

"So it would seem."

Looking down again, she said, "He was lying on the floor, exactly five feet, seven inches from his writing desk, and four feet, three inches from the balcony window."

"You measured the distance?"

Miss Fields looked up. "I always carry a measuring tape with me," she patted the handbag, "for occasions of just this sort."

"Yes. Pray, continue."

She looked down again at her notebook. "Also lying on the floor, five inches from Lord Greystoke's outstretched right hand, was a Colt .32 caliber semiautomatic pistol. A close examination of this weapon—"

"You didn't touch it?" said Marsh.

"Certainly not," said Miss Fields. "I got down on my hands and knees and I sniffed at the barrel." She looked at her notes. "A close examination of this weapon revealed that it had been fired recently. A close examination of Lord Greystoke's head revealed a hole in it, such as might have been made by the entrance of a .32 caliber slug. The hair around the hole was singed, suggesting that the muzzle of the weapon had been in proximity to the head when the gun was fired."

"Did you touch the body?"

"Briefly," she admitted. She smiled. "Well, yes, I know that I shouldn't have done so, of course, but I felt it necessary, you see, in order to determine the time of death. The body was cold, and rigor mortis had set in. I estimate that Lord Greystoke had died some six hours and thirty-five minutes before I found him. In other words, at one-thirty this morning."

"That is a very precise estimate."

Miss Fields' shoulders moved in a light, modest shrug. "I do have some small experience in these matters."

"And did that experience suggest to you that it might be advisable, at some point, to bring your discovery to the attention of the authorities?"

"It did indeed. It was quite clear to me that Lord Greystoke had been murdered, and that his murderer had attempted—rather clumsily, I might add—to make it appear that the man had committed suicide. I was about to seek out a telephone when that ridiculous Frenchman burst into the room and began to scream at me."

"Which ridiculous Frenchman?"

"That Pierre Reynard. One expects a certain amount of excitability in a Frenchman, of course, but Reynard was impossible. He stormed about the room, quite red in the face, waving his arms and screaming at the top of his lungs. And then, as though this weren't unpleasant enough, that American woman, Lulubelle Courage, the tennis player, *she* arrived and began to attack me as well."

"Attack you? Physically?"

"Verbally. To be honest, Inspector, I wish she *had* attempted a physical attack." Her eyes glinted as she smiled. "Over the years, you see, I have acquired a certain skill at jiu-jitsu."

"But why were Reynard and this Courage woman attacking you?"

"Simple jealousy, I imagine. They both fancy themselves sleuths—"

"Both of them?"

"Yes, it's absurd, of course. But there it is. And no doubt they were displeased that it was I who first stumbled upon the corpse."

"I see." Marsh glanced again at Sergeant Meadows, who shook his head in amazement. "Now, Miss Fields—"

Suddenly, the library door slammed open. In the doorway stood a small man wearing a beautifully cut three-piece black suit and, gleaming beneath the cuffs of his trousers, an immaculate pair of white spats. Tucked beneath his right arm was an ebony walking stick, and now, as he stalked forward, he swung it forward with a flourish and tapped it against the carpet. "Reynard," he announced, "will no longer be traduced by this ignoramus."

Inspector Marsh turned to Sergeant Meadows. "Sergeant, I thought that you had men watching the guests."

Standing, the sergeant set aside his notebook. "I'll handle it, sir."

The small man danced backward, toward the fireplace, swishing the walking stick through the air like a fencing foil, once, twice. "I must warn you, Monsieur. Reynard does not permit the touching of his person."

Meadows looked at Marsh, who waved him back. "You'd do well, Monsieur," said Marsh to the Frenchman, "to put down that device. Assaulting a police officer is a serious offence."

The Frenchman lowered the stick, rested its tip on the carpet, and rested his hand atop the handle. "And so is the assault upon my reputation by this *imbecile* of a woman. A face of red, she says. A waving of arms, she says. Lies, all of it. With the most icy of detachments, I calmly explained to her that her blundering about at the scene of the crime was entirely a *catastrophe*. I have, Monsieur, stumbled upon well over a thousand corpses, both here in England and on the Continent, and never have I ever seen such chaos. This numbskull had hopelessly compromised the evidence. Miles of measuring tape were draped across the body. Miles of twine, like the web of some deranged spider, connected the body to the writing table."

"You silly man," snapped Miss Fields. "You're only jealous because it was I who stumbled upon the corpse."

"Twine?" said Inspector Marsh.

"And how is it, you incompetent cow, that you *did* stumble upon the corpse before I? I had an appointment at eight- oh-five with Lord Greystoke, to discuss my book—but I was late." He tugged a gold pocket watch from his vest pocket and held it out to Marsh. "Observe, Monsieur. Someone has adjusted the hands backward by fifteen minutes, so as to prevent Reynard from meeting with Lord Greystoke at the appointed time."

Miss Fields sniffed. "You forgot to wind it, you idiot."

"Reynard *never* forgets to wind his watch. An accurate timepiece is essential to his success. No, you great nincompoop, it was you who—"

"*Enough!*" bellowed Marsh. Reynard blinked at him, apparently stunned. Marsh turned to Miss Fields. "What, pray, is this twine business?"

She waved a hand. "Nothing, Inspector, really. I was merely determining the angle at which the body must've fallen."

"And in the process," said Reynard, "she had stepped directly on the face of the corpse. The imprint of her walking shoe was clearly visible on Lord Greystoke's forehead. She had knocked over a bottle of wine, a Chateau Latour, spilling its contents across the desk, and also knocked over the wastebasket—"

"You pompous twit!" exclaimed Miss Fields. "I didn't knock over the wastebasket! The basket had been knocked over before I entered the room, as you would have known, you sniveling little dwarf, if it *had* been you who'd stumbled upon the corpse."

"*Dwarf?*" squealed Reynard. He raised his walking stick and advanced toward Miss Fields. Miss Fields tossed her handbag aside and leaped from the sofa to assume a jiujitsu fighting stance, her arms held before her in the air. Sergeant Meadows stood and moved to interpose himself between the two.

"She's right," said a voice from the doorway.

Heads swiveled.

At the door was an attractive young woman wearing a white silk blouse and a white silk skirt. Her hair was blond, cut very short, and in her right hand she held a tennis racquet. Lightly, she bounced the strings of the racquet against the palm of her left hand. She was chewing gum. "About the wastepaper basket," she said. Her accent was American. "It got knocked over before she went into the room."

"Who are you, madam," said Marsh, "and how do you know this?"

"Courage," said the woman. "Lulubelle Courage. And I know because I had myself stashed in the closet."

"Stashed. I see. May I ask why?"

"I had an appointment with Stokie at seven thirty. I—"

"By 'Stokie'," said Marsh, "you mean Lord Greystoke?"

"Right." She snapped her chewing gum. "He wanted to shoot the breeze with me, see, about a book I'm writing."

"Ah." Marsh nodded. "Miss Fields, are there, among the guests, any additional amateur sleuths?"

Miss Fields had returned to her seat on the sofa. Setting the handbag on her lap, she said. "Several, actually. There's Simon Lubner, the music critic. An absolute ninny, of course. And there's Father Greene. I shouldn't like to say anything unpleasant about a member of the priesthood, but—"

"There is also," said Reynard, "that great booby of an English lord, Wilbur Drimley. And his wife, the insufferable Edith."

"I see," said Marsh. "Sergeant, will you close the door, please, and lock it? Miss Courage, please sit there. Monsieur, please sit there. Now this is how we are going to proceed. I will ask Miss Courage some questions. She will answer them. No one will interrupt. Have I made myself clear?"

"But of course," said Reynard.

"Certainly," said Miss Fields.

"Sure," said Lulubelle Courage, and snapped her gum.

"Good," said Marsh. He glanced over to Sergeant Meadows, who had once again picked up his notebook. "Miss Courage, could you explain to me, please, what happened this morning?"

"Well, like I said," she said, tapping the tennis racquet against her knee, "Stokie wanted to see me at seven- thirty this morning. To gas with me about this book of mine. It's all about my adventures, right? Solving murder mysteries on the tennis circuit."

"And no doubt," said Marsh, "there are a great many of these."

"Hundreds. Believe me, it's a dog-eat-dog world, tennis. One time, I stumbled onto three corpses in the same day."

"Extraordinary."

"Yeah. But after a while it can really get on your nerves. That's why I've been thinking about getting into the writing game. Anyway, when I arrive at Stokie's room, no one answers the door. So before I go in, naturally, I check my watch. I always do that, just in case I stumble onto a corpse."

"*Your* watch, of course," said Reynard, with a significant glance at Miss Fields, "had not been sabotaged."

Marsh glared at him. Raising his eyebrows, Reynard held up his left hand and put the finger of his right to his pursed lips.

"And it's a good thing, too," said Miss Courage, "because I did. Stumble onto a corpse, I mean. Stokie's. He was dead meat, the poor thing, and I figure that somebody had aced him early this morning. Probably around two-thirty."

Miss Fields produced a contemptuous snort. Marsh glanced at her. Looking down, she adjusted the handbag on her lap.

"Whoever croaked him," said Miss Courage, "had tried to make it look like Stokie offed himself, but it was pretty obvious, from the way he was lying, and from where the gat was, that he'd been croaked, all right."

"The gat?"

"The roscoe," she said. "The heater."

"I believe," said Miss Fields, "that she means the pistol."

Marsh nodded. "At what point was it," he asked Miss Courage, "that you hid yourself in the closet?"

"At eight-oh-five. I checked my watch, so I know that's right. I heard someone at the door, and I figured it might be the shooter, coming back. They do that sometimes, you know—return to the scene of the crime. So I jumped into the closet, there in the entryway. And what happened, I guess, I knocked over the wastepaper basket. Anyway, so I'm inside there, right? I can see out, through these little slats in the door? And I see Miss Fields here come in. She spots the stiff—poor Stokie—lying on the carpet and right away she grabs that purse of hers and she starts hauling things out—a magnifying glass, some string—maybe a ton of string. I never saw so much string in my life. It looked like an explosion in a pasta factory. And she's got a tape measure that must be about four miles long."

Marsh said, "You remained in there the entire time that Miss Fields was ... ah ... conducting her investigation?"

"To tell the truth, I was laughing so hard I was pretty much paralyzed. You should have seen her. I mean, she was actually climbing on top of poor Stokie, so she could tie her string to the desk. A couple of times there, running back and forth, she tripped right over him. Finally, she plunks down in the chair and she grabs her purse again and pulls out a whole bunch of papers."

Marsh turned to Miss Fields.

"Tide tables," she said stiffly. "And railroad schedules." She gave Miss Courage a look that might shatter stone.

"But the sea is a good fifty miles away," said Marsh. "And there is no rail service within thirty."

"Better safe than sorry," said Miss Fields.

"Ah," said Marsh. To Miss Courage he said, "Please continue."

"So I'm in there, holding my sides and trying to keep quiet, right? Suddenly Frenchie here is in the room, screaming at Miss Fields."

"Untrue!" exclaimed Reynard. "With the most icy of detachments—"

"Yeah, well," said Miss Courage, "it sure sounded like screaming to me. And she starts screaming back, calling him a poncy frog pederast—"

"That's a lie!" said Miss Fields.

Miss Courage shrugged. "Maybe I had wax in my ears and didn't hear right. Anyway, while the two of them are going at it, I slip out of the closet and make like I'm just coming into the room."

"Mademoiselle Courage," said Reynard, smiling as he leaned slightly forward, "has neglected to explain precisely what she was doing in Lord Greystoke's room from seven-thirty, when she arrived, until eight-oh-five, when she was interrupted by the cow."

"Monsieur Reynard," said Marsh, "you are trying my patience."

"Forgive me," said Reynard. "In future I shall avoid any mention of cow."

Marsh scowled at him, and then looked at Miss Courage. "But what, in fact, *were* you doing?"

"The same thing I always do when I stumble onto a corpse. I was snooping. I mean, it was pretty obvious who aced poor Stokie, and I wanted to find some proof."

"Obvious?" said Marsh.

"Sure. Look at the evidence. The gat, the bottle of wine, the singed hair around the bullet wound. That dumb curtain, or whatever, he had draped around his middle."

"A loincloth," said Miss Fields.

"Whatever," said Miss Courage.

"And whom," Marsh asked her, "do you suspect?"

Miss Courage shook her head. "Geeze, Inspector. I'm sorry, but it wouldn't be fair for me to say. I mean, you haven't even finished your investigation."

Pierre Reynaud chuckled. "I have no doubt, Mademoiselle Courage, that you have come to some conclusion as to the identity of the murderer. I have no doubt, also, that it is mistaken."

"Oh yeah?" said Miss Courage. "And you think you know who did it?"

"*Naturellement.*"

"And would you care, Monsieur," said Marsh, "to share this knowledge with us?"

"Alas, I regret to say that I cannot. While Mademoiselle Courage is wildly inaccurate in most other respects, in this she speaks correctly. It would not, at this time, be appropriate for me to reveal the identity of the person responsible."

"What about you, Miss Fields?" asked Marsh. "Do you believe that you, too, know the identity of this person?"

"Of course," she said. "But, much as I dislike to do so, in this case I must agree with the Frenchman. And with *her*. It simply wouldn't be proper, just now, for me to reveal the killer's name."

"Is there, among amateur sleuths," Marsh asked her, genuinely curious, "some sort of code that forbids you to divulge the identity of a murderer?"

"It simply wouldn't be proper," she said.

At that moment, someone knocked on the library door.

Marsh said, "Get that, would you, Sergeant?" He looked at the others. "You do realize, I hope, that withholding information from the authorities could put all of you in a very bad light."

"Speaking for myself alone," said Reynard, "I withhold no information whatsoever. I withhold only my conclusions. And these are based upon evidence available to all. Although it is evidence, I admit, tarnished by the ineffable ineptitude of that ... personage." He nodded toward Miss Fields.

Miss Fields said, "If you hadn't interrupted me—"

"Inspector?" Sergeant Meadows, at the door.

"Yes?"

"There's someone here to see you. It may be important."

Marsh cast a baleful glance at the three people assembled before him. "Please remain where you are."

He strode across the room to the door, where Sergeant Meadows gestured for him to step outside. In the hallway, Meadows pulled the door shut. "This," he said, "is Cleeves, the butler."

Cleeves was tall and imperious, the platonic ideal of a butler. "This just arrived, sir," he said. He held out an envelope. "It is for you, apparently."

Marsh took it. The heavy envelope was addressed as follows:

To The Individual Investigating My Death
Greystoke Manor
Devon

Marsh said, "But surely there's no postal service on Sunday."

"No, sir," said Cleeves. "It must have been hand- delivered by someone. It has, as you see, no postmark. Simply that handwritten date in the corner. Yesterday's date."

"And the handwriting?"

"Is Lord Greystoke's, sir. Unmistakably. He taught himself to write, as you may know, while he was living with the great apes in Africa, and his handwriting displays several peculiarities of style which make it unique. You will notice, for example, those little smiling faces within the capital Ds. May I say something, sir?"

"Yes?"

"Well, sir, as it happens, I have a certain amount of experience with murder investigations. It has been my great honor to assist the local police with several of theirs. You have, perhaps, heard of The Middleton Muddle?"

Marsh sighed. "I'm afraid I haven't."

"Well, be that as it may, sir, I just wanted you to know that my talents, such as they are, will be at your disposal should you require them."

"Thank you, Cleeves. I shall bear that in mind."

"Will there be anything else, sir?"

"I think not. Thank you, Cleeves."

"Very good, sir."

Marsh watched the butler march away and then turned to Sergeant Meadows. "My mother wanted me to be a surgeon, you know."

"No, sir, I didn't."

Marsh nodded. He hefted the letter.

The sergeant said, "Looks like Greystoke already knew, yesterday, that someone was going to do him in."

"Umm," said Marsh, still staring at the letter.

"Who do you think they suspect?" Meadows asked him.

"God knows," said Marsh, looking up. "Perhaps none of them suspects the same individual. Perhaps they all suspect each other. An extraordinary lot, eh, Sergeant? Well. Let us see what his lordship has to say on the subject, shall we?"

Carefully he opened the envelope and removed from within it a packet of folded sheets of paper. He began to read. He frowned. He furrowed his brow. He continued to read. At last he looked up at Meadows. "You'd best call for reinforcements, Sergeant. I believe we're going to need them."

The Greystoke Letter, as it was called in the press, played an important part in the subsequent court trials. It is reproduced here in its entirety, minus its various addenda.

To Whom It May Concern:

You will forgive me, I hope, my little joke.

The act of suicide is so inherently banal that, when its inevitability became clear to me, I decided that I should attempt to enliven, as it were, my own. It was partly for this reason that I invited to Greystoke the individuals whom by now you have met; and from whom, it pleases me to think, you must by now have derived a dollop or two of entertainment. It was for this reason, too, that I stood (will be standing) in the center of my room while I perform(ed) the act, and held (will be holding) the pistol in such a way that it fell (will be falling) somewhat ambiguously to the floor. Ever since I was a lad, swinging through the trees, I have admired the intricacies of the English language.

But first things first. As a police officer, you will be understandably preoccupied by motive. Why suicide, you may well ask. To which I reply, why not?

To anyone raised by the Great Apes, as I was, the contemporary European scene, political and social, can be perceived only as depressing. Where once I was surrounded by affection, sincerity, concern, and kindness, I am now surrounded by hatred, guile, envy, and a cruelty that is, to me, quite unfathomable. Reason enough, I should think.

Additionally, however, over the years I have grown very, very tired. It is, perhaps, as simple as that.

It was partly, as I said, to enliven my ending that I invited the guests I did. But there was another, more significant reason. Like all Great Apes, I carry within myself a powerful cultural taboo which effectively prohibits self-destruction. Among us, you see, like quite a lot of other "civilized" things, it just isn't done. I realized, therefore, very early on in my planning, that in order to proceed with the act I should be required to place myself in a situation, the unpleasantness of which was so intense that suicide became not merely an escape, but a celebration.

I could, of course, have invited to the manor a group of mere writers, chosen more or less at random. I did consider this. Speaking as a publisher, I can tell you that a weekend spent in a house filled with writers, and their whining, their petty grievances, and their childish envy (which invariably masquerades as something else, usually critical judgment), is enough to encourage the average person–indeed, the average saint–to leap merrily from the lip of a nearby cliff.

But it was, for me, simply not enough. I have been around them for far too long, unfortunately. I have grown immune.

And then, in a sudden blinding flash, it occurred to me: a weekend among amateur sleuths! I have met many members of this species. For some reason they all feel that their "adventures," whether penned by themselves or by some hired hack, are worthy of publication. I do not know whether you have had any previous personal experience with them, but I can assure you that they are, individually and as a group, wonderfully intolerable.

And so I invited the assemblage among whom you have, perforce, found yourself. I am pleased to report that they have worked, as we say, a charm. By Friday evening I had developed shortness of breath and a debilitating migraine headache. By this afternoon, following the tea, I had grown nearly incoherent with rage and loathing. The end will come as an enormous relief.

I have made arrangements to have this letter delivered to you tomorrow. If, for some reason, poor Cheetah is discovered in the act, please bear in mind that he has been, over the years, a good and loyal friend, and that he has virtually no knowledge of what the letter contains.

One thing more. The people gathered here are not (as I suspect you will be unsurprised to learn) quite so noble and so morally upright as invariably they like to present themselves. To this letter I have appended proofs of this statement, proofs obtained by several quite competent (and professional) enquiry agents.

I've been dabbling, you see, in a bit of amateur sleuthing myself. But I feel certain that, in the circumstances, the Gods will forgive me.

You will learn, for example, that the inestimable Miss Fields has made, shall we say, quite a killing in Lower Wopping real estate. That the remarkable Monsieur Reynard is, curiously, without an alibi for the evening during which his erstwhile companion, Mr. Witherspoon, met his elaborate death. That the splendid Lord Wilbur Drimley, and his equally splendid wife, Edith, have nourished the gardens at Drimley Hall with a form of fertilizer, the use of which is considered, by most legal authorities, rather de trop.

You will learn, ultimately, that all of them, without exception, have been guilty of precisely the crime in which they all take such pride "investigating." Guilty, in a word, of murder.

The facts are here. Everything is documented. I wish you great fun.

Ungowah, Lord Greystoke

MISSOLONGHI

(*Alfred Hitchcock's Mystery Magazine*, October 2000)

Another story with which Sarah was involved. In fact, the story was primarily her idea. I told her that I'd like to write something about Lord Byron in Greece, and it was she who told me about Byron's stay in Venice, and about the Carbonari. Once again, Sarah read it in manuscript; by the time the magazine appeared on the stands, she was gone.

This was the last of my work that Sarah read. Not a week goes by that I don't miss her.

THE RAINS, finally, had stopped. All winter long, as the wet, ragged winds flailed at the rooftop, the Poet had longed for the Greek sunlight, for its warmth, its improbable clarity, its impossible promise. Now, with his flesh scorched by fever, his blood become acid in his veins, the light fell upon him like a hammer.

Clarity and promise lingered beyond the still-shuttered windows, while here in the room darkness prevailed. Exactly the opposite, he had at some point decided, of the way things had long ago been arranged in England.

Still, there were diversions to be enjoyed among these febrile Greek shadows.

Sometimes, for example, the room moved. It would billow outward, toward the unseen horizon, the unseen blue sky—an enormous heart slowly pulsing, he at its center, like the memory of a lover—and then slowly it would clench, contract, until the walls shuddered against his taut sheets, his trembling skin.

Sometimes, too, he saw things.

Sometimes these were blessings: an arc of familiar cheek; a spill of familiar hair; a long familiar swell of alabaster thigh, a vision so sweet it would leave him lying there breathless and aching, his spine suddenly molten.

Sometimes they were horrors: gnarled thorny hands, groping, grasping; vast looming outlandish faces, red eyes screwed into furious slits, blistered lips snarling back from putrefying black teeth.

Sometimes, and grateful for it, he wandered, he drifted, and curiously, on these wanderings he seldom found himself in Greece, with its sun and its rocks and its brave, bickering revolutionaries. Almost always he found himself back in Venice, strolling down dark narrow alleyways between ruined towers, his arm locked within Maria's, or lying beside her, the towers silently gliding by as their gondola slipped dreamlike along a cool green canal.

Red lips untouched by rouge. Almond-shaped eyes, irises so dark the pupils disappeared. Hair as black as ravens' wings, tumbling to square, bare, scented shoulders ...

Her slender hand settling at the back of his neck, like a door closing to muffle the swelter of a summer afternoon ...

Her voice: low and throaty, as soft as smoke. "*Caro mio ...*"

And now a cool touch upon his forehead.

No. Impossible.

The Poet opened his eyes.

Victor, sitting in the bedside chair, damp towel in hand, looking as splendid as if he had stepped, only a moment before, from the lawn of his Knightsbridge townhouse. Silken collar open, silken sleeves rolled back, a lock of brown hair curling from each aristocratic temple. Very dashing indeed for a wet nurse.

Victor smiled. "Good morning, George."

"Victor." His voice was frayed, rasping; not his own. He cleared it, and then, with an effort of will, an aged magician swirling on a cape, he wrapped the cloak of consciousness about himself. He could on occasion still pull off the trick, but with every performance, slowly, inevitably, the cloak was growing more threadbare and tattered. "Good morning." Better. "I was thinking of Maria."

"You called out her name."

"Did I? How very boring. First my legs, then my bowels. Now even my speech has gone antic on me."

Leaning forward, Victor stroked the towel against his cheek. "I've brought your broth." He nodded to the bowl on the nightstand, beside the earthenware basin.

Surrendering to the towel's damp, rough comfort, the Poet closed his eyes. "Broth. Delightful."

"You must regain your strength."

"Yes, of course. No one likes a feeble corpse."

"Nonsense. We'll soon have you back on your feet."

"Ah, Victor. And who speaks nonsense now?"

He opened his eyes, saw the sadness, and the knowledge, in Victor's eyes before their glance skipped away. "Who did it, do you suppose? To Maria."

Victor frowned. "The count, we always believed."

"Always believed, yes. But in retrospect, you know, I'd like to think that I chose my contessas rather more carefully than that. Do you remember the rumors we heard? Of a British spy working against the Carbonari?"

Victor smiled. "I remember thinking that you ascribed somewhat more malice to the British government than was perhaps reasonable." He held out the spoon.

"Open up."

Absurd. Bed-fed, spoon-fed, like a puling infant. "I suspect that it would be impossible, in the circumstances, to ascribe too much malice to the British government. They hate no one so much as revolutionaries. With the possible exception of poets." He smiled. "I'm a particular delight to them, I'm sure—a poet stumbling through the Greek revolution."

"Open up."

A bit of grace required here. For Victor's sake. The Poet opened his mouth, accepted the spoonful of broth, swallowed it. "Lovely," he said. "The chef has outdone himself."

"Another," said relentless Victor, spoon poised like a dagger.

"Maria's father," said the Poet, "was the head of the local Lodge. The incident destroyed him. What better way to cripple the Carbonari? Paralyze its leader, and with no one the wiser?"

"Open up."

"Do you remember Pritchard, that little swine at the consulate?"

"Pritchard? A nonentity."

"I never trusted him."

"Caro mio ..."

That perfect chin, that flawless skin. Those eyes ...

... those black eyes, their lids slightly parted, staring up at the ruined roof of the empty warehouse ...

"George?" Victor said, concern tightening his face.

The Poet tugged the cloak more tightly about himself. Drifting off, drifting off. Very bad form. "Yes, yes." He swallowed more broth. "And there were the weapons, remember. The French muskets."

"It was a long time ago, George."

"Surely, Victor, you've realized by now that time doesn't pass. People do."

He felt it then, the first breath of fever, a sensation almost pleasant, a desert breeze gently flickering along his dry skin.

He licked his lips. "She was very beautiful, wasn't she?"

"Very beautiful. Open up."

More broth. "And passionate." The breeze was growing in strength, leaching away his own.

Victor smiled. "They were all passionate, George."

"I don't mean passionate about me. Passionate about ... Venice. Passionate about ..."

"George?"

A sudden gust. The Poet toppled backward, downward, as the cloak ripped itself from his shoulders and went flapping, batlike, off into the night.

Sometimes on summer nights, when the tall windows of the room were thrown open to let in the cool air from the canal, bats would flap through them and flutter for a time up there in the shadows at the rafters.

Tonight, once again, the bats are fluttering. Beneath, in the pale yellow lamplight, the three of them sit plotting. On the table before them an empty bottle of Chianti from the count's estates, a silver salver of cheese and grapes, a porcelain platter still holding a few scraps of *carpaccio*. Conspirators ate well in those days.

"Of course you cannot come, *caro mio*," says Maria. Sitting beside him, she is wearing her famous disguise, a man's rough cotton shirt tucked into baggy woolen pantaloons, these tucked into battered workman's boots; and, with her hair still unbound, ebony and silk, no individual in the history of human labor has ever looked less like a workman. "They are French," she says. "They will shoot you, an Englishman, on sight."

"She's quite right, you know," says Victor, smiling over the snifter of brandy he holds lightly to his chest. He is sprawled back in the chair, elbows braced along its padded arms, the heels of his supple black leather boots propped up on the low table.

"It's so damnably dangerous," says the Poet.

"Not at all," says she, with galling conviction. "I know these men, and they know me."

"But I ought to go," he says. "It's *my* bloody money, after all." He hears the petulance in his voice but he cannot recant it, would not if he could. Maddening woman.

Maria is smiling. "You will get good value for your British pounds."

He feels his back go icy stiff. "That is nothing like what I meant to say, and you know it."

She places her hand upon his knee. "I do know, my sweet. It will all go well, I promise you." Of its own accord, treacherous thing, his back begins to thaw. And she senses this, for with the ease of a mother turning from the reassured child, she lifts her hand and begins to arrange her hair, drawing it back behind her perfect ears.

Watching her, head bent slightly forward, slender fingers confidently twining through that thicket of black, he realizes that no matter what happens tonight, or tomorrow, or indeed throughout the rest of time, he will remember this image until the day arrives when he can no longer remember anything at all. It is an infuriating prospect.

She turns to Victor, smiling once again. A tendril escapes her fingers, flutters to her cheek. "And you will be having an assignation? With your Austrian tart?"

Victor smiles, sips at his brandy. "Hardly a tart, you know. Sister to one of the colonel's aides."

"Consorting with the enemy, is it?" She strokes the tendril back behind her ear.

Lightly, Victor waves the snifter. "Boring from within, I prefer to think."

Her smile is teasing. "And from without as well?"

He shrugs. "A gentleman would never."

"I've met the woman," says the Poet, who, despite his affection for both of them, and his concern for her safety, has begun to feel uncomfortably like a audience. "Used in connection with her, possibly no word is more apt than 'boring.' "

Victor laughs. "But she does possess certain admirable qualities, George. She simply tends to conceal them."

"Extremely well."

"Men," says Maria, and sniffs. Holding her hair back behind her neck with her right hand, with her left hand she lifts from the sofa a wide-brimmed felt hat, black and limp. "How you must speak of me when I am gone." With a flourish she sweeps the hat over her hair. She pulls it into place and then turns to the Poet and, like a child, she cocks her head and smiles. "Yes?"

"Preposterous," he says. "Only a blind man would be duped."

"It is intended to dupe no one." She rises, strides to the mirror, the farcical boots thumping against the carpet. Peering critically into the glass she says, "The guards at the canal have been bribed." She tucks an errant strand up into the hat. "The costume is merely a sop to their conscience."

"Maria—" the Poet begins.

She turns to him suddenly, her chin raised. It is one of her operatic moments. "I must go now, *caro*," she tells him.

"I believe I ought to be leaving myself," says Victor, and pulls himself languidly to his feet. "I'll walk you to the canal," he tells Maria.

The Poet stands. "My responsibility, I think."

She rolls her eyes, more opera. "*Must* you be so childish?" She looks at Victor. "Both of you?" She walks over to the Poet, and even the absurd sound of those boots, clomp, clomp, does nothing to soothe him. There is no room for comedy here. She takes his hand. "*Caro*, I was helping the Lodge long before you arrived in Venice. They trust me. My father trusts me. How is it that you cannot?"

He tries for lightness: "I trust you implicitly, my dear. It's these French friends of yours whom I find a trifle dubious. I've always found the French a trifle dubious."

"I told you, we have dealt with them before. All will be well." She leans forward, kisses him on the cheek. He smells her familiar scent, rose petals in the moonlight. "Three hours," she says. "Giuseppe and I will bring the weapons to the warehouse on Murano, and I'll return here immediately."

"See that you do."

She laughs, her dark eyes beneath the hat's brim suddenly catching a gleam from the lamp. "Yes, my lord and master."

He smiles ruefully. "Would that I were."

She squeezes his hand. "If you were, *caro*, you should tire of me within a day." Once more she kisses his cheek. "Until later, then." She lets his hand fall and turns to Victor. "Best of luck," she says, "with the tart."

Victor smiles. "I'll give her your regards."

Almost, the Poet reaches out for her, but she is moving away, her scent already becoming a memory behind her. The two of them, he and Victor, stand there in the flickering yellow lamplight, watching her stride off into the shadows. After a glance back at them, another smile, she disappears through the door, pulling it shut behind her.

Victor turns to him. "She'll be fine. As she says, she's done this before."

The Poet nods.

"Brandy?" says Victor.

"God yes."

The room was flickering now, pale yellow in the candlelight, time had passed again as it always does, despite his hopeful lie to Victor, despite the hopeless lies he tells himself. Voices, shuttered and muffled, scurried over him; he could sense the furry pressure of them along the surface of his skin. Something was gnawing at his arm.

He realized with a small start that his eyes were open and that he was gazing at the distant gray ceiling, that he had been gazing at it, blankly, for quite some time. The wind had hurled him here, back into his sodden bed.

And then he saw them: one on either side of him, hovering like crones over a cauldron, muttering, murmuring. He could not make out what it was they said, he could not distinguish the individual words; he could only feel the prickle the words made as they fell upon his flesh. With an effort he moved his head and looked down, and he saw, at his side, in the hollow of his white, extended arm, a thin black worm sluggishly writhing. Beneath it lay a shallow metal basin half filled with ink.

And then he understood. The doctors. The incubi. They were bleeding him again.

Soon there would be nothing left. An empty husk, dry and wizened, the castaway peel of some worthless fruit.

Above him the doctors muttered. Double double toil and trouble.

Ink pattered, drip drop, drip drop, into the basin.

Every drop a word? A line? A stanza? They had taken enough to complete an epic.

Who? Who could have done it?

Pritchard. Something about Pritchard.

The wind rose again, blasting, scalding, sweeping up the debris, the refuse, tattered scraps of unwritten manuscript, discarded husks of hope, of memory ...

The brandy has done its work. It has beaten Time into submission, flattened it, leveled its peaks and valleys. He sits there in the lamplight, his back slumped against the sofa, his head precarious atop the stalk of neck. Victor is long gone, off somewhere with his pretty, boring little Austrian.

And that was ... when? An hour ago? Two?

A sound at the door. He pulls himself to his feet, wavers there for a moment, and all at once he is afraid to permit his heart to begin its beat again. Perhaps, even then, a part of him knows.

Smiling Victor saunters in, his eyebrow raised. "Rather the worse for wear, are we, George?"

The Poet lowers himself back down. "Italian brandy. Wretched stuff."

Victor glances around the room. "Maria? She's in bed?"

He shakes his head, moving it with more violence than he had intended. His brain is sloshing about in there, thick lump of clay in turgid water. "Hasn't returned yet."

Victor frowns. When he speaks, he does so slowly as though to an idiot. "But George. It's gone midnight already."

"Midnight?" Impossible.

Victor is still attempting to be reasonable. "Giuseppe, George? Has Giuseppe returned?"

A sudden chill envelopes his back. All at once his head is clear, and it is ringing. He stands. "Murano," he says. "The warehouse."

... A fumble into his coat, a race out of the house and into the street, a scramble down the alleyways, moonlight gleaming on the cobblestones, on bits of refuse, on the slick slithering tail of a scurrying rat. Around him the smell of brine and stale urine and rotten fruit. He stumbles, trips, nearly falls. Victor is there, his hand steady and strong beneath the Poet's arm. ... A boat bobbing at the quay, a handful of lire shoved at the reluctant gondolier, a clamber over the side of the boat, and they are off. But so slowly, so slowly, the whisper of the water mocking as they inch from the canal into the expanse of black, bleak, moonlit lagoon ...

"Do you know the warehouse?" Victor asks him.

"Yes. Her uncle's. On the west side of the island."

Victor, his Italian far the better, snaps directions at the gondolier.

An infinity passes. He has time to remember everything that has happened between them, and to imagine everything that might have happened to her now ...

Landfall, a flight up the pathway, around rotting coils of rope wet from the afternoon's brief but bitter rain. His head is foggy again, the brandy. Panting, he focuses on Victor's boots ahead, mottled with muck at heel and ankle, pale brown and darker brown against the black leather. Again he nearly falls.

The dark walls of the warehouse tower over them. The double doors have been left thrown open. Just outside them, unmoving, a shadow lies atop the ground. Victor squats beside it and makes a small hissing sound. He turns to the Poet. "Giuseppe. He's dead." He stands, and for a moment the two of them stare at the open door, stare into the darkness that awaits them. "George," says Victor. "We must go for help."

Without a word, without a thought, without a hope, the Poet steps toward the door.

The building's far-off wooden ceiling has collapsed in places, leaving huge rents open to the sky, some rimmed with great fangs of splintered beam. Shafts of moonlight fall from the rents to heaps of rubble on the earthen floor, brick, stone, shards and chunks of shattered glass. She is lying upon one such heap, her arms and legs outstretched as though she had been hurled there, like a doll. Beneath her breasts, along the cotton shirt, a patch of cruel black has blossomed. Her eyes are slightly opened, her lips slightly parted. She looks as though she were smiling. She looks—and the thought sends a shudder through him—as though she has just made love.

There is a howling emptiness inside of him, as vast as the universe. He cannot remember kneeling, but somehow he is on his knees beside her, and he is holding her hand. The soft flesh is growing cool.

"George." Victor's voice comes to him from a distance. Victor's hand touches his shoulder. "George, we must go. We must tell them. The Lodge. *George*."

Pritchard. Pritchard. Something about Pritchard.

"George. George, can you hear me?"

His eyelids fluttering, the Poet suddenly returned to the bed, to the room, to Greece. Victor leaned forward anxiously, his hand gripping the Poet's shoulder. "You were crying out. What is it? What's wrong?"

The Poet took a deep, tattered breath. "Pritchard." He raised his hand to Victor's, clasped it.

"Pritchard? The consular clerk?"

He nodded, released Victor's hand. "Yes ... Yes. I've been thinking of him. Whenever I recall Maria, recall what happened, for some reason my mind has always returned to Pritchard."

Victor smiled. "Pritchard makes for a rather unlikely spy."

"I believe that I now understand why he has been haunting me." He licked his lips. "Is there broth?"

"Yes, of course. I was bringing it when I heard you cry." Victor lifted the bowl from the nightstand.

"It had rained that day," said the Poet. "Do you remember?"

"George, it was so long ago ..." He held out the spoon.

"The blink of an eye, Victor." He swallowed some broth. Already the breeze was building, tugging at the corners of the cape. He would not let it take him. "By the way," he said, "is the poison in the broth or is it in the drinking water?"

Victor's face was suddenly perplexed, but around the handle of the spoon, his thin aristocratic fingers went white. "Poison?"

"It's a simple question, Victor. Logically speaking, it must be in one or the other. I incline toward the broth myself. Putting poison in the broth is somehow much more the sort of thing a British spy might do."

"George, have you lost your mind?"

A gust swept across the Poet's face, searing it. "On the contrary," he said. "As I say, it had rained that day. After it ended and I was walking to the palazzo, I happened to spy Pritchard in the square. He cut quite an amusing figure. He had fallen somewhere, and he was quite covered with mud. My mind, you see, by remembering Pritchard, was attempting to make a subtle sort of connection."

"A connection," repeated Victor.

Other winds, different winds, were beginning to howl in the distance. "To the mud on your boots. On Murano. Mud that was black, and fresh. And mud that was lighter, and old. Mud that had been left there on your earlier visit that night. When you killed Maria."

"My God, George!"

"There had been no mud on the boots earlier, before Maria left."

"George, some mud on my boots, that hardly—"

"Spare me, Victor. I haven't time. The doctors have said again and again that they cannot understand this fever. But it isn't a fever, is it, Victor? It is, rather, the work of a British spy."

"George, we've been friends for a lifetime."

"Yes. And you have taken from me the two things I most treasured—Maria, and my conception of you. And now, of course, you are taking my life. I should think that the least you could do is answer a simple question. The broth or the drinking water?"

Victor stared.

Despite the winds that screamed around him now, snapped and flapped like monstrous flames, the Poet stared back. "*Which?*"

Victor's glance dipped. Amid the winds the Poet waited.

"The broth," said Victor.

The Poet nodded. "Yes. Well. I should like some broth, please."

"George—"

"Some broth, please, Victor. If we're going to do this, we might as well do it properly." He closed his eyes. He could no longer bear to look through them.

"George, I don't expect you to understand this. But everything I've done, everything, I've done for my country."

"Oh, but I do understand." He opened his eyes. "That is precisely why I insist upon the broth. *Do it*, Victor."

Victor sat back. The winds screamed and shrieked as he dipped the spoon into the bowl, raised it, brought it toward the Poet. His hand was shaking. The Poet raised his head, moved his mouth toward the spoon, but

From deep within the blackness, beyond the scalding gales, lights flickered and flared, sometimes candles and sometimes lamps, and sometimes even suns, Northern and Southern, and he was whirling, spinning through them all, and then tumbling windblown through clammy English mists and booming Greek thunderstorms and sultry Venetian evenings and

Ah, at last ...

watching her, head bent slightly forward, slender white fingers confidently twining through that thicket of black, he realizes that no matter what happens tonight, or tomorrow, or indeed throughout the rest of time, he will remember this image until the day arrives when he can no longer remember anything at all.

The Mankiller of Poojeegai

(*Moerderishche Loewen*, Eichborn Verlag, 2000)

Thea Dorn, an editor for the German publisher, Eichborn, asked me if I'd be willing to contribute to a series of anthologies called "Astro Krimis." The idea was that there would be twelve books, each devoted to one sign of the Zodiac. I thought that this was a pretty cool idea, and I agreed. I was assigned Leo, the lion. I dusted off Berthold the Mead Master and stuck him, along with my other Neanderthals, my Cro-Magnans, and most of the remaining signs of the Zodiac, into the story. Originally published in German, it has since been published in Alfred Hitchcock's Mystery Magazine.

EVERYBODY wants to know about the Mankiller. "Tell us about the Mankiller, tell us about the Mankiller!" Sometimes I wonder—what is it with you people? Haven't you got anything better to do? Haven't you got lives?

Okay, fine. The Mankiller. Don't forget to put your donations in the hat.

It happened back in the Old Days. Looking back on those times, it seems that the sun was always shining in a bright blue cloudless sky, that the grass was always swaying in a warm sweet gentle breeze. That Life was always just about perfect.

Which is ridiculous, of course. Things seem that way now because Memory is a better storyteller than even a old pro like me. It deliberately forgets a few items, items like cave bears and saber-toothed tigers and pestilence, and it polishes up everything that's left until it's all gleaming and shiny. And if that's not story-telling, I don't know what is.

Right. The Mankiller

I was in the cave, pounding acorns, which was my share of the division of labor, or part of it. I also gathered the acorns, and, when the flour was ready, I rolled the dough and I baked the bread. Ursula, my first wife, ate the bread. That was her share.

I was just finishing up when Ursula came sauntering into the cave.

"Marta wants to see you," she said.

Inside me, I could feel my heart dislodge itself from the walls of my chest, getting ready to sink. "See me about what?" I asked.

"How should I know? Make sure you clean off before you go."

She was a beautiful woman, Ursula, with the most impressive eyebrow ridge I've ever seen, one that ran from ear to ear over her deeply-set dark brown eyes, like a ledge. Occasionally I still dream about that lovely brow of hers. But as a person, she was sometimes a bit difficult.

I stood up and I brushed flour from my arms. "Marta didn't say?"

"No. But one of those smelly Outlanders was with her. And so was your friend Berthold."

My heart sank.

"You've got flour on your chin," said Ursula.

Within fifty feet of Marta's cave, I could smell the stench of Outlander.

We didn't socialize much with the Outlanders back then. This was partly because we had some fairly strong cultural taboos against mingling with strangers—and the Outlanders were nothing if not strange—but mostly because, to put it delicately, they stank. It was a vile smell, something like cumin, but darker and stronger and more penetrating, the smell of a cumin that had grown moldy and rotten. Over the years, they've grown a little less rank. Or maybe, like all my other organs, my nose is coming up short these days.

Inside the cave, Marta was sitting on her ceremonial throne, wearing the ceremonial lion skin over her shoulders. Gunnar, her consort, was sitting on one of the rocks in front of her, and Berthold the Meadmaster was sitting on another, with that damned leather sack of his resting between his legs. A third rock was taken up by the Outlander, who was dressed in standard Outlandish garb, a pair of leather pants and a red plaid shirt. Around his wrist he wore a bracelet of black pearls. The Outlanders were big on jewelry.

Here in the Royal Chamber, the stench was a lot stronger. Gunnar, I noticed, was sniffling. He was a sensitive lad.

I nodded to Marta. "Greetings, Most Slender of Queens."

"Greetings, Doder, Son of Watt. I believe that you know Bob, the leader of the Outlanders."

I nodded to him. "Greetings, Bob."

"Hey, man," he said. "What's happening?"

Although his use of The Language was a bit peculiar, Bob spoke it surprisingly well. I've heard people say that the Outlanders are stupid. From my own personal experience, this simply isn't true. They do look odd, I admit, with those slippery white bodies and those pathetic tufts of hair sprouting from their tiny heads. And they do possess a few bizarre habits, like worshipping thunder gods and wearing clothes. And they do, of course, stink. But I've never had any doubts about their intelligence. They're the ones, after all, who invented the bow and arrow—definitely a big improvement, hunting-wise, over trying to sweet-talk a mammoth into leaping off a cliff. All in all, they're very clever fellows.

"And naturally," said Marta, "you know Gunnar."

"Greetings, Doder," said Gunnar, and coughed slightly. His eyes were watering. But so, by then, were mine. Reek was wafting from Bob like gas from a swamp.

"Greetings, Gunnar," I said.

"And Berthold is an old friend," she said.

That was an exaggeration, but I nodded. "Berthold," I said.

From his rock, Berthold smiled one of his cryptic smiles. "Berthold," said Marta, "has need of your assistance."

"In what way, Your Awesomeness?"

"There has been a tragedy among the Outlanders." She turned to Bob. "Please explain to Doder."

"The Mankiller of Poojeegai," he explained.

"What's a Poojeegai?" I asked him.

"That's the name of the village, man. Our village."

I hadn't known their name for the village. We always referred to it as The Sink of Stinks. "And what's this Mankiller?" I asked him.

"That's what we call it, man. It's a lion. It kills people. It's killed three of us already. You remember Tammy?"

"Yes." Tammy was one of their females.

"She was the first. That was last week. Over the weekend, it killed Wally the Water-bearer. And then yesterday, man, it got Art the Archer. A friend of his, Lou, went in to get him this morning, and poor Art was scattered all over the living room."

"I'm sorry to hear that," I said. "What's a living room?"

"That's the part of the house where we mostly hang out. It's just off the kitchen, usually, where we do all the cooking. You know about cooking, right?"

"Of course I know about cooking."

"Anyway, that's where Art was scattered all over."

"Terrible. But how does Berthold fit into all this?"

"Berthold's going to help us stalk the thing."

I turned to the Meadmaster. "That's very generous of you, Berthold." I turned to Marta. "Your Suppleness, I'm afraid that this time I won't be able to assist Berthold."

"And why is that?"

"I'm allergic to cats. Big cats, little cats, any kind of cat. I get hives."

"You need have no fear," she said, a remark that always strikes me, no matter who makes it, as monumentally shortsighted. "The Great Mother will protect you." Marta was the Great Mother's local representative.

"Sure, I understand that, your Slimness. But the thing is—"

"You were of great help to Berthold in the matter of The Disappearing Necklace of Pretty Blue Stones. And also in the matter of The Mysterious Destruction of Poor Ulrich." She could do that, talk in capital letters. It's something that comes easily to Queens, I've noticed.

"Yes," I said, "but—"

"The Great Mother has spoken," she said.

"Right," I said. "Absolutely." You didn't argue with the Great Mother.

Berthold stood up, lifted his leather sack, and held it out to me. "Let's be off then, shall we, Doder?"

I took the sack. It was filled with crocks, and the crocks were filled with mead. And so, usually, was Berthold.

Outside, I took a deep breath of fresh air. It wasn't as fresh as it might have been, because Bob and his fumes were travelling alongside me, but it was still better than the air inside Marta's cave. Berthold walked on the other side of Bob, sipping now and then from one of his crocks.

"Tell me something, Bob," he said. "Before the lion killed Tammy, had it bothered any of you?"

"No," said Bob. "Tammy was the first."

"And how large a lion is it?"

"Huge, man. At least eight feet long. You should see the tracks."

"Have you actually seen the lion itself?"

"Nope. No one has, except Leo."

"If my memory serves me, Bob, Leo is blind."

"Well, yeah, sure," said Bob, "in the sense that he can't see anything. But he's a soothsayer, right? And he's an expert on lions. He saw it in a vision."

"Ah. But no one has observed the lion visually?"

"Nope. For one thing, it only shows up at night, when we're all asleep. And for another thing, it's Magical."

"Magical in what way?"

"It can disappear whenever it wants to. We've tried to track it, man. But the tracks lead down to the river and then disappear. Leo says it's a Ghost Lion."

"I see." He drained the last of the mead. "Doder?" Reaching back around Bob, he handed me the empty crock. "Another, please."

"You should talk to Leo," Bob told him.

"Indeed," said Berthold.

I handed Berthold another crock. That was my share of this particular division of labor.

He pulled the cork, handed that to me, and took a drink from the crock. "Have you left Art's body as you found it?" he asked Bob.

"Sure. Everyone wanted to bury it, but I figured you'd want to see it first." Like us, the Outlanders believed that death was contagious; and, like us, they buried a body as soon as it became one–said a quick word or two, "Nice fellow, too bad," and then planted it as deep as possible.

"Excellent," said Berthold, and took another drink of mead.

We crossed the mastodon tracks and came to the river, and we walked alongside that for a while. It was a beautiful day, one of those bright polished days that Memory, in recollection, is always multiplying. The sun was shining, the sky was blue, the grasses in the meadows were shimmering. The breeze was warm and gentle, and it was probably sweet, too; but, with Bob walking beside me, I had no way of knowing.

It took us nearly four hours to reach the Outlander village, but I could smell it after three and a half. Even with Bob walking beside me.

As we approached it, we came upon an old male Outlander sitting on the river bank, a fishing pole in his hand. Fishing poles were another Outlander improvement over the traditional way of doing things. The traditional way meant standing in the stream with your hands dangling in the water, and waiting for a fish to swim between them and surrender. Not a lot of them did, usually.

He had a big head of hair for an Outlander, a bushy white mane. It swung along the shoulders of his red plaid shirt as he turned to face us. I saw that his eyes were as white as his hair.

Bob said something in Outlander gibberish, and the old male responded in kind.

"This is Leo," Bob told me. "He's our lion guy."

Berthold could speak Outlandish, and he did so now. The old male's empty eyes widened and he babbled something in return, and then the two of them were chattering merrily away. Berthold claimed that

Outlandish was a beautiful language, precise and elegant, but to me it always sounded like a box of pebbles tumbling down a hillside.

"They're talking about the lion," Bob told me.

The old male was doing more than talking now. He was making claws with his hands and sweeping them through the air. He was growling. He was hunching his shoulders and glowering right and left, his teeth bared, and then he was making claws with his hands again. Like Bob, he wore a bracelet, but his was made of lion's claws, six or seven of them that rattled as he waved his arms

It was a fine performance, and it lasted for about ten minutes. Berthold stood there, watching, sipping from time to time at his crock. Every so often Bob would translate a scrap of the old male's monologue for me. "It lives in caves at the center of the earth. ... It's angry at us because we don't offer it enough sacrifices ... It'll kill anybody who tries to find it ..."

Terrific, I thought.

Finally, the old Outlander's energy, or maybe just his story, ran out. Berthold said something else. The old male grinned, leaned forward, reached into the water, and pulled out a length of rope. Attached to the end of it was a flopping yellow fish, about two feet long. Berthold said something. The old male nodded proudly, then added a few more bits of cheerful gibberish.

"He wants to know," Bob explained to me, "if we'll all join him for dinner."

"Not if he's serving that fish," said Berthold. "It's a kraydon, and deadly poisonous."

"Yeah, I know," said Bob. "He thinks it's a trout. One of the twins will switch it on him before they cook it."

"The twins?" said Berthold.

"His daughters. Geena and Leena. They're the village virgins."

"Village virgins?" That was me, making my first contribution to the conversation

"Yeah. They're sacred. They're going to get sacrificed next year."

"Sacrificed?" I said. *"Virgins?"*

"Right," said Bob. "To the thunder god. For the crops."

"But that's–*ouch!*" Berthold had kicked me in the shin ...

"That's what?" said Bob.

"Doder meant to say, That's wonderful," said Berthold. "And personally, I think that dinner would be a splendid idea. Now, Bob, suppose you show us to Art's house."

The last time I visited the village, lively Outlanders were milling enthusiastically about, stinking the place up, naturally, but looking very colorful in their red plaid shirts, laughing and sporting with each other in that childish way they have, which Berthold always found charming and which I always found, well, childish. Today, however, the village seemed deserted. The death of three of your neighbors within a week can put a damper on your enthusiasm, even if you're an Outlander.

Art the Archer's house was on the edge of the community. Like the others, it was a rambling wooden structure. At one side was a small, fenced-in enclosure that held a threadbare goat and a very tired-looking ram. Both of them eyed us suspiciously as we walked up to the front door. By this time I was breathing entirely through my mouth.

One of the Outlanders was standing guard at the door, a short stabbing spear resting on his red plaid shoulder. He gibbered at Bob. Bob gibbered back, and then turned to me. "He's asking when they can bury him."

Berthold said something to the guard, and the guard looked from Berthold to Bob, shrugged, and stepped aside for us to enter.

Inside, the place was a mess. Like all Outlandish furniture, the stuff in Art's house was made from wood, and his chairs and tables and cabinets had been crushed and smashed, their fragments scattered around. And, as Bob had said, fragments of Art had been scattered around, too. Most of him was lying in the corner, naked, curled into a stiff ragged ball, torn and clawed, but bits and pieces of him dotted the walls, the floor, and even, in a few places, the ceiling. Flies were buzzing everywhere, tipsy, astonished at their good luck.

Berthold crossed the floor and squatted down beside the body. "Doder?" he said, holding up his empty crock.

I pulled out another crock, pulled out its cork, stepped across the room, and exchanged it for the empty one. I slipped the empty into the sack.

Berthold took a sip of mead. "What impresses you most about the body?" Berthold asked me.

"Well," I said. "For one thing, it's very dead."

He frowned sourly. "An extremely astute observation."

He glanced across the room. "What's that?" he asked, and stood and strode across the room to a shattered cabinet. Squatting down again, he lifted away some chunks of wood and revealed three golden figurines. The Outlanders were fond of gold figurines, and even I knew that each of them possessed a few. These were about two inches tall. One was a fish, one was a crab, one was a scorpion.

Berthold turned to Bob. "Are these the only figurines that Art owned?"

"He kept pretty much to himself," said Bob. "I liked Art, but I didn't know much about him. You could talk to Bill, Tammy's husband. He and Bob used to hang out together. But why're you asking, man? A lion wouldn't bother with a figurine."

"Not unless, as Leo says, it were some sort of ghost lion." He stood. "Where are the tracks you mentioned?"

"This way," said Bob, and led us out the room and through the kitchen, to a back door. "This was open," he said, "when Lou found the body." He opened the door and pointed to the ground. The earth was hard, worn down by many years of passage, but you could make out the pads of a lion's feet, and the deep indentations of its claws.

"A large one, eh, Doder?" said Berthold.

Large was an understatement. The lion that made those tracks had been enormous. "We're not really going to track this thing?"

"Not as yet. Bob, where exactly is Bill's house?"

"I can show you," said Bob.

"Thank you, but that won't be necessary. I know you must have things to do. If you'll tell me where it is, I'm sure that Doder and I can find it."

"Okay, sure. Is it all right to bury him now?"

"Certainly. Will we see you at Leo's house, for dinner?"

"Sure." And then Bob gave us directions, and Berthold and I set out for Bill's house.

As soon as we were out of earshot, Berthold said to me, "Doder. In future, unless I ask for your opinion, please keep it to yourself."

"What? You mean that thing about virgins?"

"Exactly. It's not a good idea to ridicule someone else's religion."

"Sacrificing a virgin? That's a religion?"

"How is their sacrifice any different from ours? At the next Vernal Equinox, we'll be sacrificing Gunnar."

"Yeah, sure," I said, "but that's the way things are *supposed* to happen. I mean, Gunnar's a *man*. We're talking about virgins here, two of them. All right, they're Outlanders. But, still, it's an incredible waste."

"I understand your feelings. But I'd prefer that, when anyone else is present, you keep them, and your opinions, to yourself."

"Fine," I said. "Fine."

"I'll have another crock, please." He handed me the empty one.

No one else was present, so I ventured an opinion. "You're going through those crocks pretty quickly."

"This is at least a three crock problem," he said.

I handed him another crock.

Bill's house was near the center of the village, just off the central square. It was a bit larger than Art's, and in better shape. In the enclosure at its side stood a gigantic grey bull. It glowered at us from beneath a colossal pair of horns as we approached. Just outside the house's front door was a large set of weighing scales.

"What are those for?" I asked Berthold.

"Bill is the tax collector," he said. "In exchange for a percentage of their crops, the Outlanders receive an equal weight of manure from that animal," he nodded toward the bull, "to fertilize the fields for next year."

"They hand over part of what they make, and they get bull manure in return?"

"Yes."

"And that's what they call 'agriculture'?"

"No," he said. "They call that 'politics'."

"How come you know so much about them?" I asked him. "The Outlanders."

"They intrigue me. Their enthusiasm, their love of technology. They are, I believe, the wave of the future."

"And what does that make us?"

He smiled another cryptic smile. "The wave of the past."

"You're kidding."

"As you ought to know by now, Doder," he said, "I never kid."

On that breezy note we climbed up the steps and Berthold knocked at the door. After a moment it was opened by a short Outlander male who wore the usual plaid shirt, but this one was grey rather than red. Berthold said something in Outlandish, and the male stood back and gestured for us to come in.

The interior of the "living room" was like the interior of the similar room in Art's house, but without the damage. Berthold and the Outlander chattered for a while, and then the Outlander led us back through a corridor to what was apparently a sleeping chamber.

Here, damage had been done. On the sleeping box lay a stained and torn cloth mattress, tufts of straw poking through ragged rents in the material. Deep scratches ran along the wooden wall. More dark stains covered the wooden floor.

Jabbering away, the Outlander walked to the window and opened it. Berthold asked him something, and the Outlander frowned, then went to a cabinet against the far wall and opened that. He reached in and pulled out a pair of small gold figurines, a goat and a bull. Berthold asked him some questions, the man answered them.

Berthold said something else, and the Outlander lowered his head and kept it there for a moment. When he raised it, a few tears were trickling down his cheek.

Berthold jabbered a few more words and the Outlander nodded.

Berthold turned to me. "Come along, Doder."

Outside, he handed me his empty crock. I took it, handed him a new one, and asked him, "That was Bill, Tammy's husband?"

"Yes?"

"How come the lion didn't kill him, too?"

"He was away, visiting relatives in another village."

"Lucky for him."

Berthold turned to me. "He lost his wife, Doder."

"Oh," I said. "Right." Berthold wasn't married, of course.

He took a thoughtful sip of mead.

"Did you find out anything else?" I asked him.

"One or two things. One of which is suggestive, and may even be crucial."

"Yeah? Like what?"

"All in good time." He was like that, Berthold, very secretive. By this point, as I later learned, he knew pretty much exactly what had gone on in the village. You'd think that he'd be willing to share his knowledge with the person who was carting around that damned sack of his.

But no. "First," he said, "we must speak with the relatives of Wally the Water-bearer."

And so we spoke to the relatives of Wally the Water-bearer, his aunt and uncle, inside their house, and a lot more jabbering went on. They hauled out some more gold figurines and jabbered some more, and then Berthold and I left.

"What is it with the figurines?" I asked him when we got back outside. "Why do the Outlanders keep them?"

"They represent constellations of stars. The Outlanders believe that the stars, and particular groupings of them, can affect our lives."

"How? They're just little pin holes in the Great Mother's Evening Gown."

"The Outlanders have a somewhat different belief system."

"I'll say. How come you keep asking about the figurines?"

"Each of the dead Outlanders had a collection of them. From each collection a figurine was missing."

"From Art's, too?"

"Yes, according to Bill."

"Well, obviously," I said, "the lion didn't take them."

He smiled. "Obviously," he said, "the lion did."

"And what's that supposed to mean?"

"All–"

"Yeah, right, all in good time."

"Patience, Doder."

Easy for him to say. He wasn't carrying twenty crocks of mead.

"Come," he said. "We must interview a few more Outlanders."

Which we did, three or four of them in different parts of the village. More jabbering. Finally, when we got outside the last of the houses, Berthold turned to me and said, "I believe it's time for dinner."

"You're really going to eat, in the middle of all this stink?"

"Food isn't the only thing that's served at dinner."

"Yeah? What else is?"

"Sometimes," he said, with a cryptic smile, "the Truth."

The Truth, just then, was that I wanted to take a swing at him with the sack.

The house of Leo, the lion expert, was an old one, not far from the river bank where we first met him. When we knocked on the door, it was Bob who opened it.

"Hey, man," he said to Berthold. "Come on in. How's it going?"

Leo's house, inside, was pretty much the same as all the others, except that in here, standing beside a large dining table, there was a pair of twins. They were identical young females with indentically long black hair, and they wore bracelets of lion claws, spotless leather pants, and freshly washed red plaid shirts. They were slender and sleek, and I suppose that from an Outlandish point of view they were fairly attractive. Neither of them had an eyebrow ridge like Ursula's, naturally, and I've never really been fond of hairless skin. But they were handsome enough, as specimens of their species, and it seemed a pity to me that they were going to be sacrificed next year. I was pretty sure that even among the Outlanders, there weren't that many virgins around.

"It goes well, I think, Bob," said Berthold. "And these are, of course, the twins."

"Oh yeah. This is Geena, this is Leena."

Right away, I have to admit, they surprised me. As Bob gibbered away in Outlandish, they smiled and nodded. The one of the left, Geena, said slowly but clearly, hesitating only a little, "Hey ... man." The one on the right, Leena, said, "What ... is ... happening?"

Berthold smiled. "Congratulations. Your accents are excellent."

"Thanks ... man," said Geena.

"We speak four ... distinct ... languages," said Leena.

"And all of them extremely well, I'm sure," said Berthold.

"Dinner is nearly ... ready," said Geena.

"We've got to go ... help Dad in the kitchen," said Leena.

"We'll be right back," said Geena.

As they left, Bob turned to Berthold and said, "So. When do we start stalking the lion, man?"

"I have been stalking it," said Berthold, "since I arrived here."

"Huh?"

"All in good time, Bob."

Just then, Leo entered the room and gave a hearty gibberish shout of greeting. Grinning hugely, moving here in his own home as though he weren't blind at all, he came around the table and offered his hand to Berthold, who shook it enthusiastically with his own, and then to me, who shook it. When no one was looking, I wiped mine clean on the curtain.

We all sat down at the table, and the young women served the food. There was salad and fish (trout now, and not the poisonous kraydon). Throughout the meal, the conversation was mostly small talk. The young women demonstrated their facility with The Language. Berthold and Leo jabbered away. Bob asked me why I wasn't eating, and I told him that I'd eaten a large lunch.

It was during desert—cookies and milk, which I also couldn't eat—that Berthold sat back against his chair and said to Leena, "Tell me, Leena. Which of you killed your neighbors, you or your sister?"

Bob, whose mouth was filled with milk, promptly spat it out across the table. No one was sitting opposite him, fortunately.

"Come again?" said Leena, looking confused.

"It had to be one of you," said Berthold. "One of you was seen shortly after each of the murders. None of the witnesses thought anything of it—after all, the victims were killed by a lion."

"Hey, man," said Bob. "You've got to be kidding."

"As Doder will tell you, I never kid. Doder—"

"He never kids," I said.

Berthold frowned impatiently. "Doder, when you told Marta you were allergic to cats, you were speaking the truth, were you not?"

"Absolutely." You didn't lie to the Great Mother's representative.

"How allergic are you?"

"Very. I get hives if I go into a room where a cat *used* to be."

"And yet this afternoon, when you were in a house that had apparently been visited by a lion, you had no reaction at all."

"Well, no," I admitted. I glanced over at Leena and Geena, who were exchanging puzzled looks.

"Hey, man," said Bob. "Those marks on Art's body, and the others. They were made with *claws*."

"Yes," said Berthold. "By those claws—" he pointed to Leena's bracelet. "Or by those—" he pointed to Geena's. "As were the lion tracks outside Art's house, in the earth."

Old Leo frowned, maybe sensing that the meal wasn't working out. He cocked his head and gibbered something.

"But those were *lion* tracks," said Bob.

"Either twin would have know what lion tracks look like, and how to duplicate them. Their father is, after all, the local authority on lions. Tell me this, Bob. If it was a lion who killed your neighbors, why didn't the beast eat them?"

"Well, uh ..."

"None of the victims had been eaten. No parts had been taken. A few had been redistributed, yes. But none had been removed. No, Bob. One of the sisters killed your friends, and made the death look like the work of a lion."

"Why?"

"So no one would suspect her true motive."

"Which was what?"

"Theft. The theft of a gold figurine. One was stolen from each victim."

Leo gibbered something, turning his head left and right.

Bob patted him on the back, impatiently, and asked Berthold, "Why steal a figurine?"

"To provide herself with finances."

"But neither one of them *need* finances, man. They're sacred, both of them. So long as they're here, they get everything they want."

"Yes. So long as they're here, in your village. But if one of them wanted to leave?"

"But why would either one of them want to?"

"To avoid being sacrificed."

Bob shook his head. "Oh, no, man. That can't be right. Being sacrificed, man, that's an *honor*."

Berthold smiled. "On that matter, Bob, one of the sisters disagrees with you."

"But sacrifice is a great honor," said Geena.

"A great honor," echoed Leena.

Leo gibbered. Bob patted him again and said to Berthold, "Okay, okay, look. I'm not saying you're right. But what makes you so sure it was *one* of them, and not both of them?"

"Only one of the twins was ever seen."

"What," I said, "if they took turns?" I was pretty pleased with myself for coming up with this.

"Absurd," said Berthold. "If both of were involved, they would have worked together at making the deaths seem the result of a lion attack. Two people would have been able to claw the bodies, falsify those tracks, more quickly. And both twins, in that case would have been seen, afterward. But in fact only one was seen."

He turned to Bob. "The question is, Which one? And I believe I know of a simple method by which that might be determined."

"What's that?"

"You need merely place both of them in a locked room for a period of twenty four hours, under close supervision. You see, I believe—"

"We can't do that," Bob told him.

Berthold blinked in surprise. "Why not?"

"They're sacred, man. Chosen by the thunder god. We can't do that. Lock them up. Supervise them. Not unless they break a rule."

"One of them *has* broken a rule. She's killed three of your people."

"That's what *you* say. You don't have any proof."

Leo gibbered loudly, almost a growl. Bob snapped something in Outlandish.

Berthold looked across the table at the two young females. They looked calmly back. If one of them were secretly gloating, she gave no sign of it.

Still staring at the women, Berthold said, "Bob, the villagers with whom I spoke told me that the sacredness of Leena and Geena resides entirely in their twinhood. Is that true?"

"Sure. If they weren't twins, identical and all, they'd just be normal women."

"I should think, then, that the two of them, both honored to be chosen for sacrifice, would make an effort to remain identical."

"Naturally. Didn't you see the way they ate? If one of them takes a bite of fish, then the other takes exactly the same sized bite. If one of them eats two cookies, so does the other."

"Ah." Suddenly Berthold smiled at the females. "You both claim to be innocent, is that correct?"

"Absolutely," said the two of them, in unison.

"Then neither of you would object to a small experiment which will serve to establish that innocence."

The females looked at each other, looked back at him. "Not me," said Leena. "Not me," said Geena.

"Excellent. Let us all retire, then, to Bill's house."

A few minutes later, we all stood outside Bill's house. Along the way, Bob had explained the situation to Leo, who was now gibbering angrily and waving his arms. Bob was trying to quiet him.

The sight of the twins, or maybe the sight of Berthold and me in their presence, had drawn a small crowd. They gathered in a semi-circle around us, muttering in gibberish.

Berthold walked over to the large set of scales set up beside the front door. "Geena. Please step on one side of the scale."

Geena looked at her sister, and then walked forward. The scales held two wooden plates, each suspended on ropes. Geena grasped the ropes on one side, lowered the plate they held, and stepped gingerly onto it. The plate sank to the ground.

"Leena," said Berthold. "Please step on the other."

Leena hesitated. She glanced around at the crowd.

Berthold smiled. "This will take only a moment."

Leena walked over, grabbed the second set of ropes, and stepped onto the second plate. As she sank slightly, her sister was lifted from the ground. For a moment or two, swaying slightly back and forth, the two females rose and fell in turn.

Between the two plates was an upright wooden rod that swung back and forth before a curved beam. Along the beam, at regular intervals, were lines carefully painted on the wood, to indicate by how much the items being measured might differ in weight. It was a clever piece of equipment. But, as I've said, the Outlanders were very clever fellows.

We watched as the two females bobbed for a bit, one going up as the other went down. The rod swung left and right.

No one spoke now. Bob had somehow managed to silence Leo.

At last the females, and the rod, stopped moving. The rod pointed very slightly to the left of center.

Leena weighed a fraction more than her sister.

Before any of us, except Berthold, realized what this meant, Leena leaped from her plate. Her sister shot to the ground, her knees buckling beneath her, as Leena sprang toward the street.

Bob grabbed her. She swung a fist at him. He caught that and twisted it up behind her back. Wrapping his left arm around her neck, he said to Berthold, "What? What is it?"

Geena had gotten up from the ground. She ran now to her father, who was beginning to gibber again.

"There was one thing which could ruin Leena's plan," said Berthold. "One thing which, if found, would instantly reveal her guilt."

"What?"

"The last figurine. The one she took from Art's house this morning. If the figurine were found on her person, she would be lost."

"She swallowed it," I said.

Berthold looked at me, surprised. And then he smiled. "Very good, Doder." He turned back to Bob. "She did, indeed, swallow it. If you will place her in confinement for a day or so, sooner or later the figurine—"

"I get you," said Bob, struggling to hold onto Leena. "The figurine will, uh, show up."

"Exactly."

And it did, too, as Berthold told me the next day.

The figurine, as it happened, was in the shape of a lion.

Berthold got a big kick out of that. He thought it was very ironic. He liked irony, Berthold.

But for me, the best part of the story was that it had a happy ending. Not for Leena, of course, because she was beheaded and buried before breakfast the next morning. But for Geena. With Leena gone, she was no longer a twin, and the Outlanders had to forget about sacrificing her.

No, I don't know what happened to her. Within a few months, my poor wife, Ursula, was dead and I was on my way to—

But that's another story.

On your way out, now, don't forget those donations.

Bibliography

Novels

Cocaine Blues, Dell, 1979
The Aegean Affair, Dell, 1981
Wall of Glass, St. Martin's, 1987
Miss Lizzie, St. Martin's, 1989
At Ease With The Dead, St. Martin's, 1990
Wilde West, St. Martin's, 1991
A Flower In The Desert, St. Martin's, 1992
The Hanged Man, St. Martin's, 1993
Escapade, St. Martin's, 1995
Accustomed To The Dark, St. Martin's, 1996
Masquerade, St. Martin's, 1998
Cavalcade, St. Martin's, 2005
Perfection, St. Martin's, 2006
Dead Horse, Dennis McMillan, 2006

Short Story Collections

The Gold of Mayani, Buffalo Medicine Books, 1995
The Mankiller of Poojeegai and Other Stories, Crippen and Landru, 2007

Non-fiction

Sleight of Hand, Buffalo Medicine Books, 1993

Short Stories

"Territorial Imperative," *The Magazine of Fantasy and Science Fiction*, April, 1983.

"A Conflict of Interests," *Alfred Hitchcock's Mystery Magazine* [hereafter, AHMM], November, 1982. Collected in *The Gold of Mayani*, 1995, and in *The Mankiller of Poojeegai*, 2007.

"To Catch a Wizard," AHMM, March, 1983. Collected in *The Gold of Mayani*, 1995.

"A Matter of Pride," AHMM, May, 1984. Collected in *The Mankiller of Poojeegai*, 2007.

"A Greek Game," AHMM, May, 1985. Collected in *The Mankiller of Poojeegai*, 2007.

"The Motor Coach of Allah," AHMM, December, 1985. Collected in *The Gold of Mayani*, 1995.

"Make No Mistake," AHMM, August, 1989. Collected in *The Gold of Mayani*, 1995.

"The Gold of Mayani, AHMM, Winter 1989. Collected in *The Gold of Mayani*, 1995.

"Lee Ann," *Sleight of Hand*, Buffalo Medicine Books, 1993. Collected in *The Mankiller of Poojeegai*, 2007.

"Connection Terminated," AHMM, January, 1994. Collected in *The Mankiller of Poojeegai*, 2007.

"The Cassoulet," AHMM, December, 1996. Collected in *The Mankiller of Poojeegai*, 2007.

"Murder One," *Crime Through Time II*, Berkley Prime Crime, 1998. Collected in *The Mankiller of Poojeegai*, 2007.

"Beyond the Sighs," Worldwide Publishing, 1998. Collected in *The Mankiller of Poojeegai*, 2007.

"Missolonghi," AHMM, October, 2000. Collected in *The Mankiller of Poojeegai*, 2007.

"A Mishap at The Manor," *Malice Domestic* 9, 2000. Collected in *The Mankiller of Poojeegai*, 2007.

"The Mankiller of Poojeegai," (in German) *Astrokrimis: Moerderische Loewen*, 2000; (in English) AHMM, September 2006. Collected in *The Mankiller of Poojeegai*, 2007.

"The Adventures of Col. Boone." Published as a separate chapbook to accompany the limited edition of *The Mankiller of Poojeegai*, 2007.

The Mankiller of Poojegai

The Mankiller of Poojegai and Other Mysteries by Walter Satterthwait, is set in Goudy Old Style and printed on sixty-pound Natures acid-free, recycled paper. The cover design is by Gail Cross. The first edition was printed in two forms: trade softcover, notchbound; and two hundred numbered copies sewn in cloth, signed by the author. Each of the clothbound copies includes a separate pamphlet, *The Adventures of Col. Boone.*

The Mankiller of Poojegai was printed and bound by Thomson-Shore, Inc., Dexter, Michigan and published in October 2007 by Crippen & Landru Publishers, Inc., Norfolk, Virginia.

CRIPPEN & LANDRU, PUBLISHERS
P. O. Box 9315
Norfolk, VA 23505
info@crippenlandru.com; toll-free 877 622-6656
www.crippenlandru.com

Crippen & Landru publishes first edition short-story collections by important detective and mystery writers. The following books are currently in print; see our website for full details:

REGULAR SERIES

The McCone Files by Marcia Muller. 1995. Trade softcover, $19.00.
Diagnosis: Impossible, The Problems of Dr. Sam Hawthorne by Edward D. Hoch. 1996. Trade softcover, $19.00.
Who Killed Father Christmas? by Patricia Moyes. 1996. Signed, unnumbered cloth overrun copies, $30.00.
In Kensington Gardens Once by H.R.F. Keating. 1997. Trade softcover, $12.00.
Shoveling Smoke by Margaret Maron. 1997. Trade softcover, $19.00.
The Ripper of Storyville and Other Tales of Ben Snow by Edward D. Hoch. 1997. Trade softcover. $19.00.
Renowned Be Thy Grave by P.M. Carlson. 1998. Trade softcover, $16.00.
Carpenter and Quincannon by Bill Pronzini. 1998. Trade softcover, $16.00.
Famous Blue Raincoat by Ed Gorman. 1999. Signed, unnumbered cloth overrun copies, $30.00. Trade softcover, $17.00.
The Tragedy of Errors and Others by Ellery Queen. 1999. Trade softcover, $20.00.
McCone and Friends by Marcia Muller. 2000. Trade softcover, $19.00.
Challenge the Widow Maker by Clark Howard. 2000. Trade softcover, $16.00.
Fortune's World by Michael Collins. 2000. Trade softcover, $16.00.
The Velvet Touch: Nick Velvet Stories by Edward D. Hoch. 2000. Trade softcover, 19.00.
Long Live the Dead: Tales from Black Mask by Hugh B. Cave. 2000. Trade softcover, $16.00.
Tales Out of School by Carolyn Wheat. 2000. Trade softcover, $16.00.
Stakeout on Page Street and Other DKA Files by Joe Gores. 2000. Trade softcover, $16.00.

The Celestial Buffet by Susan Dunlap. 2001. Trade softcover, $16.00.

Kisses of Death: A Nathan Heller Casebook by Max Allan Collins. 2001. Trade softcover, $19.00.

The Old Spies Club and Other Intrigues of Rand by Edward D. Hoch. 2001. Signed, unnumbered cloth overrun copies, $32.00. Trade softcover, $17.00.

Adam and Eve on a Raft by Ron Goulart. 2001. Signed, unnumbered cloth overrun copies, $32.00. Trade softcover, $17.00.

The Reluctant Detective by Michael Z. Lewin. 2001. Signed, numbered clothbound, $42.00. Trade softcover, $17.00.

Nine Sons by Wendy Hornsby. 2002. Trade softcover, $16.00.

The Curious Conspiracy by Michael Gilbert. 2002. Signed, numbered clothbound, $42.00. Trade softcover, $17.00.

The 13 Culprits by Georges Simenon, translated by Peter Schulman. 2002. Trade softcover, $16.00.

The Dark Snow by Brendan DuBois. 2002. Signed, unnumbered cloth overrun copies, $32.00. Trade softcover, $17.00.

Come Into My Parlor: Tales from Detective Fiction Weekly by Hugh B. Cave. 2002. Signed, unnumbered cloth overrun copies, $32.00. Trade softcover, $17.00.

The Iron Angel and Other Tales of the Gypsy Sleuth by Edward D. Hoch. 2003. Signed, numbered clothbound, $42.00. Trade softcover, $17.00.

Cuddy – Plus One by Jeremiah Healy. 2003. Trade softcover, $18.00.

Problems Solved by Bill Pronzini and Barry N. Malzberg. 2003. Signed, numbered clothbound, $42.00. Trade softcover, $16.00.

A Killing Climate by Eric Wright. 2003. Trade softcover, $17.00.

Lucky Dip by Liza Cody. 2003. Signed, numbered clothbound, $42.00. Trade softcover, $17.00.

Kill the Umpire: The Calls of Ed Gorgon by Jon L. Breen. 2003. Trade softcover, $17.00.

Suitable for Hanging by Margaret Maron. 2004. Trade softcover, $19.00.

Murders and Other Confusions by Kathy Lynn Emerson. 2004. Signed, numbered clothbound, $42.00. Trade softcover, $19.00.

Byline: Mickey Spillane by Mickey Spillane, edited by Lynn Myers and Max Allan Collins. 2004. Trade softcover, $20.00.

The Confessions of Owen Keane by Terence Faherty. 2005. Signed, numbered clothbound, $42.00. Trade softcover, $17.00.

The Adventure of the Murdered Moths and Other Radio Mysteries by Ellery Queen. 2005. Numbered clothbound, $45.00. Trade softcover, $20.00.

Murder, Ancient and Modern by Edward Marston. 2005. Signed, numbered clothbound, $43.00. Trade softcover, $18.00.

More Things Impossible: The Second Casebook of Dr. Sam Hawthorne by Edward D. Hoch. 2006. Signed, numbered clothbound, $43.00. Trade softcover, $18.00.

Murder, 'Orrible Murder! by Amy Myers. 2006. Signed, numbered clothbound, $43.00. Trade softcover, $18.00.

The Verdict of Us All: Stories by the Detection Club for H.R.F. Keating, edited by Peter Lovesey. 2006. Numbered clothbound, $43.00. Trade softcover, $20.00.

The Archer Files: The Complete Short Stories of Lew Archer, Private Investigator, Including Newly-Discovered Case-Notes by Ross Macdonald, edited by Tom Nolan. 2007. Numbered clothbound, $45.00. Trade softcover, $25.00.

The Mankiller of Poojeegai and Other Mysteries by Walter Satterthwait. 2007. Signed, numbered clothbound, $43.00. Trade softcover, $17.00.

FORTHCOMING TITLES IN THE REGULAR SERIES

A Pocketful of Noses: Stories of One Ganelon or Another by James Powell

Quintet: The Cases of Chase and Delacroix, by Richard A. Lupoff

Thirteen to the Gallows by John Dickson Carr and Val Gielgud, edited by Tony Medawar

A Little Intelligence by Robert Silverberg and Randall Garrett (writing as "Robert Randall")

Valentino: Film Detective by Loren D. Estleman

Once Burned: The Collected Crime Stories by S.J. Rozan

Funeral in the Fog and Other Simon Ark Tales by Edward D. Hoch

Suspense – His and Hers by Barbara and Max Allan Collins

Attitude and Other Stories of Suspense by Loren D. Estleman

Hoch's Ladies by Edward D. Hoch

14 Slayers by Paul Cain, edited by Max Allan Collins and Lynn F. Myers, Jr. Published with Black Mask Press

Tough As Nails by Frederick Nebel, edited by Rob Preston. Published with Black Mask Press

CRIPPEN & LANDRU LOST CLASSICS

Crippen & Landru is proud to publish a series of *new* short-story collections by great authors who specialized in traditional mysteries. Each book collects stories from crumbling pages of old pulp, digest, and slick magazines, and most of the stories have been "lost" since their first publication. The following books are in print:

The Newtonian Egg and Other Cases of Rolf le Roux by Peter Godfrey, introduction by Ronald Godfrey. 2002. Trade softcover, $15.00.

Murder, Mystery and Malone by Craig Rice, edited by Jeffrey A. Marks. 2002. Trade softcover, $19.00.

The Sleuth of Baghdad: The Inspector Chafik Stories, by Charles B. Child. Cloth, $27.00. 2002. Trade softcover, $17.00.

Hildegarde Withers: Uncollected Riddles by Stuart Palmer, introduction by Mrs. Stuart Palmer. 2002. Trade softcover, $19.00.

The Spotted Cat and Other Mysteries from the Casebook of Inspector Cockrill by Christianna Brand, edited by Tony Medawar. 2002. Cloth, $29.00. Trade softcover, $19.00.

Marksman and Other Stories by William Campbell Gault, edited by Bill Pronzini; afterword by Shelley Gault. 2003. Trade softcover, $19.00.

Karmesin: The World's Greatest Criminal – Or Most Outrageous Liar by Gerald Kersh, edited by Paul Duncan. 2003. Cloth, $27.00. Trade softcover, $17.00.

The Complete Curious Mr. Tarrant by C. Daly King, introduction by Edward D. Hoch. Cloth, $29.00. 2003. Trade softcover, $19.00.

The Pleasant Assassin and Other Cases of Dr. Basil Willing by Helen McCloy, introduction by B.A. Pike. 2003. Cloth, $27.00. Trade softcover, $18.00.

Murder – All Kinds by William L. DeAndrea, introduction by Jane Haddam. 2003. Cloth, $29.00. Trade softcover, $19.00.

The Avenging Chance and Other Mysteries from Roger Sheringham's Casebook by Anthony Berkeley, edited by Tony Medawar and Arthur Robinson. 2004. Cloth, $29.00. Trade softcover, $19.00.

Banner Deadlines: The Impossible Files of Senator Brooks U. Banner by Joseph Commings, edited by Robert Adey; memoir by Edward D. Hoch. 2004. Cloth, $29.00. Trade softcover, $19.00.

The Danger Zone and Other Stories by Erle Stanley Gardner, edited by Bill Pronzini. 2004. Trade softcover, $19.00.

Dr. Poggioli: Criminologist by T.S. Stribling, edited by Arthur Vidro. Cloth, $29.00. 2004. Cloth, $29.00. Trade softcover, $19.00.

The Couple Next Door: Collected Short Mysteries by Margaret Millar, edited by Tom Nolan. 2004. Trade softcover, $19.00.

Sleuth's Alchemy: Cases of Mrs. Bradley and Others by Gladys Mitchell, edited by Nicholas Fuller. 2004. Trade softcover, $19.00.

Who Was Guilty? Two Dime Novels by Philip S. Warne/Howard W. Macy, edited by Marlena E. Bremseth. 2004. Cloth, $29.00. Trade softcover, $19.00.

Slot-Machine Kelly by Michael Collins, introduction by Robert J. Randisi. Cloth, $29.00. 2004. Trade softcover, $19.00.

The Evidence of the Sword by Rafael Sabatini, edited by Jesse F. Knight. 2006. Cloth, $29.00. Trade softcover, $19.00.

The Casebook of Sidney Zoom by Erle Stanley Gardner, edited by Bill Pronzini. 2006. Cloth, $29.00. Trade softcover, $19.00.

The Detections of Francis Quarles by Julian Symons, edited by John Cooper; afterword by Kathleen Symons. 2006. Cloth, $29.00. Trade softcover, $19.00.

The Trinity Cat and Other Mysteries by Ellis Peters (Edith Pargeter), edited by Martin Edwards and Sue Feder. 2006. Trade softcover, $19.00.

The Grandfather Rastin Mysteries by Lloyd Biggle, Jr., edited by Kenneth Lloyd Biggle and Donna Biggle Emerson. 2007. Cloth, $29.00. Trade softcover, $19.00.

Masquerade: Ten Crime Stories by Max Brand, edited by William F. Nolan. 2007. Cloth, $29.00. Trade softcover, $19.00.

Dead Yesterday and Other Mysteries by Mignon G. Eberhart, edited by Rick Cypert and Kirby McCauley. Cloth, $30.00. Trade softcover, $20.00.

FORTHCOMING LOST CLASSICS

The Battles of Jericho by Hugh Pentecost, introduction by S.T. Karnick

The Minerva Club, The Department of Patterns and Other Stories by Victor Canning, edited by John Higgins

The Casebook of Gregory Hood by Anthony Boucher and Denis Green, edited by Joe R. Christopher

The Casebook of Jonas P. Jonas and Others by Elizabeth Ferrars, edited by John Cooper

Ten Thousand Blunt Instruments by Philip Wylie, edited by Bill Pronzini

The Exploits of the Patent Leather Kid by Erle Stanley Gardner, edited by Bill Pronzini

Duel of Shadows, The Barnabas Hildreth Stories by Vincent Cornier, edited by Mike Ashley

Author in Search of a Character, The Detections of Miss Phipps by Phyllis Bentley, edited by Marvin Lachman

About the Investigations of Thatcher Colt (and Others) by Anthony Abbot, edited by William Vande Water